"THIS SACRIFICE ...
WHAT EXACTLY DOES IT INVOLVE?"

"It is all very clearly explained in the traditions which have come down to us," Apu Tupa explained affably. "In order to divine which course of action to pursue, our ancestors would open the belly of a prisoner and read his or her entrails."

"Somehow I don't think our companion is going to feel honored," Manco replied dismally.

"Nonsense! It will make her very popular among the people of Contisuyu ..."

CAT•A•LYST

Also By Alan Dean Foster

THE LAST STARFIGHTER
SLIPT
GLORY LANE
MAORI
QUOZL
CYBER WAY

CAT·A·LYST

ALAN DEAN FOSTER

SEVERN
SH
HOUSE

This first hardcover edition published in Great Britain 1993 by
SEVERN HOUSE PUBLISHERS LTD of
9–15 High Street, Sutton, Surrey SM1 1DF
by arrangement with Little Brown and Company (UK) Ltd.
First published in hardcover format in the U.S.A. 1993 by
SEVERN HOUSE PUBLISHERS INC of
475 Fifth Avenue, New York, NY 10017,
by arrangement with the Berkley Publishing Group.

British Library Cataloguing in Publication Data
Foster, Alan Dean
  Cat-a-lyst. – New ed
  I. Title
  813.54 [F]

  ISBN 0-7278-4455-5

All situations in this publication are fictitious and
any resemblance to living persons is purely coincidental.

Typeset by Hewer Text Composition Services, Edinburgh.
Printed and bound in Great Britain by
Dotesios Ltd, Trowbridge, Wiltshire.

This book is dedicated to Boris Gomez Luna, David Ricalde, and Charlie Munn, three men of very different background who recognize one simple fact: it is better to keep one's neighborhood clean than to dirty it.

And for the people of Peru, who have had the wisdom to preserve the jewel of the world's rainforests, the great Manú.

And for Mittens, Saturn, Orca, Dusty, Peaches, and Daylight, who helped in the writing.

Human kind cannot bear very much reality.

T. S. ELIOT

I ───────

SPLINTERS of light flashed from the captain's buttons as he strove to peer through the roiling actinic smoke. His ears were assaulted by the screams of dying men, echoes of an insufficiently distant Hell. A shell struck nearby, showering him with clods of hot earth and fragments of torn human flesh.

"I don't see her!" He had to scream to make himself heard above the awful thunder of battle. "Regulus! Can you see anything?"

The colored soldier crouching alongside wiped at his eyes with one hand, the knuckles of the other pale where they gripped his rifle.

"No, suh! But she got to be heah somewheres, suh!" He squinted into the stinging smoke. "This be the country where I was raised and I still remembers it like the back o' mah hand. I ain't been gone North that long, suh." He gestured with the muzzle of his rifle.

"That be the old quarters over there, where I growed up. The big house be just beyond. The creek'll be to our right, with the smokehouse where they used to dry the fish. Let's try there, suh. I know the missus. She too smart to stay in the house while this fightin's goin' on."

"This is all Sherman's fault," the captain growled as he dragged the dirty, sweaty sleeve of his uniform across his forehead. The yellowish light imparted an eerie glow to his saber. "Won't be anything left of Atlanta when he gets through."

"No, suh. The general, suh, he's a hard man."

"He's fighting to win, Regulus. To win this war and keep your people free. But he's no gentleman."

"Yes, suh. Missy Amanda, suh, she might be . . ."

A feminine scream rose above the sound of exploding shells and the deadly whistle of minié balls. The soldier rose excitedly.

"That's her, suh! I'd know that precious voice anywheres!"

"Quickly now, Regulus!"

The two men scrambled down the sloping riverbank toward the slate-roofed shed that squatted by the water's edge.

The interior of the ramshackle structure had become the stage for a scene of imminent outrage. Three men—dirty, worn, conscripts all—orbited a flurry of white crinoline and silk through which flashes of red hair and smooth skin could occasionally be glimpsed. Their expressions, gaptoothed and grim, left no doubt as to their intentions. Though outnumbered and overpowered, the woman trapped in their midst was doing her best to resist their onslaught.

Sword at the ready, the captain burst into the room. "That'll do for you, you bastards." His voice and hand were steady.

The trio whirled to regard the intruder. The nearest, a tall, heavyset ruffian who might once have been a seaman, glared unrepentantly at the officer.

"This be none of your business, *sir*." He grinned nastily. "Why don't you just take that darkie with you and go on about your business, and leave us to ours?" Grunts of assent issued from his companions.

The captain returned the smile as he hefted his saber. "My intention was just to see the three of you court-martialed, but I think now that it would be only proper that I spare Mr. Lincoln's government that expense." Regulus at his side, he let out a yell and charged.

One man took a saber cut to the cheek and dropped like a stone, leaving the brigands' erstwhile spokesman to engage the captain from behind. The officer spun and parried, too late to block the scything rifle butt which struck him across the forehead. As he stumbled away from the blow he saw the third attacker taking shaky aim at the recumbent woman with his service revolver. The coward's intent was clear: no witness, no trial.

"*No!*" With a cry, Regulus threw himself forward.

The officer heard the revolver discharge as he twisted and lunged. Down went the giant, his heart pierced by the captain's blade. The private who'd wielded the unsteady pistol scrambled through the open doorway and fled.

The captain started to pursue but halted at the sight of Regulus lying sprawled near the woman's feet. A spreading crimson stain darkened the front of the corporal's uniform.

"Regulus!" Putting his sword aside, the officer knelt next to his orderly's body. "You can't die, my friend," he said more softly. "Not after all we've been through together. Not since New York."

The enlisted man's reply was hoarse, strained. "It . . . it's alright, Captain Hector, suh. It's my time, is all." He turned to gaze up into his friend's face. "It had to be this way, don't you see?"

"Oh, Regulus, I remember you, I do! I knew you'd come back!" The woman cradled the dying man's head against her crinoline-caressed bosom, tears streaming down her flushed cheeks. "Please don't die!"

Pain made the orderly flinch as he turned his head to gaze fondly up at her. "I promised your daddy, Miss Amanda, that I'd look after you if the war came. I nevah forgot that you was the one responsible for havin' me set free. If . . ." He paused. It was a long pause. The woman continued to peer expectantly down at him while the captain knelt sorrowfully at her side.

"If what, Regulus?" she finally murmured.

"Shit!" the orderly exclaimed explosively. "I can't do it!" He sat up sharply. "I can't do these lines, man! I can't identify with this part."

"Cut!" howled a new voice. The distant rumble of background explosions ceased. Fans began to chide smoke from the shed. "I said cut, dammit!"

A new figure joined the trio. The man was short, dark-eyed, swarthy, more than a tad apoplectic. "What do you mean," he inquired through clenched teeth, "you can't do these lines?"

"I'm sorry, man." Showing no effects from what had transpired earlier, the orderly stood and wiped dirt from his face. The stain on his chest had stopped spreading. "I just can't do this anymore. I mean, this dude was born a slave, right? So he gets freed, goes North, finds a decent job, joins the Union Army where he meets this white bread over here"—he gestured at the captain, who was now standing and listening quietly—"and they're the same age, right?

"This corporal, he's gone through all that hell to make it out of the South, so what does he do? He decides to play servant again to this captain so he can come all the way back to where he was a slave and throw himself in front of a bullet to save the fox whose daddy once owned him. Why? Because she had an attack of conscience and freed him? She didn't free nobody else. It just doesn't jibe, man. I can't buy it.

"I mean, this character's got a wife and kids back in New York. Sure, maybe he feels grateful to this chick." He indicated the woman in the shredded crinolines, who by now was looking thoroughly disgusted. "But he ain't gonna give his life for her. It just ain't real."

The shorter man was staring hard at him. "So now you're a writer." He glanced at the captain. "What about you, Jason? You a writer too?"

The captain raised both hands, palms outward. He'd left his sword lying on the ground. A man in his early twenties was cleaning it with a white cloth.

"Don't look at me, Nahfoud. I read my lines."

"I'm asking your opinion. You think he's right?"

Jason Carter looked past the director, to the crew bustling behind him. Men adjusted scrims and shades. Gaffers checked wires. The Steadycam team was helping the tired cameraman slip free of his harness.

"Look, I'm doing my job. Don't put me in the middle of something, okay?"

"I am so putting you."

Carter saw that Melrose was staring at him. He sighed. "Well, since you ask, no; I don't think this

guy would sacrifice himself under those circumstances. Not if he had a family. If he didn't have a—"

"There, you see?" said his fellow actor, not letting
him finish. He was more angry than grateful. "It's
like I've been saying all along. How come I gotta
die? How come it's always the black guy who's gotta
sacrifice himself? Shit, man, let *him* throw himself
in front of the damn bullet! He's the one with the
thing for the chick. Me, I'm supposed to have a wife
and two kids back in Brooklyn. Why can't the white
guy do the noble death number for a change?"

It required a visible effort for the director to control himself. "Because—that's—not—the—way—
it—is—written," he said very slowly. "That is not
what it says in the script." He smiled humorlessly.
"You remember the script, don't you? The big wad
of colored paper everyone is carrying around? The
script you read months ago and agreed to follow?"

"Look, jack," said the actor, "my agent read the
script, see? He's the one told me I should do it. I
don't want to be difficult. Soon as I heard it was a
Civil War pic I knew I wasn't bein' hired to be the
lead. Like, unless Spike Lee or one of the Hudlin
brothers is the director, no black actor is gonna get
the lead in no Civil War flick. I passed on four weeks
in Vegas to do this little epic.

"But I still don't see why I gotta die, especially
under these circumstances." He shook his head. "I
just can't do it, man. I'm an actor, but there's times
and lines a man's just gotta deal with, and this is one
of 'em. Ever since I saw *The Dirty Dozen* as a kid,
saw Jim Brown sacrifice himself to save all his white
buddies . . . I mean, I just can't do it." He brushed
past Carter and the director.

"I got some heavy thinking to do, man."

"Listen, you guys make up your minds what you wanna do, but I can't take this anymore." The woman was gathering her soiled costume around her. "All this yelling and shouting has wounded my karma enough as it is." She looked around desperately. "Where's Siddarthee? Where's my Guide?"

"Here, little one." A black-bearded scarecrow clad in a long beige robe shuffled forward to place a reassuring arm around the actress's bare shoulders. With his free hand he took one of hers.

"Everything will be all right. Just close your eyes and breathe deeply. Have good thoughts. Think of the wind in the trees, making music with the leaves."

The director muttered a curse in Arabic. "Somebody get that fake holy man off my set. We're trying to make a movie here."

"Siddarthee is no fake," said the actress with wounded dignity. "He is my Guide. If he goes, I go."

The scarecrow raised an arm heavenward, imploring in Hindi. "I do not ask for anything for myself," he added in English. To the actress he murmured, "Come, little one. We must allow time for the discordant vibrations to settle."

As he led her off the set she turned to the director and concluded sweetly, "And you tell the jerk with the revolver, the ugly little fart with the brown eyes, that if he doesn't keep his hands off my ass during shooting I'm going to kick his nuts out through his nose."

"Amanda. Dear, sweet Amanda." The director

trailed his leading lady and her mentor off the set. "These Union deserters are attempting to rape you. If you will kindly enlighten me as to how to stage such a sequence while completely avoiding physical contact I will be most happy to do so."

"That's your problem," she snapped. "You're the director. I'm just telling you that if that creep puts his hands under my costume one more time he's the one the captain and corporal are gonna have to rescue. You hear me good, Nahfoud?"

"That's in your contract too, I suppose." The director's voice faded as the trio marched in lockstep toward the actress's trailer. "That you're not supposed to be touched?"

"I can't take this, man." Melrose Fleet was leaning against a fake boulder, incinerating a cigarette. "This was supposed to be a quick shoot. They told me Nahfoud was fast. I mean, I know there's a lot of action." He saw Carter standing nearby, gestured to him.

"Those lines, man; nobody can say lines like those with a straight face today. On top of that we gotta deal with that crazy bitch and her fruitcake guru mumbling mantras while the rest of us are trying to rehearse." He flicked the cigarette butt aside, reached into his pocket, and extracted a vial.

"You want some Seconal, man?"

Carter shook his head, smiled noncommittally. Fleet nodded, popped a couple of the pills, and slipped the bottle back in his pants.

"I don't have to take this. Contract or no contract. I got a *Tony*, man. I've done Shakespeare."

Carter came over to put a hand on the other man's shoulder. "This isn't *Othello*, Mel. It's just a job."

"Yeah, I know, I know." Fleet removed his Union cap. "I know I shouldn't let it get to me. I know there's times everyone's got to be the professional regardless of personal feelings. But dammit, sometimes you gotta take a stand."

"It's just one scene," said Carter soothingly.

"It's always 'just one scene,' man," his colleague muttered. "Always just one more scene. I know it seems like I'm making a lot of noise over nothing. But you walk into a theater full of brothers and sisters and that's your face up there twenty feet wide in the dark and those words are coming out of *your* mouth, you're the one who's gotta listen to the comments afterward." He stared at Carter.

"You don't have to go through that, man. You'll never have to go through that. Look at you: big, blond, good-looking. You got a great voice, muscles, the women are fallin' all over themselves to get next to you. You can say anything you want and you'll never come off stupid."

"Maybe not," Carter replied, "but that doesn't mean there aren't plenty of times when I don't *feel* stupid."

Fleet's gaze narrowed. "I can't figure you, man. I can't figure you at all." He gestured at the outdoor set behind them. "You just walk through this like it's nothing."

"It's my profession," Carter said softly.

"That's not what I mean. You got everything, jack, but I've been watching you. You got it all and you don't seem happy. Not as happy as me, not as happy as that dumb broad with the measurements bigger than her IQ. What's with you, anyway? What're you after?"

"I'm just trying to practice my craft," Carter told him.

"Yeah, well, maybe you're right. Maybe I'm over-reacting. But sometimes you gotta overreact to get anything changed in this business. You gotta take a position."

Carter was nodding understandingly. "Sure you do. Everyone does. But you have to pick your stands carefully if you want results, and I'm not sure that this piece of carefully crafted commercial tripe is one of the right places to do it."

"Hey, whose side are you on, anyway? Mine or Nahfoud's?" Fleet nodded in the direction of the actress's trailer.

"Yours. I'm just saying that based on what I've seen of this production so far, you're not going to change anything here." He hesitated. "You know, I'd give my right arm to play in *Othello*."

"Yeah? Well, why don't you, man?"

"Nobody'll cast me. Look at me. Do you see me as Iago? It's the way I am. My face doesn't have enough 'character.' Not dirty enough. I auditioned for Shakespeare in the Park once. *Julius Caesar*. I thought they might give me a shot at Brutus.

"Know what they wanted me to play? One of the guards. They wanted to stick me in a leather bikini and armor and have me carry a spear. I had one line.

"That's why I'm in this epic. I've got the lead. I get to act, even if the words aren't by Hecht or Mankiewicz."

"Yeah, well. One line of Shakespeare versus the lead in this, I ain't sure which is better."

"I don't have any choice," Carter replied. "This is the only kind of part I can get. You at least have a choice. They hired you for your acting ability, because of that Tony." He inhaled sharply.

"Look. I'll talk to Nahfoud after he's finished with Amanda and he's settled down some. Maybe we can try something a little different."

"Oh, yeah. Like what?"

"Sound effects. Maybe we can blur some of the lines that are bothering you. Or speed the whole interchange up. You know . . . overlapping dialogue. I'll discuss it with Amanda."

"That crazy bitch? Shit, ever since she made the break from porno films she thinks she's some kind of cross between Stanwyck and Monroe. That chick is *spacey*, man."

"Maybe Nahfoud's right," said Carter. "Not only do you want to be the writer, you want to do the casting too."

Fleet started to snap off a reply, then caught himself. A sly grin started to spread across his face. "You know, Carter, you're all right. A little slow, maybe, but all right."

"She's got the best pout in the business," Carter told him. "You have to admit that much."

"Good thing, too. It's her only expression. That and total confusion."

"We have to work with her, Mel, just like we have to work with the script. Remember, the producer's nephew is the screenwriter. I'll talk to Nahfoud. I don't think this picture will hurt your career."

"We're not talking about my career, jack. We're talking pride. We're talking about my dignity as a human being."

"If pride and dignity are important to you, you ought to get out of the movie business."

"Yeah, right." Fleet chuckled softly. "Okay, man, you got a deal. You talk to Nahfoud. And if you can't do anything, hell, I don't want to get you into trouble, or hold this up any more than I have to. The sooner it's a wrap, the sooner I can get out of here. But I got my pride, man."

"There's a time for pride and a time for professionalism. Think about it."

"I will, man. You take it easy. I'm gonna get me a sandwich." Technicians and gofers gave Fleet a wide berth as he headed for the catering truck.

Carter found himself alone on the set. Behind him, workers were reinstalling the shed's breakaway wall. The long continuous sequence had been a complicated one to stage and shoot, but most of it could be salvaged since Fleet's outburst had come near the end.

His promise to his fellow actor had not been an empty one. He would talk to Nahfoud, though he didn't expect to make much headway with the director. Probably Nahfoud would reshoot the ending with Fleet's stunt double, then dub in the requisite lines later. That didn't bother Carter. By then his own involvement with the picture would be over.

He considered what to do next. If they were on a studio lot Nahfoud would probably call a break to allow everyone to cool off, but they were on location. Too expensive to call a halt. The next scene involved a tender reunion between the captain and his beloved. Given Amanda's current state of mind Carter was certain he had an afternoon full of traumatic retakes ahead of him.

As he started for the caterer he found himself beginning to shiver. The long, complicated Steady-

cam shot had exhausted him and he was still
sweating heavily. The local TV weatherman had
predicted the onset of a chilly fall for central Georgia.
As a freshening breeze cooled his face Carter could
well believe it.

He'd gone halfway when an insistent voice interrupted his reverie.

"Mr. Carter, Mr. Carter!"

Not now, he thought tiredly. Turning, he saw the
diminutive form of Trang Ho hurrying toward him.
She held her microcassette recorder out in front of
her, much as the fictional Union captain had carried
his saber. A saber, of course, was far less lethal.
He had long since come to the conclusion that the
recorder was not a separate instrument but was in
fact a small rectangular appendage of the woman's
body. Swollen and black, it protruded threateningly
from her right hand.

The tabloids she sold her stories to were invariably
not worth the trees slain to print them. Indeed, he
often wondered why they bothered with reporters
at all, since their tales were invariably based on
unauthorized photographs, pure hearsay, and innu-
endo. An actor ignored them at his peril. To do so
meant inviting a front-page story along the lines of,
"Jason Carter . . . Antisocial Star Despises Fellow
Actors! Worst Film in Cinematic History, Carter
Implies!"

You couldn't win with such people, he knew. If
you told them the truth they misquoted you; if you
told lies they printed them as the truth; and if you
said nothing at all they invented something twice
as horrible to fill the void. Privately he wondered
if the North Vietnamese still operated any of their

infamous "reeducation camps," and if they might accept someone like Trang Ho on scholarship. He knew many colleagues who would be eager to contribute to such a fund.

She caught up with him as he was filling a plastic tumbler with iced tea from the large canister marked "Sweetened."

"I hear there was some trouble on the set." Her recorder quivered beneath his lips like some exotic African parasite seeking a path to its host's innards. Her eyes were agleam. She smelled conflict, Carter knew, the way a sheepdog could smell a dead lamb half a mile away.

"Nothing happened," he muttered.

"That's not the way I heard it, Jason. I heard there was a real blowup."

"Sorry. Nobody died."

She didn't look disappointed. There were plenty of deaths in Georgia she could somehow work into a story.

"I hear that Melrose Fleet stormed off the set and refused to finish his scene."

Carter sipped tea. "It's been a tough shoot. Mel got a little tired, that's all."

He needed for this picture to end. Maybe the next one would be better, he told himself. If he kept calm and did his job, kept throwing himself wholeheartedly into crap like this, he might finally be offered something worthwhile. A role where he'd be given the chance to act instead of pose, to do something more significant than reveal his chest and declaim heroically while flashing his famous smile.

He could always black out his teeth. Envisioning Nahfoud's reaction to that made him grin.

"Something funny?" Trang Ho inquired hopefully.

"Nothing you can use." He glanced down at her. Her elfin face and stature gave her the appearance of a harmless waif, but the nonthreatening image was deceptive. Speak softly and carry a big tape recorder, he mused.

"I can use *anything*. Come on, Jason," she prodded him. "Give me something I can use. I'll be good to you. When they print the pictures I'll make sure they only show your best side."

I don't have a best side, he thought. *I don't have a bad side, either*. That's what all the cinematographers kept telling him. He wished fervently they'd quit photographing him like he was a refugee from Mount Rushmore.

"Give me a break, Trang. I've never done anything to you. I'm trying to build a career as a serious actor."

"Serious actor?" She almost but fortunately for her did not giggle. "I know your credits by heart, Carter. *The Toxic Waste Monster. Crack Slashers of Manhattan.* And what was that Academy Award winner you did last year in Italy? *Hercules Meets Jesse James* or something?"

Carter counted slowly to five. "The British don't have this problem. An actor can do Lear one week and pratfalls on *The Simples* the next. The important thing is to work."

"Sure. Listen, Carter, you help me and I help you. I'm just trying to get some ink. I get paid by the column inch and page." She looked across to the trailer which housed the film's leading lady. "Personally I consider this opus to be a step up in your career." Her voice fell to a conspiratorial murmur. "Now, if you could just give me something really interesting, something of serious import for our readers."

"Something juicy?" said Carter.

She was practically salivating. "Yeah."

"Something like, 'Jason Carter Fathers Amanda Peters's Two-headed Baby'?"

She didn't blink. "That would fly," she deadpanned. "But since I haven't seen any evidence of babies on this set, two-headed or otherwise, I'd settle for a clue to whom she's sleeping with." Black and claw-like, the recorder hovered below his chin.

"Not Nahfoud . . . she hates his guts. You? I know she's got the hots for you, Carter. Every woman in the crew has the hots for you."

"Well, I don't have the hots for anybody," he shot back. "I'm just trying to do my job."

Her eyes widened hopefully. "Fleet? Or the guy playing the big rapist, maybe?"

"I don't know whom she's sleeping with," Carter said tiredly, "and I don't care."

Mercifully the lamprey-like mouth of the recorder retreated. "And if you did you wouldn't tell me, I know. Or would you? God knows this picture could use some PR."

Carter eyed her wonderingly. "Is this what your parents became boat people for? Is this why they fled a tormenting and corrupt regime?"

"No. They did it so they could come to the land of the free and the home of the brave. So they could raise three kids on tacos and apple pie and burgers. So their daughter could graduate cum laude from UC Irvine with a degree in journalism.

"But since the editor's chair at the *New York Times* seems to be occupied right now and *The Econ-*

omist isn't hiring any overseas-based L.A. interns, this is the best their daughter can do. And you know what? I make less than the editor of the *New York Times* but a lot more than *The Economist*'s overseas interns. And I get to meet people who are much more interesting."

His felt a flicker of concern. "You think I'm interesting?"

"Not particularly. But you're about the prettiest thing I've ever seen."

"God but I'm sick of that. I want people to see me as an *actor*."

She stepped back and looked him up and down. "Well, I suppose that's not impossible. Being biond, six four, and gorgeous shouldn't be an insurmountable handicap. We all have our crosses to bear. Mine's a deadline, yours is your appearance. You do realize somewhere behind those deep blue eyes of yours that there are misguided people in this world who would not object to trading places with you?"

"I know, I know. But whether you believe me or not I'd rather not look like this."

"Not even for one hundred fifty thou per picture? You can always go do Ibsen at the local Y."

"I have," he told her.

"Sure, and twenty people came to see it. Keep plugging away, Carter. You're not such a bad guy, even if you are closemouthed. So I don't think I'll do a number on you just yet. Right now I'm more interested in Peters's mattress wars. We have a lot in common, you and I."

"We have nothing in common," Carter told her.

"No? You get the leads in the B-minus pictures, and I get to cover the stars of the B-minus pictures.

We're both working our way up. Down the coast
they're doing that space shuttle hijack picture
with Scheider and Kostner. You think I could
get assigned to that? No such luck."

"If you didn't have the morals of a cobra and the
literary aspirations of a turnip I might get to like you
a little, Ho."

"Don't," she warned him. "It's dangerous. You're
too sensitive to like me. Although if you changed
your mind about being a source I could do wonders
for your career."

"I'll handle my career just fine, thank you."

"Sure you will. What's that next picture your agency has you lined up for?" She frowned theatrically.
"Something with you and three bimbos down
in Brazil where you all lose your money, your
inhibitions, and your clothes while drifting down
some obscure tributary of the Amazon on a reject
riverboat from *The African Queen*?"

He turned away. "I haven't agreed to do that."

"Bullshit. Your agent's verbally committed you."

He whirled on her. "How do you find these things
out?"

"Hey, it's my job." She pocketed her recorder.
"Think about it, Carter. You give me something
and I'll see you get some good space. If not," and
she was grinning as she strolled away, "I'll just have
to make do with the best I can."

Carter followed her with his eyes. Her petite Asian
shape was quite attractive. But when considering
poisonous creatures one always had to keep in mind
the general rule that the smaller they were, the more
toxic.

The crew did their best to ignore the muffled

shouts emanating from the vicinity of Peters's trailer, indication that Nahfoud's ongoing conversation
with his leading lady was proceeding in a manner
less than smooth.

He was abruptly aware that people were pointing at him. A cluster of tourists, well dressed and
privileged, was visiting the set. He smiled back automatically, provoking disparate responses from the
women in the group. It was so easy for him, a talent
he'd discovered and grown bored with in his teens.

He drank his tea and like a good team player
let them snap pictures until their guide, someone
from the film's PR team, urged them along. Then
he headed for his own trailer.

It was not as big as Peters's. That was specified
in the contracts, along with everything else down
to how many oxygen molecules per day were to
be allotted to each performer. He didn't care. He
would've been happy to sleep in a tent in the Georgia
woods.

Something shiny in the grass caught his attention.
At first he thought it might be a piece of jewelry, but
when he knelt he saw it was a metal disc two inches
in diameter. As he picked it up the afternoon light
cued a rainbow on its surface.

He wiped dirt from both sides. It didn't look bent
or otherwise damaged. Interestingly enough, there
was no label.

A quick look around showed no one nearby examining the ground for lost property or asking anxious questions of the crew. As he continued toward
his trailer he showed the disc to everyone he encountered. No one admitted to having lost anything
like it, nor did they know anyone who had.

Gathering clouds had begun to shed afternoon rain
by the time he reached his home away from home.
A low rumble reverberated through the damp air,
though whether it came from overhead or from the
direction of Peters's abode he couldn't say. It might
well have been Nahfoud: even if he managed to
mollify his leading lady there would be no more
shooting today. The light was gone.

Carter was glad of the respite. He could relax and
read. The rain on the roof was imitating a snare drum
on uppers as he carefully put the unlabeled compact
disc on the kitchenette table and went to ferret out
a magazine.

II ─────────

O'LAL had been aware of the disturbance for some time. It was subtle in character, unmistakable in nature. Something was very wrong with The Way Things Were. The shift in the plenal equilibrium was sufficient to alarm her, though it was premature to consider alerting any Others. Not that anyone could be spared to assist her anyway. The Monitors were spread too thin as it was, and this world was her responsibility.

The exquisite delicacy of the disturbance suggested that whoever was responsible was aware of the serious nature of the interference they were causing. As presently constituted it was impossible for her to trace it without revealing herself, and that of course she could not do. Not without damaging the course of social evolution on the very world whose development she was charged with safeguarding. Over the centuries she had grown very protective of her simple charges.

Now someone was trying to make trouble.

No reason yet for serious concern. The interference was still little more than a tremulous suggestion of unease sliding across her field of perception. Its source might be wholly natural in nature, distorted by some causational trick of mutaphysical mimicry. No need to panic.

21

But when it did not vanish and continued to perpetuate itself on her consciousness she began to believe that another Shihararaneth was responsible. It had the distinctive thrust of the Kind. Yet all of the Shihararaneth in this Quadrant were accounted for. So her instincts must necessarily be playing her false.

Only, she didn't think so.

One of the primitive Kind sauntered across her physical plane of perception. Non-Shihar, it resembled her closely. It paused to consider her, able to utilize only a tiny fraction of that great range of cognizance which characterized the mature Shihararaneth. The root Kind of this world were still evolving, still maturing. They had a long ways to travel before approaching the level of the Monitors.

Though beginning to properly comprehend their surroundings and their environment, their first hesitant explorations of the spacetime continuum still exceeded their capacity for deductive cognition. Mastery of both was required to qualify for true sentience.

They were still restricted to those places where matter had concentrated itself sufficiently to generate retentive gravitation, unlike the Shihararaneth, who could travel through progressively less organized reality with ease.

Such jumps remained beyond the ability of the primitive locals. Occasionally, haltingly, one of them would stumble clumsily between the planes of existence and emerge safely elsewhere without knowledge of how it had accomplished the mature feat of transposition. They invariably survived such accidents of maturity undamaged but confused.

So she was not surprised when the male confronting her made an inquisitive noise and started to approach. His eyes were intent on hers: the true Shihar stare, she was pleased to note, though devoid of adequate accompanying intelligence. She gazed back appraisingly.

He was a handsome specimen, lean and muscular. A pity she was not one of those who enjoyed dallying with primitives. Its attitude signaled a confused mix of hostility, curiosity, and lust, a not uncommon combination among undeveloped elemental Kind.

When it was very close she tensed, chose her angle of departure carefully, and jumped. She passed above and beyond, vanishing into the open place the primitive could sense but not enter. She felt the curved plane she'd chosen slip glutinously beneath her, the one above brush lightly at her head. Up and down had no meaning during the jump, directions having become momentarily as irrelevant as gravity.

Greatly puzzled, the immature Kind blinked and looked around wildly for the one he'd been stalking. There was no sign of her. O'lal had jumped from one reality nexus to another by means of a gap in real space. For a mature Shihar such dissimilarities were easy to negotiate.

She emerged near in time but quite a distance away in space, landing neatly on her feet in another city on the other side of the world. This time no one saw her, though on several occasions she had been observed. It did not matter. Unequipped to correctly interpret her means of locomotion, the primitives of this world satisfied themselves with comforting rationalizations. Besides, the elemental Kind they shared this world with occasionally made similar if undirected voyages. So O'lal's arrival provoked no comment.

More than ever, she was convinced that the persistent disturbance was the product of a fully mature Shihar. It clung to the fringes of her consciousness, refusing to go away. She'd been feeling it now for years. Each time she had tried to pursue, it had fled, its echoes dissipating untraceably in the pockets of emptiness that occupied the plenum between ordinary mass, mocking her attempts to carry out her monitoring functions. She was persistent and dedicated, but not even the most experienced Monitor could capture a taunt.

Nor could she expend very much energy tracking disquieting phantoms. Too many other tasks made demands on her time and talents. There were the immature Shihar of this world to nurture, and the promising Others to guide and cajole toward civilization. Yet the disturbance never left her entirely, and occasional widely spaced reminders of its presence served to keep her alert for any chance to pounce.

Somewhere an unregistered Shihar was biding its time, planning disruption, intending inimical influence. It was her task to ensure that did not take place while simultaneously preserving her anonymity.

So much work to be done, so many seemingly inconsequential yet vital details to attend to. Endless was the task of Monitor, yet also endlessly rewarding. Not one but two species benefited from her untiring attention: the domestic immature Kind, and the Others. The rewards of monitoring lay in watching her charges progress.

She had no intention of seeing her hard-won accomplishments jeopardized by some unregistered, mischievous Renegade.

Somewhere there must be a god, Jason thought, who looks after fools, idiots, and suicidal film directors. Not only did the cloud cover break and the rain stop falling, so did most of the crap.

After a lengthy conversation with his agent, a gentleman of no taste and impeccable credentials within the field who expounded tersely to his client on the virtues of working in any capacity as opposed to not working at all, Melrose Fleet returned to the set to deliver the remainder of his lines with a subservient aplomb that left even jaded crew members applauding.

Amanda Peters (nee Ethel Berkowitz of Tope, Oklahoma) executed her final scenes with vigor and style, managing to appear at once distraught waif, noble southern belle, and period costume nymphomaniac. The fact that her three erstwhile attackers concluded their parts with their parts more the worse for wear than hers constituted a kind of poetic justice, not to mention license. Once the director had been assured by his sound man that her occasional out-of-character four-letter outbursts could be easily edited out of the live track, he pronounced himself delighted.

As for the lingering clouds, they provided the kind of diffuse dramatic lighting the best matte artists could not have surpassed. Only after the final covering shots were in the can did the rain return, in the form of a deluge heavy enough to have extinguished the real burning of Atlanta had it fallen a hundred and some years earlier.

Carter made his way through the rain toward the wardrobe trailer. Inside, he slipped behind a privacy screen and began removing his costume. Along with those which had garbed the rest of the cast it would be carefully packed and returned to Los Angeles, preserved and numbered in case reshooting or sequels were required.

After dressing in jeans, sweatshirt, and sneakers, he stepped out and passed the Union uniform one piece at a time to the diminutive woman waiting behind a narrow counter. She chatted as she checked each piece against the readout on her laptop.

"Bet y'all are glad this shoot is over." Her consonants twanged against her palate as if someone were using the letters for guitar picks. Texas, Carter thought. He'd never asked her but the accent was pretty easy to slot.

He shrugged. "The usual disagreements over artistic interpretation."

She let out a derisive snort. "Artistic copulation, you mean. But you stayed clear of what was flyin', didn't you? That's the best thing you got goin' for you in this business, cuddles. Not your looks, not your voice. You got equilibrium. Always say that no matter what his profession, a body's got to maintain its equilibrium." She tucked his officer's hat into a plastic bag that had his name scrawled on it.

"Gonna keep everybody around for another week, I hear. Try and get some close-ups and two-shots with backgrounds, make the editors happy. Then we're outta here." She smiled up at him. She was in her fifties, he suspected. Country-pretty, not Hollywood. Marjorie Ashwood was part flirt, part grandma, all professional. She could whip up a new costume on the computer laser cutter in the back of the trailer faster than most seamstresses could alter a hem.

His reciprocal smile turned to a wince when she added, "Goin' to do a pic in South America, I hear."

"Possibly," he mumbled.

"Some kind of river epic?"

"I'd rather not discuss it. It's still in the talking stage."

"You don't have to explain." She was buttoning the officer's jacket she'd hung on a plastic hanger. "This is ol' Marj you're talking to, remember?" When the jacket was ready she pushed a button that revolved the wardrobe rack, hung the jacket alongside its identical twins. The rack was crammed full. Period pictures demanded extensive wardrobes and experienced wardrobe masters to look after them.

As she clipped the pants to a second hanger something slipped from a front pocket. Catching it before it hit the floor, she held it up to the light.

"What's this?"

"Oh, I forgot about that." He pulled his rain poncho from his carry pack. "Found it in the grass today. Asked around but nobody claimed it." He looked thoughtful. "There were a bunch of gawkers around earlier. Some studio flunky was escorting them. Maybe one of them lost it. There's no label."

"I can see that." Light refracted from the argent slice as she turned it over in her fingers. "This size, it's probably a storage disc. Funny there's no label. Maybe it peeled off." Her eyebrows lifted. "Want to see what's on it?"

Her eyes were blue but paler than his. "That's private property. I don't know if we should do that."

"Hell, it's probably a bootleg copy of some con-

cert. Illegal on the face of it. We might find some
identification. Then you could have the pleasure of
returning it to its rightful owner."

"Why me?"

"Because it wouldn't mean anything coming from
me. You, on the other hand, might make a lifelong
fan." She turned and sat down at her tiny work-
station. "Here, let's see."

The laptop whined as she powered it up and slid
the disc into the two-inch slot. A couple of keys got
her out of her cadcam costume program and into a
search utility. Carter waited patiently.

"That oriental gal was in earlier looking for you."
Ashwood spoke as she teased keys. "The reporter?"

"Trang Ho. The term 'reporter' doesn't apply to
her. She's a professional snoop."

"That a fact? I'd almost think she had a thing for
you."

"She's like that with everybody. Not that she
wouldn't sleep with me, but it'd be to get a story,
not sex."

"I know the type. She gets her orgasms from
gossip." The comment did not surprise Carter.
Despite her grandmotherly attributes, Ashwood had
an earthy sense of humor. And she'd worked in film
for thirty years.

"She tried pumping me a few times, too."

"You didn't give her any material?"

"Me?" Ashwood glanced up at him. "I got a pen-
sion comin' someday soon, good-lookin'. I'm not
about to jeopardize that by whisperin' rumors somebody might trace back to me." She leaned toward
the screen, squinting over her half-bifocals. "This is
interestin'."

"What?" He tried to see around her.

"Come look for yourself."

He raised the divider and peered over her shoulder, frowning. "You know I don't know anything about computers, Marjorie. I'm not one of these actors who want to direct, produce, light the set, and run the camera. I'm about as technically oriented as a geranium. I don't see anything."

"That's because there's nothin' to see. The contents of this disc are protected. System's too elaborate for this to be a cheap bootleg copy of a concert. What we got here is some serious information storage." She fiddled with the keys. Words and images flashed across the screen.

"What are you doing?"

"Just hackin' around. Ah, here we go. The codes ain't real complicated. Just enough to discourage the casual prober. I never was the casual type."

"Isn't this invasion of privacy or something?" Carter was uneasy.

"Naw. If this was major stuff, government or internat, I wouldn't have been able to get in so easy. Not with a commercial search program. See?" She pointed triumphantly. "Owner's name and address. We done a good thing, good-lookin'. Says there's a reward for safe return, too." Her fingers hovered above the keyboard. "Now let's see what he's so anxious to have back."

Carter put a hand on her shoulder. "We don't have to do that, Marjorie. It might be personal. Family records, tax information . . . We don't know."

"Aren't you even a little curious?"

"Not really."

"Reward's a thousand bucks." She tapped the

screen. "It's a Georgia address. Can't be that far. I don't know where Brunswick is but we can find it on a map. Why don't you come with me? I'll split the reward with you."

"I don't need the money, Marjorie." He smiled down at her. The offer to share indicated just how unaffected by Hollywood Marjorie Ashwood was.

"I won't force it on you, but I'd enjoy your company. We can split the driving, if not the reward. C'mon, cuddles. I can hang out the window and pretend you're my gigolo. You can spare an old gal some time. Tomorrow's Saturday. No work 'til Monday no matter what our phay-roh decides."

"Nahfoud said something about looking at rushes," Carter replied lamely.

Ashwood made a rude noise. "Uh-huh. And the first thing he's gonna do is ask the *actors* for their opinions. Get real, good-lookin'."

Carter considered. His instinctive first thought was that despite the difference in their ages she might be looking for an opportunity to put the make on him now that their professional relationship was about to end. He decided that wasn't the case. If that was what Marjorie Ashwood wanted, she would've put the question to him directly, and before now.

"Let's find out where this place is first," he said.

"You got it, gorgeous."

She returned the laptop to the main menu, withdrew the disc, and pulled up a resident atlas. By zip code, it placed the address on the disc on the south Georgia coast.

"Pretty good drive," he commented. "Any farther south and you'd be in Florida."

"Okay by me. I've always wanted to see more

of the South. Never worked this part of the country before." She favored him with another of her maternal, impish grins. "I'm not as widely traveled as some folks."

"Very funny. I don't pick the locations of the pictures I make."

"Then you'll come along? We will make an interestin' couple. Unsettle the natives."

It would be nice to get away from the intense atmosphere that surrounded the production, he thought. See some new country, meet some new people. The Teamsters he usually hung out with probably had plans of their own for the weekend. And he'd heard that the Georgia coast was real pretty.

"Why not?" He buttoned up his poncho. "I'll rent a car."

"I'll let you," she said agreeably.

III _____

THEY clung to 95 all the way to the coast, picking up Interstate 16 just north of Savannah. From there it was a straight shot southward.

Much of the town of Brunswick was obscured by dense forest which was a never-ending source of wonder to a visitor from Southern California. Piney woods dominated the terrain in every direction except east, where tidal flats and rush-choked waterways separated the coast from a verdant necklace of barrier islands.

The address led them to a cluster of private postal boxes. Only Ashwood's insistence and Carter's wheedling succeeded in prying the location of the owner's actual residence from the reluctant but slightly awed franchise operator.

"Can't get a reward from a post office box," Ashwood pointed out.

The disc's owner lived not on the mainland but on nearby Sea Island, which was itself a suburb of Saint Simon Island. Directions sent them across a busy causeway, through housing developments and compact shopping centers, across a second much smaller causeway, until they eventually found themselves driving down an unexpectedly beautiful avenue lined with enormous live oaks.

Spanish moss dripped atmospherically from the vaulting branches. Stunted streets named for local flowers, birds, and animals ran perpendicular toward the mainland or Atlantic Ocean. The houses themselves consisted of everything from fifties ranch-style homes to rambling Castilian mansions and concrete bastions ajut with Bauhaus flourishes.

Robin Lane contained only four homes. The last, of brick and glass, faced the surf. Vehicular approach to the house was barred by a gray wrought-iron gate. From what little he knew of such matters, Carter thought the house architecturally unimaginative and pedestrian in execution.

"Not a bad place," he commented, damning it with faint praise.

Ashwood let out a grunt. "Be the caretaker's shack in Beverly Hills. I reckon it's what passes for fancy around here."

An intercom was mounted on the pillar immediately to the right of the gate. Ashwood rolled down her window, leaned out, and addressed the pickup. Following a brief delay a male voice replied.

"Who is it?" The voice was richly nasal, with a drawl than hinted strongly of New England rather than southern origins, Carter decided.

"My name's Ashwood. Got a friend with me. Were y'all by any chance floatin' around the Macon area the other day?"

Another pause, then, "Who are you people, and what do you want? I'm a . . ."

" . . . very busy man," Ashwood finished for him. "I know, you men are always 'very busy.' Just answer one question for us. Did you visit a movie set and lose something?"

No pause this time. "You found my property?"

"What kind of property?"

"A small storage CD," the voice replied impatiently. "Obviously you found it, or you would not have been able to find me. Just a moment."

The disembodied twang was replaced by the whirr of a hidden motor as the heavy gate was drawn aside.

"Park by the main door, please. I will meet you there."

"Not so fast," said Ashwood. "How do we know y'all are the owner and not just somebody house-sittin'? Are you," she hesitated briefly, remembering, "Bruton Fewick?"

"*Fee*-wick," the voice snapped. "Not Few-ick. I am."

As Carter drove up, Fewick came lumbering lightly down the front steps, moving with unusual grace for someone with the build of a resurrected zeppelin. He had wavy blond hair, hazel eyes, and the look and demeanor of a demented baby. He was also much younger than Carter expected, thirty at most.

"I am very grateful to you." Definitely New England, Carter thought. As an actor he picked up on accents right away. "I have been working with the material on that disc for some time and, silly me, neglected to back up everything." He turned. "Please, come inside."

Must be valuable, Ashwood told herself, *for him to have been carryin' it around with him*. To Carter she added in a whisper, "Maybe we can get two thousand out of him."

"Marjorie." Carter shook his head disapprovingly.

He expected servants, but there were no other signs of life as Fewick led them through the house and into a combination library-study.

"Stupid of me," their host was saying, "keeping that on my person."

"Yeah, it was." Ashwood feigned interest in the crowded bookshelves that lined the walls.

"You must know something of how RW-CDs function because you got in deep enough to unearth my name and address."

"I work with optical storage myself," she told him. *He looks like a surfing snowman*, she thought. *Only pink instead of white.* All he needed was black eyes instead of brown and a carrot sticking out of his mouth. Instead of waddling when he walked, as she would have expected, he covered ground with a sort of athletic mince.

Unlike his companion, Carter found the room fascinating. The only time he'd ever seen more books in a private residence was in the mansion of a major producer who'd been considering him for a role. Every book there had looked brand-new, probably because not one of them had been touched by human hands since they'd left the bindery. In contrast Fewick's all looked thoroughly perused, unevenly packed on their shelves, sometimes stacked in horizontal haste instead of having being returned to their proper niches.

A huge antique desk dominated one corner of the room near a window that overlooked sand and salt grass. Gilt decorated its clawed feet and edges. Two other tables stood nearby. The top of one was inclined forty-five degrees and displayed sheets of paper. It was illuminated from within. The other was

home to more than a dozen wide, shallow drawers of
the type one might find in the office of a professional
cartographer.

Sculptures and other arcane objects were scattered
about the room: on shelves, pedestals, the carpeted
floor. Carter found himself standing next to a
gargoylish human figure which had been boldly
hacked from black wood. Decorated with feathers
and beads, its cowrie-shell eyes seemed to follow
him around the room. He thought the fist-sized
ball of amber on the desk much more attractive,
despite the dozen or so insects entombed within.
It rested next to a small solid sterling sculpture
of a nude woman and a swan, whom the artist
had captured in the middle of an act not likely to be depicted anytime soon on the Disney
Channel.

"Lotta books," Ashwood observed. "You read 'em
all?"

"At least in part," Fewick replied pleasantly.

Carter turned from the desk. "Mind my asking
what kind of business you're in?"

Fewick beamed. "Why, the best sort of business
there is." A gargled, choking noise emerged from
his throat, which, since he was evincing no obvious signs of external distress, could be nothing
other than a laugh. "My parents are obscene-
ly wealthy. They are also painfully sophisticated, extremely intelligent, and dull as dishwater.
Which is why, as soon as I came into my inher-
itance from my grandparents, who were, if anything, even duller people, I immediately moved
out of the family manse and set myself up down
here."

"Where's home?" Ashwood asked him.

"Boston. Have you ever been to Boston, Mr. . . . ?"

"Jason Carter. I'm from Minnesota myself. About fifty miles west of Minneapolis. A town called . . ."

"How extremely interesting," Fewick said with unseemly haste. As their host smiled it struck the actor that he wasn't being intentionally rude. It was simply his manner. At least he was straightforward, which was more than could be said for the average executive producer or axe-murderer.

"If you would be so kind as to restore my property to me?"

Ashwood removed the plastic-wrapped CD from her purse and handed it over. Fewick took it delicately, holding it by the edges.

"Thank you," he told her with feeling.

"Why is it so important?" Ashwood asked him, tact being one of the few four-letter words with which she was not comfortable.

Instead of replying, Fewick went to his desk and opened a side drawer. The disc slipped into a vacant slot alongside dozens of others. The storage capacity represented by the contents of that single drawer, Carter knew, must be immense.

"There was something on there about a reward?" Ashwood said pointedly.

Fewick shut the drawer. "Oh, that's old information. I should have erased that long ago."

Her expression narrowed and she adopted a tone that startled Carter. Suddenly she didn't sound like good old Marj, the wardrobe lady.

"Old information? You handled that sucker like it was yesterday's prostate scan." Her voice softened. "Besides, would you really try to cheat an old lady?"

"Oh, very well." He sighed. "I suppose that to your way of thinking you have gone to some trouble. I will give you . . . a hundred dollars."

"The disc said a thousand."

"Two hundred, then." A large rust-colored tomcat suddenly materialized atop the desk. Carter decided it had been sleeping in the leg space beneath. It rubbed up against Fewick, who reached down to stroke its back. Half-closed Persian eyes regarded the visitors.

"This is Moe." Their host was enjoying himself, Carter saw.

"Nine hundred," said Ashwood.

"Three." Fewick continued to stroke the cat. "My best friend. Have you ever noticed how much nicer cats are than humans? I truly believe they are our only equals." He eyed the immovable Ashwood. "Unlike Moe, I do not have a lot of time to waste in play. Five hundred."

Ashwood muttered something under her breath. "All right."

Fewick had a very small mouth which all but disappeared behind bunched cheeks when he smiled. Seating himself behind the desk, he wrote out a check, then rose to hand it to Ashwood. She was watching him warily.

"How do I know you won't stop payment on this soon as we're out the door?"

Fewick clasped his hands together delightedly. "What delicious cynicism! Madam, I could easily have given you nothing. This I offer for your time and out of the goodness of my heart."

"I have this feeling that your heart is full of goo, not goodness."

Fewick pursed his incongruously small lips. "You wound me deeply."

"I 'wound you deeply'? Y'all been watchin' too many bad movies, bubbles. You need to get clear o' this mausoleum more and out into the real world."

"Marjorie!"

"It is quite all right, Mr. Carter," Fewick assured him. "My verbal affectations reflect an admiration for a world of elegance lost to time. I am inured to criticism of both my speech and appearance. That explained, you will both now do me the courtesy of departing."

"Did you have to insult him, Marjorie?" Carter slid behind the wheel of the rented car, turned the ignition.

"Nope. But it sure was fun. The cheap son of a bitch promised a thousand bucks reward. He got off on cheating us." She held up the check. "I had half a mind to wad this up and throw it back in his face. Fortunately the other half of my mind stayed in control." She dropped the check into her purse. "Hey, how about we go back through Valdosta? We got time."

"What's in Valdosta?" He turned out of the driveway and onto the main street.

"I dunno. But the name always intrigued me."

As the wrought-iron gate closed, the rotund shape standing at the second-floor window lowered the drape it had been holding aside and returned to the gilded desk. Seating himself, Bruton Fewick opened the file drawer and carefully removed the prodigal disc.

It slid easily into a slot in the side of the computer that emerged on command from within the desk.

Not until several complex passwords had been processed did the screen fill with precious information. Only when he was certain nothing had been damaged did he allow himself to relax.

He'd been utilizing the research library at the University of Georgia when an acquaintance had mentioned that there might be an open spot on a forthcoming excursion to a nearby movie set. The result of letting himself be talked into participating had been near disaster. Months of work, of reading and poring over maps, would have been lost forever if not for the resourcefulness of the simple people who had found his disc.

Now his efforts were about to enter a new stage. It was time to begin final preparations. He could have survived the loss of the disc, but it would have set him back many months, and after years of research and toil the delay would have been painful.

Soon the whole world would know his name, would stand in awe of his accomplishments. Especially his parents, who had barely condescended to speak to him ever since he'd announced his intention while a junior at college to pursue a field of endeavor outside the family business.

He stroked the big tom, listening to it purr contentedly. He had the cat to thank for that. It was Moe who had accidentally dislodged the book in his father's library which had so intrigued the studious young Bruton and changed the course of his life. Prior to that he had been at best an indifferent student. Subsequent to his change of direction he had applied himself to his studies with a vengeance.

It did not bother him that his parents disapproved. Their attitude toward their only son had always been lukewarm at best. They had raised him as one might a pedigreed dog for which they had overpaid, cozening but rarely touching, admiring formally while still regarding him with a distinct air of vague disappointment.

That would change with the fulfillment of his work. They would have no choice but to admire and recognize his achievements because their snooty society friends certainly would. He smiled down at Moe, mentally thanking the cat yet again for the providential accident which had so changed his life. Fewick had encountered the stray on campus and it had immediately attached itself to the hefty pre-law student. They'd been together ever since.

We're both outcasts, he thought. *We belong together*.

Pulling a book from the pile on his desk he began comparing its contents with notes recorded on the disc. Soon his parents would be able to ignore him no longer. They would have to admit that he'd been right all along, that they'd been wrong. His growing fame would soon eclipse their anger and disappointment.

Even his haughty, supercilious father would be forced to confess that having a famous archaeologist in the family might not be such a bad thing after all.

The Renegade was reasonably content. While another creature might have reacted ebulliently now that plans long in the making were nearing fruition, he remained restrained. His sense of time was very different from that of the ordinary sentient.

Not that he wasn't enjoying the game. In the end, it was all that made existence worthwhile. If not for it, he surely would have expired long ago of inconceivable ennui.

Events were progressing according to plan despite the presence of the Monitor. Her futile attempts to locate him and put a stop to his activities only added to his enjoyment. Nothing was going to interfere with his little amusement. Boredom could be allayed only by the introduction of unexpected anomalies into the developmental scheme, and if millions died as a result, well, it promised some real excitement at last. He looked forward eagerly to the culmination of his gambit.

Slip-sliding boredly through the planes of existence had led him to stumble on this unique opportunity to unhinge normality. He had immediately grasped the dynamic possibilities. Only recently had the local Monitor even begun to sense his presence. Her subsequent attempts to confront him were a continuing source of amusement.

He had been patient and would continue to be so. Of course, there was always the possibility of local interference, but he was confident he could cope with that without revealing himself. The local sentients were entertaining but not very perceptive. They no more suspected his existence than they did that of the Monitor. Their tendency to spend so much of their time looking inward was one of the things that made them so much fun to play with.

Nothing would stop him. He had committed too much time, too much effort, to allow that to happen. The key to local destabilization was a gift from a sardonic cosmos, one that he intended to put to optimal use.

If developed to its utmost it might even provide him with a power base with which to challenge stabilities elsewhere. That would truly complicate the work of the Monitors. A pity none of the other Shihararaneth shared his passion for chaos and disruption. He found their obsession with ordered progress and evolution sickening. It was up to him alone to do something about it.

Even if it did mean having to start small.

IV⸺

THE pat on his backside didn't startle Carter. Years in the business had resigned him to uninvited contact. But the identity of the perpetrator did surprise him.

Marjorie Ashwood was grinning up at him, a drink clutched loosely in one hand. Not the cheap champagne the producers had magnanimously provided for the wrap party, but hard liquor the hue of burnt acorns. She was happy, not drunk.

"Hi, good-lookin'."

"Hello, Marjorie."

She gave him a conspiratorial wink. "*I* gotta secret. Wanna know my secret?"

"I don't know, Marj." He replied carefully, wondering what she was getting at. If she'd been any younger he'd have known automatically, but that conclusion didn't fit the maternal if testy image he'd formed of the wardrobe mistress.

"Hey!" The complaint reached him above the din of the party.

He looked back at his companion of the moment, an actress who'd played one of the picture's numerous accessory southern belles. Watery champagne notwithstanding, she was far more tipsy than Ashwood. Beautiful blue eyes, severely glazed, stared back at him. She was swaying on her feet,

45

and not for emphasis. Her body didn't need any extra emphasis.

He regarded her tolerantly. In addition to the champagne, she'd been indulging in some controlled substance of unknown potential. Her current equilibrium was about as stable as her speech.

"Get rid of the old bag, Jase, and let's go." Her speech was heavily slurred. She reached out to grab his hand.

He pulled away. "Not now, Kimmie."

She frowned at him. "Don' tell me you'd rather be with that . . ."

"I don't want to be with anyone," he said sharply. "I'm really tired and I've got to catch a plane tomorrow."

She gave it one last try. "You can sleep on the plane. You don't wanna sleep here. This is partytime."

"I'm kind of partied out, Kimmie." He smiled apologetically and walked away from her. Her frustrated muttering was quickly swallowed by the noise of the crowd.

Ashwood was there to intercept him on the far side of the hall, away from the open bar.

"Thanks for rescuing me," he told her.

She sipped at her glass as she observed the milling crowd of crew and performers. "Most guys your age would think of it as interference, not a rescue."

"I know, but I get so damned tired of women looking at me like that."

"Awww. Poor boy." She patted him on the cheek, having to stand on tiptoes to reach his face. "Life's such a trial for you."

"You don't have to patronize me," he grumbled. "I didn't say I didn't like who I was, just that that sort of thing gets old when you have to deal with it day after day."

"Still want to see my secret?"

"Oh, all right. What's your secret, Marjorie?"

"Y'all have to come out to the trailer."

"Whoa. I just got through thanking you for rescuing me from one situation."

"It's nothin' like that, handsome. Not that I'd be averse, mind. You really are a beautiful young man. But I promise that's not what I've got in mind."

He dismissed the party. "Why not? This was old before it got started."

They exited the hall and found themselves in the courtyard of the rambling suburban motel in which cast and crew had been housed. He followed Ashwood along a concrete walkway, past the pool, and up one flight of stairs. While his guide fumbled with her room key he wondered if she was being straight with him. He looked worriedly in both directions, wondering where Trang Ho was. This kind of publicity he didn't need.

The room had been cleaned earlier. Two fully packed large suitcases lay open on the bed. Piled on the small dinette-style table were several boxes and the wardrobe mistress's laptop. She sat down and turned it on.

As she worked, words appeared and scrolled up the screen. They were accompanied by drawings and maps.

"There it is," she told him. "This is my secret."

"You're going too fast for me to read anything."

She looked up at him. "Remember the disc we returned last week?" He nodded. "When some sucker offers a reward for the return of information, wouldn't you be curious to know what it consisted of?"

He should've guessed. "Marjorie . . . you didn't copy his disc?"

"Just as a precaution. Don't look at me like that, gorgeous. I could've kept the original. And don't tell me you ain't interested."

"I'm not." He moved to leave.

"Well, since you ask," she said slyly, "taken as a whole, I think it's some kinda treasure map."

He halted, turned. "You've been using my rejected scripts for reading material."

"Are you sayin' there's no such thing as treasure?"

"What kind of treasure?"

She looked back at the screen. "Well, it don't exactly *say* that there's a treasure. But it hints, and gives directions." She smiled brightly. "And I'm gonna go find it."

He gaped at her. "What about your work?"

"The next picture I'm contracted for don't start principal photography for six months yet. I'll just tell my people not to sign me up for anything interim. I was plannin' on taking a little vacation anyways."

He couldn't keep from asking, "Where's this treasure supposed to be, anyway? Off the coast here?" Like anyone else who watched TV he knew all about the Spanish galleons that had been salvaged off the Florida Keys.

"Wrong coast. We're talking South America. Peru, to be exact."

Carter considered. "You don't want to go there. It's swarming with drug runners and Maoist guerrillas who think Stalin was a raving liberal."

"Listen to me, sonny-boy." She switched to the voice she'd utilized briefly in Bruton Fewick's study. "There's plenty you don't know about me. To you I'm just Granny Marj, the lady who darns your jockey shorts. But before I started stitchin' I did other things. I can take care of myself."

"That so? What did you do that qualifies you for a trip like this?"

She backed off abruptly, as though she might already have said too much. "Let's just say it involved a lot of travelin' around, and that I learned how to handle myself on the road. I'm only tellin' you any of this because I thought you deserved to know, you havin' found the disc an' all. Now go back to your party. Go on." She waved at him as if trying to shoo a puppy.

He didn't stir. "My next film, *if* I decide to sign the contract, doesn't start for a number of months either. It's supposed to shoot in the Amazon somewhere. I wonder if Manaus is close to Peru?"

She made a face. "Not hardly." She tapped the screen. "Where I'm going there won't be any air-conditioned, bugproof rooms or eager gofers waiting on call with iced drinks."

"It would still be like research for the picture."

"What would be like research?" she asked guardedly.

"If I went with you. You can't really be thinking of going by yourself."

"Matter of fact that's just what I was thinkin'."

"I could help. Except . . . I'm up for a lead in an Ibsen revival in New York. If I get the part that'll tie me down until the next picture. If I don't . . . how do I get hold of you?"

She ripped a page from a notepad in one of the open boxes next to the laptop, scrawled numbers. "This is my home phone. I'm in the Valley. I ain't gonna wait around for you."

He pocketed the slip. "I still think you're crazy for even thinking about doing something like this on your own."

"Me, I think it's the people who don't do stuff like this who are the crazy ones. I'm fifty-three. What am I, saving myself for the Miss Senior America contest? You go do your Ibsen and let me worry about me."

"You're a nice lady, Marjorie. I'd hate to think I had a part in you doing anything that got you hurt."

"Thanks for the concern, cuddles." She walked him to the door. "But I usually ain't the one who ends up hurt."

He didn't get the part. His reading was as good as that of any of the actors who auditioned, and he had his growing marquee value going for him. But the producers were of the subspecies that concerned itself more with notices than box office, and they ultimately decided that casting hunky Jason Carter in the role of a mentally tormented intellectual was a cultural risk they weren't prepared to take.

On the day after his latest rejection he picked up the phone and dialed the number he'd brought from Georgia. He was puzzled to learn that it had been disconnected. That was nothing compared to his surprise when upon further investigation he learned that it had not been in service for almost a year, which implied that Marjorie Ashwood had deliberately given him a wrong number.

He was simultaneously confused and angry, sufficiently so to begin calling all over L.A. in search of her business manager.

When he finally tracked him down the man was reluctant to provide any information.

"I'm telling you," Carter said smoothly, "she *told* me to call."

"She didn't say anything about you to me." There was hesitation at the other end. "Tell you what: I'll call her and tell her you called."

"I can't spare the time. We worked together on her last picture," he said imploringly. "I was the lead."

"Wait a minute. Jason Carter. Yeah, I know you. You were in that Old World summer hit last year, *Black Steel Guts* or something."

Carter winced. The man was not talking Ibsen.

"Sure, I know you." The manager evinced some interest for the first time since he'd answered his phone. "You played the big cop who crashed the police car into the truckload of chemicals at the end."

"I want to surprise her." Carter was at his most persuasive. "I'm in New York. I promise you, I'll give her several days' notice before I show up."

The man sounded wary again. "What's the big rush?"

"I might have a job for her."

"Are you putting me on? The only time an actor wants to discuss wardrobe is when his costume binds in the crotch."

"It's just that we got along so well on my last film and . . . Look, if you don't want to give me her number, we'll just forget it, okay?"

"Hold on." Clearly the man was torn between propriety and greed. "If you just want to talk to her . . ."

"That's all I want to do."

"Okay. But don't tell her where you got the number. Even though I'm acting in her own best interests."

"No problem," Carter assured him.

As soon as he was off the phone he called a service he knew and used the telephone number the manager had given him to trace Ashwood's address.

He was in L.A. the next day. After a brief stop at his own place up in the hills he rolled out the Corvette and crossed down into the Valley. Eventually he found himself in a quaint foothill neighborhood where the trees had matured almost as fast as the property values.

The startled look on Ashwood's face when she opened the door was worth the trouble it had taken to find her. She recovered quickly, though.

"Hello, cuddles."

"Can I come in?"

"Sure, why not?"

The older home was furnished with overstuffed furniture and modest bric-a-brac. On the way to the den they passed a small study whose walls were completely covered with autographed photos of the actors and actresses she had dressed over the years.

"How'd you find me?" She sat down in a big flesh-toned armchair.

"I'm not as dumb as people think. Does it matter?"

"I reckon not."

"I thought you'd be in South America by now."

She shook her head. "Can't leave for another week. There's preparations to be made, packing to be done. It ain't like I'm goin' down to La Jolla for the weekend."

Carter sat on the edge of the couch. "I still want to go."

"I don't recall invitin' you." She stared hard at him, taking the measure of something more critical than his chest dimensions. "It'd be nice to have company, though, and the muggers'd be less likely to pick on me with you hangin' around, but you could be a hindrance, too. How spoiled are you, handsome?"

"I'm not spoiled at all," he said angrily. "I don't mind roughing it. And I could use the break from work. Might even get a treatment out of it," he added, thereby contradicting himself.

"I dunno." She still looked dubious. "Where I'm fixin' to go y'all won't be able to use your credit cards, your reputation won't get you out of any scrapes, and you're gonna need a strong constitution and a stronger stomach."

"Are you saying *you'll* be able to handle it and I won't?"

"Okay," she said tightly, "you're in. You found me. That shows resourcefulness and independence. Just keep in mind there's probably nothing to this.

"You'll have to get your own kit together. I've got other things to do. We leave this comin' Sunday. Varig's only got one flight a week out of LAX and I ain't gonna miss it."

She tried to brief him during the long flight, extrapolating upon the maps and information she'd copied out. He'd never been much on geography and recognized little of what she showed him. But the name of one tiny town in the region they were to enter jogged his memory.

"Fitzcarrald?"

"What about it?" she said.

"Herzog made a movie about a guy named Fitzcarraldo. Kinski was in it. They shot most of it on location. Horrible conditions. I didn't know it was a real place."

"This ain't a movie, hotshot, and where we're goin' there won't be any towns." She traced a huge section of map. "This whole area's called the Infierno Verde. The Green Hell." She grinned. "You can always hop a turnaround flight after we land."

V

THEY didn't linger long in Lima, hanging around the foggy airport only until they could recover their luggage and catch the first flight to Cuzco on an antique Aeroperu 707.

That's when they learned that their confirmed onward reservations meant nothing. Fortunately a few persuasive words from Carter to the female sump block of a scheduling clerk cleared the way, leaving Ashwood to grudgingly admit as how her companion might be of some use on the journey after all.

Nothing fell off the flying vibrator during the short flight, and the landing was smoother than it should have been, given the powerful crosswinds that usually scoured the high Andean plateau. The air on the tarmac was thin but free of the familiar pollutants. To the east the snowy peaks of the Andes delineated a pale horizon.

By afternoon they were both slightly woozy and nauseous. Their hotel provided cups of coca tea, the traditional remedy for altitude sickness. Carter drank only after being assured that there wasn't enough serious stimulant in the brew to get a gerbil high. Within a few hours they felt well enough to try dinner.

Still, lingering aftereffects compelled him to keep

his eyes averted from Ashwood as she hungrily de-
voured a disgustingly rare chunk of steak.

She smirked across the table at him. "Remind me
again later how fortunate I am to have you along."
He responded with a wan smile. "Hey, if you want
to puke, feel free. But not while I'm eating, okay?"
She put her knife and fork down and rose.

"I'm goin' up to my room. Y'all ought to get some
sleep. Tomorrow we've got to try and find us a guide
who won't lead us around in circles to run up his
bill."

"I'm not sleepy," he told her. "Mom."

She started to respond, caught herself. "All right,
sonny-boy. Truce. Do whatever you want, so long
as you're ready to go at sunup. But if you're plannin'
on waiting around to sign autographs, you're wastin'
your time. There's no audience here for y'all."

But she was wrong.

The woman who approached the table half an hour
later did not ask for an autograph, nor did she gape
simperingly at him as so many of his female fans
were wont to do. Staring boldly and not waiting for
permission, she sat down in the chair Ashwood had
vacated.

The salubrious effects of the hot tea having banished the last traces of dizziness, he found himself
debating whether to follow Ashwood's advice and
do the sensible thing or let his present situation continue to evolve. The woman was extraordinarily tall,
almost his height. She towered over everyone else
in the hotel. Her features were classical Castilian,
her eyes saturnine. Shoulder-length black hair, black
eyes, a slim upper body, and slightly wide hips com-
pleted his initial impression. Her attitude was a not

unattractive mix of the sophisticated and the girl-
ish: a twelve-year-old trapped in the body of an Amazon.

"*Buenos* . . . good evening," he ventured. His
Spanish bordered on the nonexistent. As it hap-
pened, his linguistic ignorance was not a hindrance.
Her English was fluent, mellifluously accented.

"I'm Francesca. I live here. You don't. You're a
norteamericano."

"That's right." He was used to forwardness in
women.

"You a tourist?"

"Yes."

"You just get in?" She lit a cigarette. Everyone here
smoked, he'd noticed. "I don' mean to pry. You don'
have to talk to me if you don' want to." Her gestures,
like her speech, were abrupt, hyperactive. "I'm not a
whore. I just like talking to people. You here to see
the ruins?"

Her energy was formidable. "Yes." It was easier
to let her ramble on like a runaway rocket than try
to interject more than a simple acknowledgment or
denial.

"I live here. Cuzco's my home. What do you do?"

"I'm an actor."

She nodded. "When I first see you I think that
might be it. You are very good to look at."

"Thanks. You're quite a knockout yourself."

She smiled, cocked her head sideways. "Mutual
admiration is good." She eyed the plate in front of
her. "You not alone."

"I'm traveling with a friend." He saw no reason
to elaborate.

"I unnerstand." She looked around the nearly de-

serted dining room. "I come in here a lot, to talk
with people. Cuzco is very provincial. The people
here are either very poor or think they are very
rich. Those who think they are rich are arrogant.
Arrogance makes them dull. Tourists carry a different kind of baggage with them and can be so much
more interesting. So I spend my free time visiting
the hotels. It lets me practice my English."

Her earlier disclaimer seemed to be the truth. An
hour of casual conversation included nothing to suggest that she was in fact a loquacious nocturnal capi-
talist who was simply biding her time prior to ven-
turing the expected proposition.

"I don' have the money to travel," she was telling
him as they both nursed local coffee. "So I watch the
television and read magazines. But it's better to talk
with someone who has actually been such places as
Paris or New York or Buenos Aires than jus' to read
about them."

He checked his watch. "Then I hope I've been
informative as well as entertaining. I've enjoyed your
company, Francesca."

She ignored the hint, leaning forward across the
table. "So tell me: what you gonna do while you in
Cuzco? You mus' go up to Sacsayhuaman, of course,
and there are many interesting buildings around the
Plaza de Armas."

"My companion is doing all the planning," he told
her.

"I unnerstand. Are you goin' down into the selva,
the jungle, at all?"

"We might," he murmured diffidently. "Like I
said, my friend is handling our itinerary."

"You really don' want to go there. It is miserable,

hot, and the insects will have you for breakfast if the snakes don' kill you first." She shook her head. "I don' understan' tourists. Machu Picchu, Cuzco, that I understan'. But why anyone would want to pile into a plane and go to Puerto Maldonado to sweat like pigs to see some macaws, that is jus' crazy. We who live here have more sense than that." She stared evenly at him.

"The only people who go into the selva do so for money: gold prospectors, oil engineers, poachers. An' all of them would rather be someplace else. For many of them the selva is their last chance. Why would anyone go there who doesn' have to?"

"Why do people go to zoos?" Carter finished his coffee. "As for me, I'm one of those people who like looking at animals."

She shook her head disparagingly. "The animals in the selva don' just look back. Most of them bite. Take my advice and look at the ruins instead. It's safer." She rose and he reflexively echoed the movement. It wasn't often he had the chance to say good night to a dinner companion eye-to-eye.

"Maybe I see you around Cuzco," she told him. "You goin' to be at this hotel for a while?"

"As far as I know," he replied truthfully.

"Okay. You don' mind my talking to you, do you? All I want is to talk, not to sleep with you."

Her bluntness delighted him. "Fine by me. The altitude makes me dizzy anyway."

"I could make you dizzier." She favored him with a strange, tight little smile. "But that I can have anytime. Good conversation is much harder to come by. Maybe I see you here again tomorrow night."

"Maybe. Good night."

"Buenas noches."

He followed her with his eyes as she marched out of the restaurant. So did the maître d' and the remaining waiter. So did the clerk at the front desk. With her beauty, height, and regal bearing she would have turned heads in Manhattan.

It was exhausting simply to sit and listen to her and he discovered that he was suddenly very tired. The elevator carried him to the third and top floor. There was no action from the phone, no knock on the door as he undressed and readied himself for bed. The flight from Lima, the altitude, and the tea combined to counteract the effects of the after-dinner coffee and he quickly fell into a deep and dreamless sleep.

He sensed the movement before he came fully awake: something small and active in the darkness at the foot of his bed. The rapid return of consciousness was accompanied by memories of every television documentary he'd ever seen on South American wildlife: enormous snakes, smaller venomous reptiles, giant bird-eating spiders, and lethal scorpions. They crawled and slithered through his mind in rapid succession, as clear and sharp and immediate as if he were scrolling through a CD-ROM encyclopedia.

Blinking furiously to clear sleep from his eyes, he lifted his head just enough to see a dark silhouette fumbling under the blanket near his feet. Uttering a silent curse, he jerked his body into a sitting position, back against the headboard, his knees drawn up close to his chest. Swinging his legs to his right he slipped out of the bed and looked around wildly for a weapon.

Clutching the dressing-table chair in one hand he

cautiously approached the foot of the bed. By now his eyes had grown accustomed to the dim light. With his free hand he snatched convulsively at the blanket, prepared to retreat into the bathroom if necessary, and yanked it aside.

A dark, four-legged shape exploded off the sheet and vanished under the dresser.

Carter let out a long, relieved sigh and put the chair down, embarrassed at his initial panic. Slipping into his robe, he got down on hands and knees to peer beneath the dresser. A pair of bright close-set eyes stared back at him.

"It's okay," he murmured. "Believe me, kitty, you surprised me more than I surprised you. Come on," he said coaxingly. "Come on out. I won't hurt you."

His persistence finally drew forth a querulous *meow*, followed by the emergence of a dainty black and white feline form. At first he thought it was only a kitten, later saw that it was simply a very small but fully adult female.

The head jerked back as he reached for it, then slowly slipped beneath his patient fingers. Soon he was stroking the animal as though he'd known it for years. The cat slid her spine contentedly back and forth against his hand. Nor did she offer any resistance when he picked her up and placed her in his lap as he sat down in the chair. She turned a few circles, finally collapsing into a black and white spiral against his robe as he scratched her behind her ears.

"Now, how did you get in here?" He glanced at the window which opened onto the cylindrical three-story-high atrium. "Did you come in that way?"

The animal wore no collar, which didn't surprise

him. A third-world city like Cuzco would be full of
strays. Despite that and some basic scruffiness she
was pretty clean. He could find no evidence of injury
or infection and at this altitude fleas would find it
hard to make a living.

Calling the front desk never crossed his mind. If
the animal wasn't a house cat the appalled staff
would instantly put her back on the street, if not
worse. He didn't want to see that happen. Though
he'd always liked animals, as a traveling adult he'd
never had the time to take care of one.

A sharp rap on the door punctuated Ashwood's
query. "You up, cuddles?"

"Yeah! Just be a minute, Marjorie." He rose and
gently set the cat on his abandoned pillow. "Be quiet
now," he instructed the animal softly as he headed
for the door.

Ashwood stood in the hall, fully dressed and anxious to go. "Y'all ain't ready. You were supposed to
be ready."

"Sorry. My wake-up call was unexpectedly early."

"Who was it? The basketball player? Look, I don't
care what you do on your own, Carter, but if you
plan on stickin' with me on this little hike you *will*
be ready each morning to depart on time."

"Actually a lady is involved, but not the one you're
thinking of." He smiled. "Why don't you come in
and say good morning to her?"

Ashwood was taken aback. "Hey, I don't have the
slightest interest in your . . ."

"Don't be shy, Marjorie." He grabbed her wrist
and pulled her in.

Ashwood looked around warily. "Where is she?"

"In the bed. Where else?" Carter's smile widened.

His companion looked in spite of herself. Then she muttered something under her breath. "Oh, you should definitely be doing stand-up, Carter. Where'd that come from?"

"I have no idea. I thought maybe through the inside window." He sat down by the head of the bed and began stroking the animal. It stirred in its sleep. "She got under the foot of my blanket and woke me up. I want to tell you, I nearly made it back to Lima without the plane."

"What are you gonna do with it?" Ashwood shifted impatiently from one foot to the other. "We've got to get moving."

"Well, I'm not just going to dump her out on the street. Poor people elsewhere eat dogs. No telling what they eat here. If I just leave her, the hotel's liable to have her put down."

"So what's left? You gonna take her with us?" She meant the suggestion as sarcasm.

It had a different effect on her young companion. "Why not?" he replied defiantly, as if the thought had already occurred to him. "I could sure use an alternative to your company."

Ashwood held her temper. "You can't take a house cat into the jungle."

"Why not? She's small, doesn't weigh much. I'll carry her in my pack."

"You're crazy. Something down there'll make a meal of her. This is a domesticated animal we're talkin' about, Jason." She sounded disgusted. "Big tough actor, the guy who carries the machine gun in one hand and the grenade launcher in the other, and you're gonna nursemaid a cat through the jungle?"

"Watch me."

"When'd you decide to do this?"

"Spur of the moment. I've never done anything like it before, so why not do it now?"

"I can't stop y'all. But I don't want to hear about it when things get tough, you understand? The cat has any problems, they're your problems."

"That's what I had in mind." He gazed fondly at his newfound friend. The cat lifted its head, eyes shut with pleasure at his touch. "Pretty bold of her sneaking in here like this. I think I'll call her Macho."

Ashwood rolled her eyes. "You can't call her Macho if she's a female. Call her Macha if you have to. And you'd better hope she keeps quiet while we're out or the hotel will make *machaca* out of her."

Carter rose and latched the interior window, barring the only exit. "I'm sure she'll sleep 'til we get back." He glanced across at the animal. "You'll be quiet, won't you?" The only response was a continuing sessile purr.

"God," Ashwood muttered. "When we get down into the lowlands you gonna talk to the snakes and piranhas too?"

"If I think there's any chance of getting an answer," he shot back.

"Throw on some clothes and let's move."

They made inquiries at the hotel desk, at the American Express office down the street, and around town. An English-speaking cop finally directed them to the offices of the Organización por la Conservación de la Selva Sur, on the north side of the Plaza de Armas. A busy researcher juggling a handful of slides told them to try another room in the same building.

The guide's office was a tiny, jumbled mess. Gear and books crowded the battered desk into a corner and all but obscured the famous view of the ancient cathedral across the plaza. A telephone and an antique manual typewriter clung precariously to one side of the desk.

The office's single occupant was a soft-voiced, swarthy young man with lively eyes and delicate features. He stood barely five seven and looked much too young to be a representative of his chosen profession. His English was excellent, but that was to be expected, Carter mused.

"Your timing is not good," he informed his visitors. "I'm supposed to go to Lima to check out some new equipment. I'm not really interested right now in going into the selva."

"What would it take to get you to change your mind, sonny?" Ashwood added something in rapid-fire Spanish and Carter eyed her in surprise. Obviously pleased, the guide replied in his own language.

Their haggling gave Carter time to study the contents of the office. He found a stack of high-quality eight-by-ten photos: greenery, something that looked like a black alligator with a dragon's tail, a pair of impossibly large otters, and a jaguar napping in a tree.

After Ashwood and the man settled on a price there were handshakes all around, at which point Carter learned that henceforth they would be trusting themselves to the expertise of one Igor von Mannheim de Soto.

"We're really going into unexplored jungle with a guide named Igor?" Carter whispered to his companion.

"You've lived in L.A. too long," Ashwood admonished him. "South America isn't any more ethnically homogeneous than the North. So there's German and Russian in the kid's family. It's his competency that concerns me, not his genealogy."

"You never told me you spoke Spanish."

She ignored the observation. "He says he grew up in the Madre de Dios district and knows it the way you'd know Beverly Hills. He's been guiding since he was fifteen."

"That's right," agreed Igor, blandly indifferent to his new employer's outright appraisal of his qualifications.

"He's fresh enough to be enthusiastic and crazy enough to take us wherever we want to go. Aren't you, sonny?"

"Sure. You said that you want to see ruins. What you really mean is that you want me to help you try to find Paititi."

Ashwood gaped at him. "Now, what makes you think that's what we want?"

He sat on the edge of his desk. "Because every *norteamericano* who comes to this part of the world and says they want to go looking for ruins really means they want to try and find Paititi. People have been doing that since Pizarro's time."

Carter pursed his lips. "Actually I thought we were looking for—"

"Treasure," said Igor, interrupting. "There is no treasure. Everyone wants to believe there is. I know better."

"How do you know that?" Carter wondered aloud.

"Because if there was any treasure the conquistadores would have found it centuries ago. Pizarro's men could smell gold, like dogs can smell carrion."

"How come you know all about this?" Ashwood asked him.

The young man slid off the desk and fumbled at an overloaded, collapsing bookcase that was now wholly supported by its literary content. He extracted a dusty volume and flipped through it as he spoke.

"The Spaniards could not find Paititi because it doesn't exist. It is a legend. Not that they didn't try. They tortured and killed a lot of Incas. People unable to provide information they didn't have died because of honest ignorance. In 1912 your Mr. Hiram Bingham found the city of Machu Picchu up above the town of Agua Caliente. A lot of people think that was the city that gave rise to the stories about Paititi. But Bingham found no gold. Just a lot of old buildings that were falling down.

"It's pretty. I like to go there myself sometimes and stay the night, after most of the tourists have left. But treasure?" He smiled.

"How can you be so sure Machu Picchu is Paititi?" Ashwood asked him.

The young man looked at her. "I didn't say that it was. Only that it makes good sense. Hundreds of prospectors, poachers, scientists, and crazy people have kept after it for years without finding anything. That does not mean it isn't there." He shrugged. "For the right price I am happy to help anyone look.

"What I can promise you is that you will enjoy the wildlife. There are more species in the Manú basin than anywhere else on the planet."

"We're not interested in animals," Ashwood said sharply. Igor's blithe negativity had clearly upset her. "Maybe that bloated Brahmin was just playing at what he was doing," she muttered thoughtfully.

Carter wasn't as disturbed as his companion. After all, he'd come for the experience, not for treasure. He'd be perfectly happy to spend their time in the selva looking for animals . . . though Igor's declaration did take the edge off his expectations.

Ashwood wasn't ready to concede. "We have reason to believe that this place really exists . . . or that there's something down there, anyway."

"Of course you do." Igor adopted a conciliatory tone. "If you didn't you would not have come all this way and spent so much money."

"You're a very mature young man." She regarded him shrewdly.

Another shrug. "You grow up fast in the selva or you do not grow up at all." His voice didn't change nor did his expression harden, but the feeling of inner strength he projected was unmistakable. It was the same kind of strength that enabled other young men to survive on the streets of Beirut . . . or New York. The characters Carter portrayed often displayed it on screen. It was much less common in real life.

He waited while they hammered out the rest of the details. Boats had to be arranged, food and medicines stocked, the land cruiser checked out. Ashwood grumbled at but acquiesced to the immutable costs.

"D'you want us to sign some kind of contract?" she asked him when they finished.

"There are no lawyers in the selva," he told her. "It is very much like your old western frontier. People tend to use things other than words to settle disagreements. Payment in advance will be sufficient. I won't cheat you. My reputation is worth more to me than your traveler's checks."

"Tell me something." She looked into his face. "How many other crazy gringos have you taken in search of Paititi?"

"Does that matter?"

"I suppose not. Are you familiar with the Pinipini River?"

He showed some surprise. "You have done research. Very few people have been up that way. The river tends to parallel the foothills, and the country is very bad. Where the foothills meet the lowlands you get vertical jungle. I have camped at its mouth where it joins the Upper Madre de Dios. There are no maps of the river itself and the aerial survey goes back to the 1930s.

"Where are you staying?"

"Hotel de Oro," Ashwood told him.

"Decent enough. Watch your wallets, especially when you are around children. Pickpocketing is one of the few growth industries in central Peru. I will have everything ready for us in two days. One to assemble everything, the second to make sure I haven't forgotten anything. There are no stores, no telephones, where we are going. We must take everything with us." He looked at each of them in turn.

"I tell you now, if you have any second thoughts about this I will refund your money and help you to make reservations for the flight back to Lima. Where we are going we will be entirely on our own. You must trust me completely. Do not be fooled by my age. I will keep taking you wherever you want to go, keep you alive, and bring you safely back out. If you expect comfort or a semblance of civilization then you have come to the wrong part of the world."

"Maybe I ain't been in your jungle before, sonny," Ashwood told him, "but I can take care of myself. You just hold up your end of this little jaunt and we'll handle ours."

VI _____

CARTER was helping Igor secure the last strap atop the battered land cruiser while Ashwood sat in the front passenger's seat, studying the little folder of information she'd put together and muttering to herself.

The actor snapped down the lock-tight and walked around behind the vehicle.

"Are you so sure that this place doesn't exist?"

"I told you." Igor strained at the nylon. "I rule nothing out. I just say that reason is against it." He secured the last strap, wiped his hands on his pants. "But the Spaniards took hundreds of ships full of gold, silver, and emeralds out of South America. There is no guarantee that they got everything. Only that if they did not, the Incas have surely hid the remainder very well.

"For me the treasure of the selva lies in the uniqueness of its plants and animals, not any lost gold."

Carter helped him wrestle a large ice chest into the back of the land cruiser. "Marjorie's not much into nature. But I'm different. So when we pass something interesting I hope you'll point it out to me."

De Soto smiled up at him. "I could not do otherwise. Knowing that someone is interested will make the journey more enjoyable." He prepared to lift and shut the vehicle's tailgate. "That is everything."

"Not quite." Carter hustled back into the hotel, returned a few moments later with a small wood and wire box. Igor eyed it uncertainly.

"You are going to take a cat with you?"

Carter gently placed the box and its dozing occupant atop the ice chest. "Why not? She won't be any trouble."

"But why?"

Somewhat to his surprise Carter had no ready answer. "I dunno. Maybe because Marjorie said I couldn't get away with it. She's fun to tease. Besides, if I leave Macha here I have a strong feeling she won't last very long in the city."

"The selva will not be any kinder to her."

"Maybe not, but I will. She'll be my responsibility. I've already tried her in my backpack and she just curls up on my towel and goes to sleep. She'll be good company at night."

Igor looked dubious. "Wait 'til she hears her first jaguar."

The ride over the crest of the Andes was as beautiful as it was bumpy. At twelve thousand feet Carter was astonished to see terraced hillsides rising hundreds of feet above the floor of the valley through which the single dirt road wound its uncertain way.

They passed through ramshackle, windswept towns with names like Paucartambo and Acjanaco, whose inhabitants eyed them with quiet curiosity. Dark-eyed laughing children ran alongside the road, giggling and gesturing until the land cruiser was out of sight.

As they began to descend trees appeared; in clusters at first, then in rolling, cresting green waves that came sweeping up the side of the mountain. Carter had never seen so much green.

They ate lunch in the clouds, swathed in the swirling mists that nourished a unique habitat Igor referred to as cloud forest. A clear stream ran down the side of the road, spilling over to fill the slightest depression, each pothole a thriving miniature ecology. Innumerable small waterfalls cascaded off steep slopes, nurturing wild orchids, mosses, and bromeliads.

Igor sat on a folding chair and munched a chicken wing. "There are very few places like this left on the planet. The creatures that live here, like the spectacled bear, are solitary and secretive. Even the birds are hushed."

Carter watched Macha hunt tadpoles in a pothole. She stayed close to the land cruiser and gave no sign of wanting to wander off. They had not seen another vehicle since they'd left Paucartambo.

"What d'you think, Marjorie? Isn't it beautiful?"

She held her sandwich in one hand and slapped at the back of her neck with the other. "Ain't had time to look. Been too busy killing things."

Igor did not smile. "The first mosquitoes. Scouts and outriders, come to greet you."

"I put repellent on everywhere," she told him, taking another swing at her neck.

"It does not matter. The more you slap on, the better the bugs will like it. They look forward to their predinner cocktails." He walked back to the land cruiser and rummaged around inside until he emerged with a pink bottle.

"Try this. It helps some people more than others. The best defense is to wear long pants and long-sleeved shirts, two pairs each. Make sure you keep the legs of your pants tucked into your shoes." He handed Marjorie the bottle. "Long hair is a help."

She took the container. "You're twenty years late with that advice."

As they continued to descend, the road narrowed still further, until they were driving with sheer cliff to their left and an equally precipitous drop-off on their right. Mist obscured any view, for which Carter was grateful. There were no guardrails and in many places not much road.

Forty-five minutes were wasted when they met a small logging truck inching its way upward. It took that long to find a spot where the truck could pass, and there was a horrible moment when the rear right wheel of the land cruiser actually hung out over empty space, the jungle a thousand feet or more below. But the truck finally sneaked past and they continued on downward. In twelve hours of continuous driving it was the only vehicle they encountered after leaving the Andean crest.

By evening they found themselves bouncing over hills and ruts, across fast-running streams, through mud that would have swallowed the car of a driver less knowledgeable and skilled than Igor. Trees hung over the narrow road, blotting out what sunlight the pouring rain did not already obscure and making Carter feel as if they were driving down a dark green tunnel.

It was pitch-black out when, exhausted and filthy, they finally reached the tiny Indian community of Pilcopata. Even children and chickens had taken shelter from the steady downpour. Ghostly figures darted past the land cruiser's headlights.

Igor vanished into the storm, reappeared moments later. The fact that he was drenched to the skin did not seem to bother him.

"There is an old tea plantation across the river. They keep a few beds available for the scientists and naturalists who come this way."

"We're gonna cross a river in *this*?" Carter could see Marjorie Ashwood's lust for Inca treasure beginning to fade. "What about the car?"

"It stays here. From this point on we go by boat or on foot. You are welcome to sleep here if you prefer the backseat of the car to a dry bed with clean linen."

Mumbling under her breath, Ashwood climbed out into the rain. Carter carefully eased the sleeping Macha into his waterproof backpack and hefted it high on his broad shoulders. Together they followed their guide's flashlight through the darkness.

By morning the rain had stopped. The plantation's owner hosted a surprisingly luxurious breakfast. Exotic cries from the surrounding jungle punctuated their conversation as they ate, the raucous concert dominated by the oleaginous warble of the oropendula birds.

They were on the river by eight o'clock, speeding over clear shallows in the largest dugout canoe Carter had ever seen. Set on a ridiculously long shaft, the prop of the old Evinrude engine powered them smoothly downstream. There were no seats. Ashwood and Carter made themselves as comfortable as they could atop the piles of supplies.

Igor's chief boatman, Pierre, had appeared magically at daybreak, accompanied by a stocky mestizo porter named Christopher. Apparently Hispanic names were less than universally popular in this part of the world.

The following day Igor directed his men to pull inshore. A short hike brought them face-to-face with a large rock outcropping which was covered with drawings.

"Ancient petroglyphs," Igor explained. Ashwood glanced around, saw that they were alone.

"Where are your people?"

"They won't come here," their guide explained. "Pusharo is a sacred place to them. Come and see."

He led them around the side of the site. Beneath a protective granite overhang the rock wall was completely covered with bizarre drawings and carvings. Many had an incomplete look to them, as if the artist had given up in exhaustion or despair and moved on to another section of stone to try and realize his intention anew. Those that did look finished resembled nothing Carter or Ashwood had ever seen. They said as much.

Igor smiled. "Do not let it discourage you. Nobody knew there were any such ancient drawings down in the jungle until Padre Vincente Cenitagoya found these in 1921. There has yet to be any systematic scientific study made of them. Nothing is known of their origins or makers and they resemble nothing the Incas did. You are free to interpret what you see however you think fit." He studied the wall.

"Myself, they speak to me of mystery and ancient days." He touched smooth gray stone. "This here is clearly a human face, but this object next to it utterly confuses me. Many of the shapes are unrecognizable." He moved to his left. "I call this one 'sun-in-a-box.' It is fun to make up interpretations for them."

There were hundreds of drawings, seemingly scattered at random across the outcropping. The visitors were turning to leave when Ashwood suddenly stopped and pointed.

"Wait a minute! There's one I recognize."

Their guide's eyebrows lifted. "You recognize it?"

"Yes. I have a drawing of it. I'm sure I do."

Igor considered. "If that is so," he said slowly, "then perhaps we may stumble across something of interest to you after all." A yowl drew their attention away from the petroglyphs. Carter looked anxiously in the direction of the river.

"The people who live in this country do not eat cats," Igor hastened to reassure him as they started back the way they'd come.

They spent the night in tents on the shore, heading up another, smaller river the next morning. While Carter was having a marvelous time, Ashwood was somewhat less than enthused. At least when they were out in the river, he pointed out to her, the bugs didn't harry them. She was not mollified.

Igor consulted frequently with her on directions, once angling the dugout to scoot up a tributary whose existence Carter had not even suspected, so dense was the vegetation crowded along the bank. They would keep to the water for as long as possible.

It was the height of the dry season, Igor informed them. Most of the year the terrain they were currently traversing was impassable: the land impossibly boggy and muddy, the rivers wild with froth and huge trees whose root systems had been washed away by the floods.

They supplemented their supplies with fresh catfish and piranha, the white meat of the latter reticulate with small bones and tasting vaguely of trout. When Igor and his men jumped eagerly into the river at precisely five-fifteen every evening (when the day mosquitoes clocked out) and splashed around delightedly for ten minutes to emerge before five-thirty (when the night mosquitoes clocked in) Carter was at first reluctant to follow their example despite the temptation of a cool bath. Accumulated sweat and grime finally induced him and his companion to take the plunge. As Igor had promised, the piranhas did not bite. But their curious nibbling kept him from relaxing as he stood in the shallows and soaped himself off.

Days later when the stream had grown too narrow to navigate they beached the dugout and hefted packs. In the thick heat and cloying humidity Carter was sure that his weighed only slightly less than his thirty-six-inch T.V. back home. Macha had miraculously acquired the dimensions and mass of the jaguar they'd heard briefly the previous night. But he said nothing, nor did Ashwood. Pierre bid them goodbye. He would remain behind with the boats, awaiting their return.

By the end of the first hour Carter found himself envying the boatman. As for himself, he could think of nothing but the hotel back in Cuzco: of air-conditioning and cubed ice, of the refreshing high-pressure shower and lemon-scented bed linen. He had long since stopped slapping at the voracious insects which worried his exposed skin, relying on the dense gelatinous layer of insecticide he slathered on every morning to protect him. This it did with greatly varying degrees of efficacy. Those insects that somehow managed to bite him right through his denim jeans he could only ignore.

Igor had spoken of diseases endemic to the Infierno Verde which not only had no known cure, they had yet to be named. Carter tried very hard not to think of such things.

Instead he concentrated on the green conflagration through which they stumbled. Igor's and Christopher's machetes rose and fell in rhythm, excavating a path where none existed.

By late afternoon his legs were throbbing, his feet aching. When Igor announced that it was time to take a break Carter started toward a circular clearing from which rose a single small tree, intending to use it as a backrest. The guide practically tackled him from behind.

"Stay away from that."

"Why?" Carter scanned the ground. "There're no bugs here, no rocks."

"Precisely." Igor gestured at the tree. "That's a palo santo."

The six-inch-thick bole looked innocuous enough to Carter, and he said so.

"Look at the ground again," Igor advised him. "See how clean it is? Not only are there no insects here, there is very little leaf litter and no young plants. Nothing living."

Despite the heat Carter felt a chill. "So?"

The guide had him approach the tree . . . carefully. "See these venous lines running across the bark? They are ant tunnels. The tree provides them for the ants, who make their homes within. In return, the ants cut down any competing plants that try to take root near their home, and kill any creatures which come too close. See?"

He tapped lightly on the trunk with the butt of his machete. Within seconds the gray bark was swarming with angry quarter-inch-long, rust-red ants that came pouring out of holes in the vein-like tunnels.

"They don't look like much," was Ashwood's comment. "Not as threatening as the army ants you've showed us or those huge black solitary hunters."

Carter let out a scream and jumped several inches off the ground, clutching at his left wrist. On the back of his hand a single ant had pierced the skin with its stinger. It was wiggling and twisting like a living drill, trying to drive the tiny weapon ever deeper into the invader. Several slaps were required to dislodge it. Instantly a small red circle began to form around the minuscule hole.

De Soto examined the skin, his expression as phlegmatic as ever. "It must have fallen off a branch." Carter immediately looked upward and began backing away.

"I got stung by a yellow jacket once," the actor muttered. "This is worse. How can such a tiny little creature hurt so bad?"

"Their poison is very strong," Igor explained. "The Machiguenga Indians who live in this region will punish a severe offender by tying him face-first to one of these trees. When they return the following morning the victim is always dead."

"I think I'll go sit in a nice mud puddle somewhere," Ashwood declared with alacrity. They left the sunny, bug-free clearing to its owners.

After another day of oppressive heat, choking humidity, stinging plants, and maddeningly persistent biting insects Igor matter-of-factly announced that from that point on, progress was likely to become difficult.

"I know that in this day and age it's hard to believe, but we really are entering unexplored territory. Only true fools leave the rivers to travel this country on foot." He smiled. "I greet my fellow fools." Turning, he gestured toward the jungle ahead. "Nobody in their right mind comes here for a hike. Too steep and slippery. Maybe we'll see something interesting. New species are being discovered in this country all the time."

"What about Indians?" Carter asked as they resumed their advance.

"There are still tribes in the Manú district who've had only the most marginal contact with civilization, people whose languages are not understood. I do not think we are likely to encounter a previously untouched tribe, but it is possible."

When it wasn't raining they could see through breaks in the trees. They were climbing a green wall, ascending by means of switchbacks and angles, only to descend the opposite side, wade a creek, and start the process all over again. It was painfully slow and miserably uncomfortable. The blue sky overhead seemed an abstract unattainable ideal, pure and unsullied by drifting spores and bugs.

Carter could see why no one would want to visit such a place: not prospectors, not poachers, no one. It was ruggedly inaccessible. Even if you found anything worthwhile it would be hell packing it out.

Two days later they encountered the Indian. He

did not fit the image Carter had constructed during idle moments of speculation.

Certainly he was old. His skin resembled a banana peel that had been left too long in the sun. Their appearance startled him erect and Carter estimated he was barely five feet tall. His attire consisted of a pair of fraying khaki shorts and an equally thread-bare undershirt. A temporary structure of saplings and palm leaves stood behind him. Off to one side unidentifiable skinned animals and a couple of neatly filleted fish dangled from a horizontal limb supported by crossed poles set in the ground. They had been recently cut.

"Poacher?" Ashwood wondered aloud.

"We'll see." Their guide stepped forward and addressed the old man in a peculiar singsong tongue. He responded haltingly, shaking his head. Igor tried again.

Eventually he returned, some strain on his face. "He's not a poacher. Says his name is Minga. Claims to be a local shaman. He lives by himself and people come to him when they need help. He's been as far as Shintuya. That's an advanced Indian settlement farther down the Alto Madre de Dios. What's interesting is that while his speech is similar to that of the Machiguengas there are also significant differences. But we can understand each other.

"He says there are no villages near here and that no one else camps in this vicinity. That I can believe." His eyes shifted from Carter to Ashwood. "I told him what you told me: that we were looking for a place where two pillars of rock almost meet to form an arch. He says he's been all over this country and that he knows of only one such spot that might fit the description. Also that he is the only human who's ever been there."

"Can he, will he, take us?" Ashwood inquired anxiously.

Igor nodded. "He wants to be paid in something real. He knows about paper money but doesn't trust it. Intis or dollars, it is all the same to him. I have a couple of small solar-powered flashlights. I think he will accept one of those."

"What do you think?" Ashwood stared at the skinny old man. "Is he just telling us a story to get the flashlight?"

"There is no way of knowing except to follow him. I do not think he'll lead us around in circles. Whether he actually knows of such a place remains to be seen."

"Has he ever heard of Paititi?"

"I will ask him." Igor did so. When he turned back to them there was a hint of excitement in his voice. "He does not know the name, but he claims that there is a place near the notched rocks where the stones have been carved by the gods."

"The gods?" Carter asked.

"These jungle Indians remember nothing of the Incas or their civilization. Or it might be nothing more than a rockfall that he finds interesting. Again, the only way to find out is to go and have a look."

"Promise to give him the flashlight," Ashwood decided, "but only after he's led us to the place."

VII

FOUR days later they reached and passed the notched rocks, a place where a swift-running stream had cut its way through softer limestone. There was no path, no trail, and Carter found it difficult to believe that the old Indian had any specific destination in mind.

They continued to climb and descend, slipping over mossy boulders and clutching at dangling vines for balance. Throughout, he marveled at Ashwood's endurance. She complained endlessly but never asked for an extra rest stop. The march would have defeated a much younger woman, and many younger men. Only Macha traveled without complaint.

The old man slipped between trees and vines as if oiled, pausing frequently and impatiently while Igor and Christopher hacked a wider following trail through the selva.

Three additional days of arduous walking brought them to a place of rocks that was clearly no mass of collapsed hillside.

The crumbling wall that lined the mountainside was festooned with creepers and epiphytes, its outlines barely discernible beneath the greenery. Several low-ceilinged, dark openings were visible in the dangerously unstable barrier. From the air the ancient construction would have been invisible.

A few petroglyphs could be seen beneath the attacking lichens. They were similar but not necessarily kin to those of distant Pusharo. There was no sign of any gold or silver, no pillaged temples or granaries. As a ruin the place was singularly unimpressive. If they were standing on the site of a lost city, Carter decided, its municipal boundaries about equaled those of a full-service car wash.

He found he was too tired to be disappointed. Right then he would have given a gold idol for ten minutes in a real bathtub.

An exhausted Ashwood finally had to stop picking at the wall and sit down, slumping against the badly pitted stone.

"It don't make any sense. Why would a geek like Fewick go to so much trouble to try an' find a place like this?"

"Probably for the same reason as us." After checking to make certain it wasn't a palo santo, Carter cleared a place to sit beneath a short, leafy tree. Removing his pack, he watched while a curious Macha hopped out and began to explore the nearby undergrowth. "Because he wanted to believe there was something here."

"Well, we sure have gone an' saved him a lot of trouble," Ashwood groused. "When we get home the first thing I'm gonna do is write an' tell him to save his energy. I'm gonna be completely truthful an' upfront about it. Maybe that way he'll think I'm lyin' and waste the money to come here himself."

Even the indefatigable Igor was tired, Carter saw. His long-sleeved cotton shirt hung as dark and damp on him as an oil field washrag. There wasn't a dry spot on anyone's body. In that respect the tormenting bugs were useful: they kept his mind off the humidity and the mold he was sure was beginning to grow between his toes.

He was ready to go home. The novelty of traveling through strange country, of seeing and hearing exotic birds and monkeys and other creatures, had long since worn off. He was anxious to reacquaint himself with the mundanity of indoor plumbing.

Exhausted as she was, Marjorie Ashwood was still reluctant to accept the reality of what they'd found.

"Are you sure this is all of it?" She looked at Igor, then their aged guide. "Ask him."

Igor did so and the Indian replied. "He says these are the only god-works in this area."

"What about those openings?" Ashwood refused to let it go. "We can't leave without seein' if there's anything inside. There might be caves, or rooms."

Igor was sipping from a plastic water bottle. "You may explore them all you wish. I will not go in there."

"Why not?" Carter inquired.

Their guide put the bottle aside. "The Manú is home to some very interesting snakes, Mr. Carter. Bushmaster, fer-de-lance, assorted vipers, all quite aggressive, each more poisonous than the next. They love dark places. I gladly leave such regions to them." He eyed Ashwood. "If you want to go exploring such habitats I wish you good luck. I do not think you will find any gold. I don't think there was ever any gold to be found.

"Paititi is one of those wonderful myths that sprout from hope and avarice and are nurtured by people whose lust for lost places and great secrets obscures their vision. You paid me to bring you to this place. That I have done. Your company has been less than a constant enjoyment to me. I would have much preferred to guide a group of naturalists or photographers.

"Our supplies are limited and we have been fortunate in the weather. I have no intention of pushing our luck for little reward. We will camp here tonight. You may spend one day surveying this site. The day after tomorrow I will discharge the remainder of my professional obligation by leading you safely back to the river and thence on to Boca Manú, where you have the choice of returning the way we came or chartering a plane to take you to Puerto Maldonado and from there back to Cuzco. Then, God willing, I will have a little time to do some studies on my own, without having to guide anyone anyplace.

"That is what I work for. I do not know what you work for. If you came hoping for gold you will at least return with wisdom."

"I didn't really expect to find any treasure," Carter told him.

"Well, I did, dammit!" Ashwood followed her disclosure with a stream of colorfully embroidered language which Carter listened to admiringly and Igor added to his store of knowledge.

When she began to wind down, Carter put an arm around her shoulders. "Chill out, Marjorie. We came here without any guarantees." Something was rubbing against his ankles. Looking down, he saw that Macha had returned from her brief exploration of the campsite and was now demanding a share of his attention. She was the only member of the expedition who wasn't sweating profusely.

Igor was helping Christopher break out the tents.

Leaving Ashwood to her muttering, Carter sat and allowed Macha to curl up in his lap. It really was a beautiful place, he mused as he examined his surroundings. If only something could be done about the climate and the insects.

Ashwood removed a flashlight from her pack. "Y'all can sit on your butts if you want to. I'm gonna have a look inside."

"Marjorie," Carter cautioned her, "what about what Igor said?"

"I ain't afraid of no damn snakes," she sniffed. "Hell, I grew up in Texas. I was raised around snakes."

He pretended to be surprised. "Texas? I thought you were from California."

"Yeah, well, there's quite a bit I ain't told you about myself, sonny-boy. Just don't worry about me. I'll watch my step."

"I don't think there are any rattlers here, Marjorie. You won't get any warning."

"I just want to have a look. So I don't carry any second thoughts away from this place. If I don't find anything I'll be the first one up and ready to leave tomorrow."

Carter let out a sigh and gently eased Macha out of his lap. "Guess I'll come with you."

"You don't have to. I'm a lot slimmer and smaller than you and if there are narrow passageways I'll just leave you behind. If I find any big openings I'll give you a holler, okay?"

"I guess. But I don't like it."

"Hey, I told you before we left that I wouldn't tolerate any of that protective macho crap, remember? I can damn well take care of myself."

"Okay, okay." He made placating gestures. "Do all the crawling around you want. Find the biggest bushmaster in Peru and bring him out in your teeth. It's no skin off my nose."

She nodded and turned to examine the crumbling wall. Of the three openings, the farthest away seemed to be the largest. The entrance to a lost temple it wasn't. Anyone could see that whatever kind of outpost this had been, it had never served as home to more than a few people at a time, if ever.

"Don't you think that if there was anything of value around here he would already have found it?" Carter indicated the old Indian who had led them to the site.

"Not necessarily." Ashwood was making her way along the wall, toward the farthermost opening. "Remember how the porters refused to go up to Pusharo? This is another place of the gods. I doubt the old boy's even been inside."

"Well, you can find out, and then you can tell all of us." Carter was unpacking his sleeping bag.

She straightened. "If I break a leg or fall down some old shaft you'll come and get me, won't you?"

Carter ignored her with great deliberation.

"Get up!"

Carter tried to turn over. Even with his knees drawn up to his chest the small tent was still barely big enough to cover him. He half opened one eye and squinted down past his feet. It was barely light outside. What the hell was going on?

"I'm not ready to get up."

Someone kicked at the soles of his feet. Hard. "Get up and come out."

He blinked, realizing that the voice was new to him. The English was even more heavily accented than Igor's.

Sitting up, he slipped into his shirts and pants, tugged on his boots. Macha was standing near his feet, ears alert, her tail twitching like a nervous metronome. The tent rattled around him as he repeatedly bumped into the stays. Unzipping the mosquito netting, he pushed aside the rain flap and crawled out, still half asleep.

In the dim light of early morning he saw Igor and Christopher seated next to the remnants of last night's campfire. Ashwood stood in front of her tent, looking angry and unhappy.

Three strangers confronted them. No, that wasn't quite correct. Two of them were strangers. One he recognized.

Bruton Fewick was sweating profusely. The automatic pistol looked distinctly out of place in his pudgy fingers. It shifted to cover Carter as he emerged from his shelter.

"I was beginning to wonder if you were going to take my instructions seriously, Mr. Carter. I thought actors were accustomed to rising early."

"Only when you have an early call." Carter buckled the belt of his pants. "The rest of the time you learn to sleep in."

"I am sorry to have to rouse you. If it is any consolation you should know that your presence here is equally distressing to me."

"Screw you," Ashwood told him.

Fewick's eyebrows lifted and he brushed blond hair from his forehead. "You know, Ms. Ashwood, you are an extremely foul-mouthed old lady. If you persist in insulting me I may be forced to shoot you."

"Very melodramatic. You're not gonna hurt anybody."

"Really? I thought you were a seamstress. I didn't realize you were prescient as well. How did you find this place?" Ashwood simply smiled at him.

"Suddenly you prefer not to talk? Well, I suppose I can imagine a scenario. You had my disc. You copied it, despite the fact that it was private property, and decided to usurp my life's work."

"You ain't lived long enough to have a life's work." Ashwood's fists were clenched. "What you got in mind for us, Few-ick?"

"*Fee*-wick. If you don't give me any trouble and you in particular can keep a civil tongue in your head, I probably won't shoot you, for all that your presence here complicates my life. Even though you are thieves I did not come all this way for revenge."

"Your research only led us as far as the notched rocks," Carter said. "How did you make it the rest of the way?" He indicated the old Indian, who sat off to one side observing the proceedings with detached interest while amusing himself by making drawings in the dirt with a pointed stick. "Minga there said he was the only person who'd ever visited this spot."

Fewick frowned. "You don't say." Turning, he addressed his two porters in fluent Spanish.

Carter tensed. He knew some martial arts, and Fewick's physical reactions were likely to be slow. Still he hesitated. The pistol Fewick clutched was no prop.

One of the porters turned and shouted something into the trees. A third Indian emerged, older than the pair who were shouldering Fewick's supplies.

At his appearance Minga rose and tossed his stick aside. Simultaneously Fewick's guide caught sight of what was obviously an old friend. The two men embraced formally and walked back to Minga's pallet of leaves, chatting earnestly while utterly ignoring everyone else.

"I thought you said he was the only one who knew how to find this place?" Ashwood asked their guide.

Igor shrugged. "That is what he told me. Sometimes truth in the selva is as scarce as ice."

"You don't need that." Carter indicated Fewick's pistol. "There's nothing here worth shooting someone over. If it's right of discovery you're concerned about, I could care less."

"Same here," said Ashwood.

"That remains to be seen. In the meantime I will keep my gun, Mr. Carter. If I were to put it aside that would leave you with the option of beating me up, which I am certain you could do very effectively. Now, if you will please seat yourselves I will have my people bind you except for your man, who may depart if he so desires. My concerns do not extend to the locals."

Igor murmured something to Christopher, who looked reluctant but finally nodded. Still reluctantly, he gathered his pack and with a last backward glance at his friend and employer hurried off into the jungle.

"He'll bring back help," Carter said.

"Oh, I doubt that." Fewick watched as his porters securely bound the two men and Ashwood. "The local people owe Europeans no allegiance. They might have some loyalty to him," and he indicated

Igor, "but not enough to risk involvement in Anglo affairs. I'm confident that he'll return to his family and forget all about this as quickly as possible." He settled himself against a tree.

"You say there's nothing here worth being shot for. I therefore take it that you have found nothing of value?"

"You can bet your ass on that," Ashwood told him with relish. "There ain't no lost city here, no Inca treasure. Nothin' but that damn wall."

"I can see this was never a city site. A runner's outpost, perhaps. As to treasure, that remains to be seen."

"You don't seem upset," Carter commented.

"Why should I be? You are the ones who came expecting to find gold and emeralds. Myself, I am an archaeologist. Money I have already. I searched for Paititi in hopes of securing enough material for a monograph or two, perhaps even a cover of the *American Journal of Archaeology*. A validation of my choice of profession. Something to shove in my parents' faces that screams, 'I am a success without you, without family connections!' " He indicated the crumbling wall, the isolated petroglyphs.

"This may look like nothing to you, but to me it is real treasure. An undiscovered, undescribed site. Already I suspect the presence of non-Inca influences. Chimu, perhaps, or even Moche. I expect to find artifacts, but they need not be gold."

"Then why treat us like this?" Ashwood struggled against her bonds. "We'll leave quietly and you can poke around here all you want."

"I will probably do just that . . . eventually," he told her. "For a while, though, I must insist that you remain, until I have quantified sufficient work for preliminary publication. I cannot chance you returning to Lima to blab to the first reporter you encounter. Forgive my caution, but this is the discovery of a lifetime. I cannot put it at risk. One word would be sufficient to bring an avalanche of would-be treasure-hunters down on this place, who would quickly destroy anything of scientific value.

"Meanwhile you must bear with me. Try to relax. You will be properly looked after and when I am finished you will be released. Until then I fear you must indulge my paranoia."

Fewick had more to say but the conversation was interrupted by violent yowling and spitting from the vicinity of his baggage.

"Now what?" Fewick directed his query toward the noise. "Moe, what's got into you?"

"Moe?" Ashwood gaped at their captor. "You hauled that big tom all the way from Georgia?"

"Of course. Moe accompanies me wherever I go." Fewick motioned to one of his porters. "Well, don't just stand there. Let him out."

Nodding, the porter moved to open the lid of a box which had been strapped to his pack. The bulky four-legged shape which emerged took off in the direction of Carter's tent.

"Macha!" Carter yelled in sudden realization.

The tom hit the front of the tent like a rusty cannonball as Fewick stared at Carter. "You also have a cat with you?"

"I found her in Cuzco," Carter said anxiously as spitting, yowling sounds came from the tent. "I thought she'd be safer with me and that after we finished here I might be able to get her back into the States."

As they stared, Carter's cat emerged from the back of the tent and raced off into the forest. The tom followed a moment later, in active pursuit.

"A fellow admirer of felines. My opinion of you, Mr. Carter, is elevated. A 'her,' you say." He grinned.

"I do not think Moe will damage her."

"What if they don't come back?"

"Moe will. While I cannot vouch for your animal I would not worry myself overmuch. If you have been feeding her she will surely return. They are simply being cats. They will sort things out between themselves, without our unnecessary intervention in their affairs.

"Now, if you will excuse me I shall begin my work." After handing the pistol to one of his men and leaving him to watch the prisoners, Fewick extracted a small camera from one pack and began taking pictures of the wall, beginning at one end and working his way methodically toward the other.

"If he does find any gold we're liable to be in for trouble," Ashwood muttered after lunch. "That's what worries me. He could shoot us and leave us here and no one would ever find the bodies."

"Take it easy, Marjorie," Carter told her. "I don't think Fewick's the killing type."

"Is that so? Well, let me tell you, cuddles, that where gold is concerned all bets are off."

"And how would you know anything about that?" Carter inquired challengingly.

"Because I've seen what happens when folks have the chance to acquire large amounts of unearned income." She was quiet for a long time, as if considering whether to say anything more.

Finally she looked up at him, twisting against her restraints. "I don't suppose y'all ever heard of the Breckenridge Massacre?"

"No." He eyed her strangely.

"I ain't surprised. That was back in the . . . well, too long ago for you to remember. There was a bank, and a holdup that didn't work out the way it was supposed to. A couple of dumb local yokels were in the wrong place at the wrong time and got their stupid selves killed. The papers called it the Breckenridge Massacre. One fool went to prison, the other got himself caught under an eighteen-wheeler tryin' to outrun the cops.

"The only one who got away was the gal waitin' back at the motel with three first-class airline tickets to Brazil. When she saw on the news that her boyfriend had not only screwed up but been turned into ground chuck on U.S. 180, she beat it back to Dallas, cashed in the tickets, and lit out for parts unknown. They never did find her."

Carter stared numbly at his companion.

"Yeah, me. The cash from those tickets gave me a stake. I'd always been pretty handy with a sewing machine. I ended up in L.A., learned how to use a laser cutter and computer designer, and wandered into the film business. It keeps me movin' around, which lets me sleep easier. I think the Texas cops gave up on me years ago anyway, but I don't take any chances. Life's worked out pretty good for me." She shook her head at the memories.

"That was . . . thirty-five years ago, sweet man. Been clean ever since. But before that I had a pretty rough time of it. I once saw a guy shoot another for

the ten bucks in his pocket. So I know how large
sums of money you don't have to work for can
change folks." She looked back over her shoulder.

"I don't give a damn how much cash Fewick says
he has. If he finds anything convertible I think we'd
better start worryin'."

"Did you ever shoot anybody, Marjorie?" Carter
asked her quietly.

Her gaze didn't swerve from his. "Let's just say
that if you can get that gun away from Fewick, I'll
be able to make good use of it."

With so much reality to monitor and so few Shihararaneth able to undertake the task it wasn't sur-
prising that it had taken O'lal so long to resolve the
pattern of the Renegade's disruption. With nothing
to begin with save constantly shifting suspicions and
suggestions of abnormality it was a wonder she had
been able to construct a trail at all.

She still did not know the Renegade's precise intentions. Those remained far more nebulous than
his purpose. But to a Shihararaneth maliciousness
was a physical reality which could be sensed and
measured, and there was no denying the degree to
which it dominated the Renegade's actions.

Patient observation and calculation had paid off. It
was clear she had surprised him, just as it developed
that he was stronger than she'd anticipated. That did
not matter. It was not necessary that she defeat him;
only that she disrupt his plans.

His astonishment at her appearance was simultaneous proof of his vulnerability and arrogance.
Obviously he had expected his manipulations to
proceed undisturbed. The confrontation had rattled

him, unsettled his intricate construction. No matter what happened now, his plans could not move forward in the intended vacuum.

Instinctively he'd attacked. She'd reacted with the skill of long practice, leaping easily between two colliding planes of existence, slipping beyond his grasp before he could so much as touch her. To a Monitor gravity is but a minor encumbrance. It did not slow her.

She wove and danced through glistening spaces, perceptions wide open, avoiding both his frustrated grasp and the isolated tendrils of intrusive mass which occasionally brushed against her being. He struck and she pirouetted neatly beyond his reach, sliding down a viscous hint of shining place whose existence he had not suspected. Knowing this world's geometry better than he, she could continue the dance until she exhausted him. Nor could he reveal himself on a physical plane without risking damage from the primitive fauna around them.

She did not have to kill. All she had to do was keep him occupied until his carefully constructed design collapsed of its own unwieldiness. Then, with the world entrusted to her charge safe once more, she could deal with him as an individual.

U'chak knew that his frustration and anger were making him clumsy, affecting his reflexes. The Monitor was toying with him, teasing him, staying temptingly close yet just out of his reach. No matter how he anticipated, she did him one better. It quickly became clear he was not going to be able to run her down.

Her appearance at a critical juncture in his plans had been a shock and he berated himself for overconfidence. Failure was in sight, if not imminent. Fortunately he had been able to work some hasty damage control, but the sequence was far from favorably reconstructed and might still abort itself at any moment. Nor could he devote himself wholeheartedly to its repair. Not with the Monitor present.

Distressingly he had been forced to improvise. That automatically bent advantage the Monitor's way. All was not yet lost, however. Though fractured by unexpected intrusion, the destructive sequence he had devised remained in forward, if jarred motion.

He consoled himself with the knowledge that his present difficulties were the result of an accident and not the Monitor's direct intuition. It had allowed her to proceed without disclosing her existence to the native fauna, which revelation could be as dangerously disruptive to their development as his own intentions. It was a caveat he'd counted on to help preserve his own anonymity, a component vital to success if one considered the unpredictable and often dangerous nature of the local fauna.

There was nothing for it but to proceed as best he could, occupying the Monitor's attention and hoping that the very beings he intended to affect would continue along the path he had chosen for them. Any misstep could prove costly.

O'lal sensed the Renegade's loss of confidence and knew she had disrupted his scheme. All without revealing herself and thereby adversely impacting the creatures she had been assigned to monitor. She kept ahead of his pursuit, exhilarating in it, knowing that while he was occupied with her he could not directly influence the reality around him. Bereft of his subtle manipulations, his inimical design would undoubtedly collapse before any serious damage could be done. And having found him, she could put a categorical end to his intrusions, harrying him until he fled beyond easy return to this world.

What neither Shihararaneth expected or foresaw was the introduction of a startling new element into the equation. Thrust and parry they might, but while they did so reality was not frozen in stasis. It maintained a momentum of its own, one which might influence events either way.

Patience was demanded. There were limits to what even the Shihararaneth could do. Both Monitor and Renegade observed and analyzed, trying to determine how best to make the unexpected serve their own special requirements.

U'chak was hopeful. Disruption was generally to his advantage. It suited his temperament and intent far more than that of the Monitor.

With luck he might yet ride wondrous Chaos across this dull, boring world.

VIII

CARTER had fought his bonds all morning without achieving anything more than a cramp in his shoulders.

Ashwood rolled over as her captors returned from their digging. She was stiff, dirty, and angry.

"Find any gold?" she asked sarcastically as Fewick returned from his probing of the first of the three openings in the ancient wall.

"No," he told her blandly. "Not much of anything. A few petroglyphs whose designs are new to me, some pottery shards, the remains of an old fire pit. Of course we have just begun. Great discoveries are not made in a day. Archaeology is a time-consuming science." He sat down on a smooth rock while his porters began to prepare a meal.

"Are we to eat?" Igor inquired.

"Certainly. My desire is to immobilize you, not starve you. After my men and I have eaten, you will be released one at a time. I will sit here with my little gun and watch until all of you are finished. Isn't that nice of me?"

"How long do y'all intend on keepin' us like this?" Ashwood asked him. "Are we expected to sleep with our arms and legs tied?"

Fewick pursed his lips. "I fear you are in for several

uncomfortable nights. I do apologize."

"So do I." The admonition did not come from
Fewick's porters, nor from the pair of elderly Machiguenga who sat off to one side cooking something
unappetizing over their own fire.

"I wouldn' do that," the voice said more sharply when Fewick reached for the pistol holstered at
his belt.

"Who the devil are you?" Fewick looked toward
the trees as his fingers halted a couple of inches
above the butt of the gun.

A tall, leonine figure emerged from the brush. "My
name is Francesca da Rimini."

Carter gaped at the unexpected arrival. Noting his
reaction, Igor and Ashwood tried furiously to figure
out what they were so obviously missing. Fewick's
porters retreated from the confrontation while the
two old Indian guides hardly bothered to look up
from their cookfire.

Fewick's gaze narrowed. His hand remained in
the vicinity of his gun. "*Francesca da Rimini* is a
Russian opera."

"Well, I not a Russian opera," the Amazon replied
dryly. "My parents, they had poor imaginations but
a good radio."

"I am sorry, but that does not impress me."

"Perhaps this will." She turned and whistled
into the trees. In response to her signal three
dark-skinned men emerged from the forest's edge.
Two were twins, Carter saw. They wore identical
clothing, carried identical backpacks, and more
important, clutched identical AK-47s. If they were
porters, Carter thought, they were extremely successful ones. Instead of T-shirts and frayed shorts

they wore expensive twill pants and shirts, and their jungle boots looked brand-new.

The third individual wore tattered jeans holed at the knees and a badly worn short-sleeved shirt. He looked to be in his teens.

Ashwood leaned toward Carter, whispering curiously. "That the same Amazon?"

"I met her our first night in Cuzco, after you went to bed," the actor replied.

Ashwood's eyes rolled heavenward. "Lemme guess. You told her our plans, right?"

"I did not." Carter was feeling the prize fool. "She was very nice and just wanted to talk. I told her we were tourists."

"Uh-huh. I mean, that's obvious, isn't it?"

"Look, it's not my fault if she drew other conclusions. Maybe she's here to rescue us."

"Right," said Ashwood tersely. "Just like my ol' flame Billy-Bob Postin went to robbin' banks because he never got that scholarship to Princeton." She made a rude noise.

"I'll relieve you of this." Towering over Fewick, Da Rimini removed the pistol from his holster and stepped back. The two men behind her relaxed.

"These are the Fernández brothers." She indicated her companions. "That Manco on the left. You can tell them apart because his brother, Blanco, is a little taller and uglier." The individual thus described smiled agreeably. "We are old friends."

The young Indian who'd accompanied Da Rimini strode apologetically past her and the captives, offering a raised hand and a few words by way of greeting. Minga and his dinner companion glanced up from their fire and responded unenthusiastically.

The youngster took a seat across from his elders, whereupon the trio began chatting in low tones.

"Lemme guess," said Ashwood sarcastically. "That boy's the only one, the only one in the world, who knows the location of the lost city of Paititi and could guide you to it."

"Not exactly." Da Rimini had a wild look in her eyes. She no longer acted the oversized ingenue Carter had met in Cuzco. It took a very special, very unusual woman, he thought, to plunge into the selva with two heavily armed men hoping to find . . . what? "But he did know that his uncle had taken some white men in search of his grandfather, and how to track them."

Carter found that her darting gaze and quirky gestures were making him more nervous than the AK-47s. The supercilious Bruton Fewick might be obsessed, but at least he wasn't unbalanced. The more Carter saw and heard of her, the less assured he was of Francesca da Rimini's state of mind. How would she react to the discovery that the fabled lost city of Paititi consisted of a single crumbling wall, some overgrown paving stones, and three holes in the ground?

"You I know, Jason Carter. Your outfitter, Igor von Mannheim de Soto, I also recognize, and the ugly old woman is clearly the friend you mentioned." Ashwood tensed but said nothing. Da Rimini's gaze danced over Fewick. "But who is this unpleasant fat man?"

"His name's Bruton Fewick. He's kind of an archaeologist. He's the one who first figured out where this place was. Marjorie and I, we sort of appropriated the information from him and got here first. He didn't like that, which is why we're tied up."

"That is correct," said Fewick with misplaced self-importance. "I am the official discoverer of Paititi. The rest of you are nothing more than intellectual interlopers."

Da Rimini responded by continuing to treat him with all the deference she would an ant. She glared at the disintegrating wall. "*This* is Paititi? This is all there is? Where is the city? Where is the lost gold of Atahualpa?"

"This is a priceless archaeological site," Fewick informed her. "That is gold enough."

She glared murderously at him. "Don' joke with me, *gordo*. Not after what I gone through to get here."

"I believe it may have been an Incan runners' station," he added stiffly.

She brushed the suggestion aside. "All the runner's stations are up in the mountains. The jungle would have slowed communication, not speed it up, and the selva tribes were hostile to the Incas."

"There's no treasure here." Despite the delicate situation in which she found herself, Ashwood couldn't pass up an opportunity to sneer. "You blew it, sister. The only ones who'll make money on this little hike are the locals." With a jerk of her head she indicated the three guides seated around the cookfire.

"We'll see." Da Rimini was gazing fixedly at the wall. "There has to be treasure here. There *must* be treasure!"

"Not necessarily," Fewick began. The archaeologist's ingenuousness made Carter wince. "If one considers the available literature it is clear that—"

"Shut up! Shut up, *cállese usted!*" Da Rimini slammed the barrel of the pistol across Fewick's face.

Carter's guts twisted but he said nothing. Fewick hadn't welcomed his predecessors with open arms, but neither had he hurt them.

The archaeologist stumbled backward but did not fall. A trickle of blood started from where his lip had been split.

"Tie him with the others!"

Blanco Fernández slipped his rifle over his shoulder and moved to comply. As he did so Da Rimini spoke sharply to Fewick's porters. With admirable alacrity, they grabbed what supplies they could carry and beat it into the jungle.

While Da Rimini angrily studied the unimpressive wall, Carter studied her. She had her hair secured with a single elastic band and her clothing was soaked through. Standing there clutching Fewick's pistol she looked like she was auditioning for a part in a cheapie Filipino adventure epic. Except that the gun she held wasn't packed with blanks. The hint of madness in her eye did much to mitigate her physical attractiveness.

Meanwhile her guide, his uncle, and his grandfather nattered on, oblivious to the inexplicable doings of the Europeans who had variously employed them.

"What do you intend to do with us?" Igor inquired.

Her response was rather less considered than Fewick's had been.

"Why, I'm going to kill you, of course. Did you think we carried these guns all this way to hunt hoatzins? But you will live for a while. We want that one," and she gestured at Fewick, "in case there is information to decipher, and the rest of you to help with any digging."

"What if there are no secrets here?" Carter asked her. "What if there is no treasure?"

Her lower lip pushed out slightly. "If we find the treasure I am going to shoot you to protect it. If we don' I will shoot you out of disappointment. Or perhaps I will have you tied to palo santo trees. Have you been introduced to the charms of the palo santo?"

Within the limitations imposed by his current posture Carter adopted his best leading-man pose. "I thought you liked me."

"You very pretty, but I prefer my men determined, with a little more here." She tapped the side of her head. "Like the Fernández brothers." Behind her, Manco Fernández shifted his AK-47 and grinned.

Carter was dubious as he studied the two older, unattractive men. Then he noted anew the fancy jungle attire, the expensive weapons. "Money," he said. "You're with them because they have money."

"It don' disinterest me," she replied amiably. "We understan' each other, Manco and Blanco and I. *Sí,* they have money. But not nearly enough for them, or me. So when I tol' them that I knew of some rich *norteamericanos* who were goin' to go looking for Paititi, they were anxious to come with me to see for themselves. This is not the first time we have done this, but it is the first time anybody has found something for us."

"Hey, I recognize that one!" Manco Fernández was looking at Carter. "He's an actor. I saw him at the Odeon in Miraflores, in *Prison Planet. Santa María,* what a stinker of a picture!"

Carter sighed. "Don't expect me to give you your money back."

Ashwood regarded the critic. "What do you boys do for fun when you're not working as spear-chuckers for Fran the Giant?"

Self-importance colored Manco's reply. "We are bottlers."

"Pardon?" said a confused Carter.

The man straightened proudly. "Surely you have been in Peru long enough to have heard of Inca Cola."

"Oh God." Ashwood rolled her eyes.

"No, I haven't." Carter felt like he was acting a role in one of the screenplays his agent received on a regular basis from an eager slaughterhouse worker in Kansas City.

"It's not cola like in Coca or Pepsi." Blanco Fernández tied the last of his knots. "Actually it uses a grapefruit base. My brother an' I," he declared smugly, "own the concession for most of central Peru an' the whole selva region as far north as Iquitos."

"We have big plans," Manco announced. "My brother an' I are three-quarter Indio, one-quarter Spanish. All our lives we resent the way the Spanish imposed their culture on our people and destroyed much of our heritage. It has always been our dream to emphasize that culture in a contemporary way. For that we need much money. Hard currency, not intis. The profit margin in soda bottling is thin."

"We have accumulated some dollars but not near-ly enough," Blanco added. "As you may know, there is a vast international black market for primitive art."

"Oh no," said Fewick, blithely disregarding his

precarious position. "Any artifacts found here belong to the Peruvian government."

"We will put them at the service of the Peruvian people," Manco Fernández replied sharply. "The *true* Peruvian people. *Los Indios*. Some we will keep for future display and education, but we will sell what we must to raise the money we need for our great project." He lifted his gaze to the ancient wall and its indecipherable petroglyphs.

"Paititi has been a legend for so long, it is the ideal place to make our beginning."

"Beginning of what?" Igor asked.

Manco looked down at the guide. "Our dream, which is to promulgate our native heritage. To restore its influence throughout the modern world. To make it come alive for people everywhere, not just narrow-minded men who live in dry, dusty books." He glanced disdainfully at the sullen Fewick.

"My brother and I," he continued proudly, "have made a study of the success of American popular culture, which has spread itself to every corner of the globe. We have tried to learn the secrets of its success so that we may apply them to our own culture. Now we believe that we have learned enough to proceed. We have formulated an unbeatable plan . . . all that remains is to find a means of financing it.

"Not only will we spread our influence throughout the world, we will make money while doing so. This is our sacred trust."

"Mind if I ask you a question?" Carter shifted his position on the hard ground. "Why do you call it Inca Cola if there's no cola in it?"

Manco Fernández eyed him pityingly. "Do you know nothing of marketing strategy? And you call yourself an *American*. All the great soft drinks are named 'something' cola. What does it matter what it contains? All that is important is if people buy it or not."

"What's this 'great project'?" Ashwood asked in spite of herself.

"A museum!" Fewick bestirred himself. "To showcase the great traditions of Inca culture, to display in a modern setting the grand achievements of your ancestors. Yes, I can understand, even sympathize with that."

"A museum will be a part of the complex," Manco admitted. "A small part. It is evident you too know nothing of marketing. Do you not study your own society?"

"Complex?" Carter said.

"We are going to build a vast park here on the site of Paititi. It will include a museum, *sí*. Also a part of the rainforest, preserved for all to see. Sanitized and cleansed of insects, naturally." His gaze rose as he focused on his distant vision. "And rides, lots of rides. And shops, and theaters, and concession stands and fast-foot outlets!" His voice deepened with the sheer majesty of it.

"Shooting galleries where people can fire back at the hated conquistadores! An amphitheater where the festival of Inti Raymi can be performed every day. A selva water park! A petting zoo!

"Today Paititi, tomorrow Rio and Buenos Aires. Then on to the United States and Europe and Japan. It will be called"—his voice shook with emotion—"*Incaworld*!"

In the dazed silence that followed, Igor de Soto said softly, "Some of us prefer the selva the way it is."

Manco regarded him pityingly. "Ah; *un verdadés loco.* You are a crazy greenie. I might have guessed."

"What makes you think you can get people to come to this sauna that bites, even if you put a roof over the whole thing and air-condition it?" Ashwood wanted to know.

Fernández wore the look of the calculatedly mad. "Marketing."

"You're crazy, all of you. Not that it matters. There ain't no treasure here."

"Shut up, old woman!" Da Rimini snapped at her.

Ashwood glared. "Don't call me an old woman, she-weed. If my hands weren't tied . . ."

Though Da Rimini had twenty years and plenty of pounds on Ashwood, Carter didn't think he'd care to bet against his companion in a fair fight.

The Amazon, however, wasn't interested in a fight of any kind. Not while her associates wielded automatic weapons.

"You can't kill all of us," Ashwood insisted.

Da Rimini feigned astonishment. "Why not? No one will find you out here. After we bury you the ants and other scavengers will reduce you to bones inside a week."

"You know," Carter said tersely, "you were a lousy date."

She ignored him as she began unpacking their supplies. "You don' mind if we use your tools, do you? They are just lying here doin' nothing." She hefted a flashlight and pick while Blanco Fernández unfolded a collapsible shovel.

"*Incaworld!*" A startled Manco whirled and aimed the muzzle of his gun in the direction of the unexpected shriek. Everyone else turned to look.

"Fabulous concept, truly real. Visionary!" A figure stepped out of the trees.

Carter slumped. Evidently a callous God intended to visit one final ignominy upon him.

"Wonderful idea!" Trang Ho advanced, holding her microcassette recorder out in front of her. She was barely sweating. "Marvelous!"

Da Rimini noted Carter's reaction. "Who is this . . . person?" she asked warily.

"Her name's Trang Ho," Carter muttered. "She's a free-lance journalist . . . and I use the term advisedly."

Ignoring the AK-47, Ho thrust the recorder at Manco Fernández's face. "Sir, would you tell my readers more about your fantastic plans!"

The gun muzzle dipped. "You are really interested, aren't you?"

"Of course. You give me information, I give you a story."

Fernández's reply was interrupted by Da Rimini, who was studying the jungle from which the diminutive Vietnamese had emerged. "Where's your guide? Where's the rest of your party?"

"Oh, I came alone," Trang Ho informed her cheerfully.

Manco eyed her in disbelief. "You followed us by yourself?"

"I always work alone." She started slipping off her modest pack. "Excuse me. This is getting heavy."

"How did you track us?" Blanco asked.

"Are you kidding, man? I'll track a story *anywhere*. Besides, it was like following a bulldozer. And my people were raised in the fetid, steaming jungles of Southeast Asia."

"Yeah, but you were raised in Canoga Park," Carter reminded her.

"Well," she said defensively, "L.A.'s kind of a jungle."

"You want to help publicize our plans?" Manco inquired uncertainly.

"All that I can. In return for exclusive publication rights, of course."

Ashwood raised her voice. "While you were taking notes did you happen to hear that these people plan to kill all of us?"

"Do you think I'd miss anything as dramatic as that?" Ho was clearly insulted. "That has nothing to do with me. With a little rewriting it will only add punch to my articles."

"Now, wait a minute," Carter began, trying to rise.

Da Rimini was studying the latest arrival to what was becoming a very crowded lost city. "You mean this, don' you?"

"Certainly. As Jason Carter can attest, I have no morals whatsoever and my employers have less." She smiled exuberantly. "If we did, our business wouldn't exist." She turned to Carter. "I am sorry, but look at it this way: think of the press you'll get. People will forget all the lousy pictures you've made in the rush to immortalize you. I'll personally see to it that whoever they cast in the film version of your life is a better actor than you are."

"You're not just going to watch them shoot us," he declared uneasily.

"Of course I am. They have two very large automatic weapons. I have a little knife. What else can I do?"

"Then you'll report them if you make it back to Lima," Ashwood said.

"Why should I? You'll already be dead. It would be a waste of a great story."

"Justice would be served," Fewick pointed out.

"I'm not in the business of serving justice," Ho informed him. "I'm a *reporter*, for Buddha's sake! If I were anything less than a total pragmatist I never would have been able to lift myself out of the stinking, crowded L.A. Vietnamese ghetto."

"I heard that your father was vice-president of a major bank," Carter said.

"Details." She turned back to Manco. "I think your Incaworld is a terrific idea."

No one had noticed that the three Indians, disgusted with what was taking place and disliking a crowd, had quietly picked up their few belongings and slipped away into the selva.

While Trang Ho followed Blanco Fernández and Da Rimini toward the nearest opening in the wall, Manco found himself a resting place and relaxed, cradling his rifle in his lap. Carter found himself watching the jungle. By this time he half expected someone to emerge in Trang Ho's wake, but the passing hours brought forth only bird noises and the rustling sounds made by secretive, unseen creatures.

"I wonder if that big tom of yours hurt Macha," he said.

"Moe's not a vicious animal." Fewick regarded the verdure. "Is yours spayed?"

"I've no idea, but I'd doubt it."

"I never had the heart to have Moe neutered, so it is possible they are enjoying this sojourn more than we."

"Anybody got any suggestions?" Ashwood murmured softly so that Manco Fernández would not overhear.

"There was a palo santo not far back along our trail," Igor told them. "If one stood with his back to the tree, the ants would come out and eat through the ropes. Unfortunately they might also eat much of one's hands before weakening the ropes sufficiently for one to break free."

"Good suggestion," Ashwood observed. "We'll wait for you to get back."

It was late afternoon when screams erupted from the vicinity of the third and farthest opening in the Inca wall.

"Cave-in?" Ashwood ventured hopefully.

Igor twisted to look. "I'm afraid not."

Da Rimini and Blanco Fernández were running toward the campsite. Trang Ho followed, her half-frame camera working furiously. Even at a distance the glint of sunlight on metal was impossible to mistake.

Manco rose to stare. The prisoners tried to.

Blanco had slung his rifle. Now he passed the contents of his cupped palms to his brother. Hairpins, pieces of necklace, earrings, and household utensils tumbled to the ground, overflowing from Fernández's hands.

Every one of them was fashioned of dull, yellow gold.

"That's nothing." Da Rimini's expression was wild. "Look at this." She unwrapped the towel from the object she was carrying. It caught the setting sun along with everyone's breath.

The plate was half an inch thick and eighteen

inches in diameter, solid gold, inscribed with designs and symbols inlaid with turquoise. The raised outer rim was lined with twenty-one emeralds, each the size of a silver dollar.

"That's it." Ashwood straightened. "They'll kill us for sure now."

Da Rimini gazed haughtily down at Fewick. "*Mira*! There is more inside, much more. You did not have enough confidence in your own research." She glanced over her shoulder.

"The last opening leads to a small cave, the far end of which is lined with broken stone. It was a wall which had collapsed, perhaps from an earthquake. We dug and broke through to another, much bigger cave. The floor is of Inca stonework. So are the bins which are filled to overflowing with artifacts like this!" She turned the plate and it threw sunlight into the trees.

"We left in a hurry to bring Manco the news, but I saw at least one clay pot full of emeralds, another of gold figurines. We did not walk the length of the cavern but we saw enough to know that this is truly the Paititi of legend. This is the place where the Incas hid the treasure the conquistadores never found. Riches beyond imagining."

Manco Fernández held a necklace of heavy gold up to the setting sun. "*Incaworld*!" he proclaimed, his fingers clenching around the strand. Visions of millions of eager visitors filled his thoughts, and they were all buying Inca Cola and fried chicken and T-shirts.

The following day the prisoners were herded into the cave. Not so they could view the treasure, but because it made it easier for their captors to keep an

eye on them. Though they could see little because
the Fernández brothers were using the lights, Fewick, at least, was ecstatic.

"This is unprecedented." Blanco Fernández directed them to a depression in the floor and ordered
them to sit. "The quality of the stonework both
underfoot and in the bins is superb. The Incas were
not known for building underground."

"What I would like to know," said Igor, "is what
happened to the people who built this place and hid
this treasure here?"

Fewick considered. "Perhaps they left to join in
the fight against the Spaniards and the location was
lost as the builders were killed. Or as the empire dis-
integrated they may have intermarried with the jungle peoples, or been wiped out by them. The fallen
wall sealed this part of the cave, and in any case the
local Indians would be reluctant to enter an obviously sacred place. Though clearly not to visit the
site."

They were forced to sit there most of the day while
their captors loaded backpacks with the choicest
artifacts and jewels. The only consolation was that
it was much cooler inside the cave than out in the
sun.

When they decided they could carry no more, Carter knew, Da Rimini would carry out her sentence.
Oddly he found himself worrying not for himself but
for Macha, who had not returned since being chased
into the jungle by Fewick's cat.

"Hey, what's this?" Concern resounded from the
depths of the cavern and he recognized the voice of
Manco Fernández. By sitting erect and straining he
could just make out the man's light, bobbing in the

distance like an inquisitive will-o'-the-wisp.

"*Qué hay?*" Blanco shouted.

"Come and see." His brother's voice echoed off the dark stone walls. Da Rimini and Manco took flashlight and lantern and moved to comply. The occasional flare of Trang Ho's camera accompanied them like a parasitic firefly.

Left alone in the darkness, Carter whispered to Igor. "Turn your back to mine and let me work on your ropes."

It was not to be. Da Rimini soon returned and the two men had to separate hurriedly. Her light blinded them.

"We have found something puzzling." The beam of the flashlight focused on Fewick. "You are the archaeologist. You mus' explain this thing to us."

"Why should I help you?" Fewick shot back, with a resolve that made Carter proud.

"Because if you do not I will shoot off your left testicle."

Fewick struggled to his feet. "Always ready to aid a lady in need of assistance."

Da Rimini wasn't about to leave the prisoners alone for any length of time. "The rest of you come too."

At the far end of the cavern a perfectly circular platform of exquisitely dressed stone surmounted the paving. Atop the platform and fashioned of identical gray stone was a small circular building whose walls inclined inward. The structure was roofless and airy, the curving wall punctured by traditional trapezoidal Inca-style windows. In order to enter, one had to step around a single oddly carved rectangular block of stone that must have weighed several tons.

"It looks just like the intihuatana," Fewick exclaimed in surprise.

"The what?" Ashwood asked, puzzled.

"An altar stone at Machu Picchu which is hewn out of the mountain itself. Its four corners point to the four points of the compass. The name means 'the place where the sun is tied,' or more colloquially, 'the hitching post of the sun.' " He frowned. "But there is no sun here."

"This isn't what you were brought to look at." An impatient Da Rimini prodded them forward.

They entered the little building and found themselves looking at a gigantic egg.

IX———

THE egg was twice the size of Fewick's belly, which was saying something. Four legs of what appeared to be rutilated blue ceramic raised it two feet off the stone floor.

"It won't move," Manco Fernández informed them. "I tried."

The top and upper two thirds of the egg were completely covered with carvings and inscriptions. They resembled neither the Pusharo petroglyphs nor those which decorated the wall outside the cave. In the artificial light its surface shone like a pearl, lustrous and full of reticent whorls of iridescence.

"If I am to examine it properly I will need my hands free," Fewick declared firmly.

"All right." Da Rimini nodded to Blanco, who released the archaeologist. "But don' try nothin'."

Fewick favored her with a wan smile, then approached the egg and cautiously ran his fingers across the engraved surface. "It feels sticky in places, glassy-smooth in others. Most peculiar. If it is an Inca artifact it is unique." He glanced at the entrance to the circular shelter. "Clearly a connection exists between this object and the replica of the intihuatana, but what it might be quite escapes me."

"Never mind that." Da Rimini's hands were in

constant motion, piercing the air like psychotic hummingbirds. "Is it valuable? Some kind of enormous gemstone, perhaps?"

"I am not a geologist." Fewick gazed in fascination at the glistening, milky-white engraved ovoid. "Superficially it much resembles chalcedony, but the presence of iridescence suggests a different composition. It is not a moonstone. Quartz crystals larger than this have been found in Minas Gerais province in Brazil, but that is a long ways from here. Until now, the crystal skull of the Mayas has been the largest artifact of its type found in Mesoamerica. This is bigger, but less spectacular."

"It mus' still be valuable." Da Rimini blinked in irritation as Trang Ho's camera flashed.

"Wonderful," the reporter was bubbling. "Another major discovery. I'll get a series out of this trip, and maybe a book."

"I hope y'all get a rare disease," Ashwood told her. "An' if you set that thing off in my face one more time, tied or not, so help me I'll . . ."

Oblivious, Ho continued to take pictures from different angles.

"Well, if it is a kind of gemstone we will find out when we come back to this place," Da Rimini declared.

Manco Fernández was reluctant to leave. "You are sure you cannot make sense of this, gringo?" He was running his fingers over the deep engravings that covered the upper third of the object.

"I note a few similarities to other Peruvian petroglyphs, but that is all. The majority of designs are unknown to me."

"That is all right." He spoke proudly. "It is a good

conversation piece. We will put it in front of the log ride at the park."

"What's that?" His brother suddenly whirled and lowered the muzzle of his AK-47. Then he relaxed and smiled. "Crazy gringos and their pets."

Fewick knelt and welcomed his cat into his arms. "You finally got lonely out there, did you, Moe?" He glanced up at Blanco. "Getting nervous, are we?" The brother grunted.

A worried Carter looked back toward the entrance to the cave. There was no sign of Macha.

Da Rimini was watching Fewick, a disgusted look on her face. "How touching." She kicked out at the tom, who easily avoided her foot and landed atop the ovoid. It paced there, watching her.

"You know," said Ashwood conversationally, "you really are a first-class bitch."

The Amazon ignored her, tapped the enigmatic egg. "I agree that this is interesting, but no matter how valuable it may be, it is too big for us to carry."

"If we only knew what these meant." Manco used a finger to trace one of the indentations cut into the side of the artifact. "They might tell us much about our ancestors." Moe leaned over, sniffing at him.

The egg began to hum.

It was a steady susurration, unvarying in pitch, that rose rapidly in volume until it was as loud as a human voice. Manco Fernández let out a startled oath and jerked his hand away from the vitreous surface he'd been caressing as if he'd been burned. Da Rimini's gaze narrowed.

Moe continued to pace unconcernedly atop the object. Only when it began to glow with an intense white light did the cat leap lithely to the ground. It rubbed against Fewick's ankles, purring softly.

Ashwood was the only one with enough sense to make a dash for the exit. She didn't get very far, as the light simultaneously intensified and expanded to soundlessly engulf them all.

Carter blinked, having lost both footing and vision for an instant. Now he steadied himself, trying to focus on his surroundings.

The light had faded as quickly as a burst from Trang Ho's flash. The egg was still there, resting immovably on its four peculiar blue supports. Everyone had kept their feet and several were rubbing at their outraged eyes.

"*Madre de Dios*," Da Rimini mumbled. "What happened?"

Fewick was shaking his head, blinking at the floor. "That is not a gemstone. It is a device of some kind."

"That is crazy," said Da Rimini. Holding the fluorescent lantern high while keeping a wary eye on the now quiescent ovoid, she started backing out of the room. "We have enough treasure. Let's finish our business here an' leave this place."

Outside the circular stone chamber, Manco Fernández stepped around the intihuatana before halting uncertainly. He played the flashlight he was carrying over the walls of the cave.

"This does not look right."

"What are you babbling about?" Da Rimini looked back at him. "Hurry up."

"No." He stepped up alongside her. "It is different somehow. See there?"

With his light he illuminated one of the bins which lined the right-hand side of the cave. Carter stared.

The stonework was the same, but he did not remember the intricate inscriptions which covered much of the rock nor the complex bas-reliefs.

Ignoring the guns, Fewick let out an excited cry and rushed forward to run trembling fingers over the inscriptions. "Writing! Do you realize what this means? It has always been believed that the Incas never developed writing." His voice rose triumphantly. "This means the Baxter Prize for certain, perhaps even a Nobel!"

Ashwood was frowning. "I don' recall seein' any writing when we come in." She sniffed at the air. "Don' it seem drier in here than before?"

Manco Fernández's fears vanished in light of the discovery his brother made next. While Fewick wept over the unprecedented inscriptions, Blanco tried the handle of the wooden door which barred the way into the modest structure. When it refused to open he hammered on the catch with the butt of his rifle.

On the third try the ancient, desiccated latch gave way. So did the entire door, which buckled in the middle. The contents of the structure buried Blanco before he could get clear, flooding outward and carrying him partway across the floor.

When the avalanche finally ceased, Blanco lay flailing wildly in a sea of gold.

Gold plates and cups, gold strips and bars, necklaces and rings and earrings of gold and silver. The glistening bounty multiplied the light of the lantern and sent it careening joyfully across the dark stone walls and ceiling.

Like everyone else Carter was stunned speechless. The small high-walled bin probably held several tons of gold. And there were other bins, similarly shaped and secured, lining the right-hand side of the cave for a distance of at least fifty yards.

He peered past the last. No entrance, no small circle of sunlight, greeted his gaze. He checked his watch. It was still late afternoon. The sun should still be up. For that matter, he did not remember that any of the small bins they had passed on their way in had been secured with wooden doors.

Trang Ho was of similar mind. "We have come out somewhere else from where we started. This is wonderful!" She began taking pictures like mad. "This is marvelous, this is fantastic!"

"This sucks," muttered Ashwood.

Da Rimini looked from where the Fernández brothers were cavorting like children in the golden talus back to the circular temple room which held the egg.

"I don' understand. What's going on?"

"Trang Ho is correct." Fewick turned reluctantly from his beloved inscriptions while Moe regarded the whooping Fernández brothers thoughtfully. "That flash of light moved us from the cave we had been inside to this one." He nodded in the direction of the now quiescent ovoid. "It is a transportation device of some kind. A transmitter of matter. A means of travel." He glanced down at the floor. "Somehow Moe activated it when he was walking around on top."

"You are talking of magical things," she said nervously.

"Not magic. Science. The Incas had advanced to the point of performing brain surgery, trepanning. Although I can scarce credit it, this is something they must have discovered at the last minute, probably after Pizarro defeated Atahualpa. Evidently they utilized it to save the last of their treasure from the conquistadores."

"That's a lot to swallow," Carter commented.

"I am open to alternate explanations." Fewick leaned back. "The ceiling is twenty feet higher than before. I wonder where we are."

"In one of the caves reached by one of the other two openings?" Ashwood suggested.

Da Rimini shook her head. "We tried them first. Both were dead ends."

"Or better sealed," Ashwood argued. "Don't y'all think you ought to see if there's a way out?" She was smiling wolfishly. "If there ain't we could be trapped in here forever. That'd be nice an' cozy."

"Shut your mouth." Da Rimini was clearly unnerved as she turned to yell at her companions. "We need to find the exit, you idiots! There'll be plenty of time for play later."

It occurred to Carter that he could ram the preoccupied Da Rimini from behind and knock her to the floor. The Fernández brothers were busy swimming in their gold. Unfortunately that plan required that Fewick, as the only one with his hands free, recover his pistol from the Amazon and use it if necessary. Which meant, Carter decided sorrowfully, that it was no plan at all.

If he could only get one hand free.

Everyone waited while the brothers explored the cave. Two hours later they returned, considerably less animated than they had been earlier. Manco shook his head.

"We could find no way out."

"There are big tunnels but they all lead downward," Blanco added with a slight shudder. "We did not go very far into any of them."

"There has to be a way out," the frustrated Da Rimini exclaimed.

"Not necessarily." Fewick sat quietly by the lantern, stroking Moe. The cat lay contentedly in his lap. "What better hiding place for a great treasure than a cave with only *that* as the way in and out?" He nodded in the direction of the ovoid.

Ashwood made a noise. "Are you thinkin' of tryin' to use that whatever-it-is again?"

"Why not? If it was used to bring this gold here, then people had to be moving back and forth. We have no reason to suppose it only operates in one direction."

"Then we could take some of this gold with us." Da Rimini looked thoughtful.

"Hey," said Carter warningly, "whose side are you on, Fewick?"

The archaeologist eyed him noncommittally. "Why, the same side I have always been on, my thespianic friend. The side of knowledge." He glanced at Da Rimini. "This is a primitive site. If there is another way out of here I am the individual most likely to find it. However, if you wish my help I must ask that you return my pistol to me." He paused. "I would decide quickly. The batteries in these lights will not last forever."

Da Rimini hesitated, glanced at her partners. Manco Fernández nodded. "Very well. But if you try anything you die."

"Concisely put." He smiled and set Moe aside.

"Bastard," Ashwood muttered.

"I beg to disagree," he responded. "I am legitimate, if not popular." He accepted his pistol from Da Rimini, made sure the safety was off, and slipped it back into his holster.

"Get up," Da Rimini told her three remaining prisoners. "You are coming with us. I don' trust leaving you alone."

So much for him and Igor working on each other's bonds, Carter thought disappointedly. They stumbled up the tunnel, following their captors.

Sure enough, Fewick found a path where no one else would have thought to look. It began beneath a half-collapsed lintel and led off to the right. In spite of the fate which probably awaited them, Carter found that he was eager for fresh air and the sight of the sun again. If they had to die he much preferred to do so out in the open. And if they were lucky an opportunity to escape might yet present itself.

The paved path ended in a solid rock wall.

Fewick made no attempt to conceal his disappointment. "This is not what I expected."

"It not very useful, either," growled Da Rimini.

"That's because your eyes ain't no sharper than your brain." Ashwood stepped forward and nodded at a corner of the wall.

Set in a small carved recess was a miniature of the mysterious ovoid. It sported a much duller sheen than its larger relative and was no more than a couple of inches tall. Only two grooves marred its otherwise perfectly smooth surface.

Manco reached for it, only to find that it was fastened securely into the stone. He glanced back at Da Rimini.

"Try it," she said.

He nodded, considered for a moment, then ran two

fingers down the pair of engravings. His effort was
rewarded by a grinding noise that made everyone
retreat several steps.

A portion of the wall slid aside, creating an opening just wide enough for one person to slip through.
Accompanied by a cool breeze, evening light poured
into the passageway. They filed out under Manco
Fernández's watchful eye.

The jungle was gone.

They found themselves standing on a rocky hillside. Brush and small trees grew in isolated clumps,
hiding the well-concealed entrance from view. Not
that there was anyone around to notice it.

Spread out before them lay a vast barren plain.
To the north they could make out a few cultivated
fields scattered around a small river. A single smoky
tendril curled through the clear air, marking the
location of some unseen habitation. Other than the
smoke, the only sign of life was a small single-engine
plane which was slowly circling the plain at high
altitude.

The sharp-eyed Igor was the first to notice what
the plane's occupants were examining. As soon as
he pointed it out, Manco Fernández let out a startled
oath in Spanish.

"Nazca. *Por Dios*, we've come to Nazca!"

"What's that?" Carter asked him. Fewick looked
at the actor and shook his head sadly.

"An archaeological site of some repute," he explained dryly. "It predates the Incas by some hundreds of years." He squinted at the buzzing plane.
"People come here to view the massive figures and
lines the Nazca 'drew' on this plain by moving dark
rock and gravel aside to reveal the lighter rock under-

neath. Many of the drawings can only properly be viewed from high above. It is an interesting phenomenon for which multiple explanations have been advanced."

"Von Daniken," said Ashwood.

"Oh, come now," Fewick admonished her.

"Who's Von Daniken?" Carter inquired ingenuously.

"Don't tell me you've never heard of Von Daniken?" Ashwood stared at him in disbelief.

Carter shrugged slightly. "Actually, no."

"Erich von Daniken? *'Hubcaps of the Gods,'* or whatever? One o' his theories claimed that these here Nazca lines were made by the locals to help extraterrestrials' spaceships land here."

"Every one of his claims has been explained away," Fewick insisted.

"So I've heard." She looked back over her shoulder, at the entrance to the cave. "Now somebody's gonna have to explain away that matter transmitter. Or are you gonna tell me it was a Kodak moment that brought us all the way here across the Andes from Paititi?"

"The two phenomena are not related," Fewick muttered.

"Where is here, anyway?" Carter asked.

Igor was studying the plane, wondering if its occupants might spot them standing there among the trees. "More than two hundred miles southwest of the Manú, where we were. Close to the ocean."

Ashwood continued to taunt the archaeologist. "C'mon, Fewick. Tell me again there ain't no connection. Tell me how the Incas went and built themselves a matter transmitter."

The whirr of the motor drive on Trang Ho's camera provided quiet mechanical counterpoint to the hum of the observation plane's engine. Igor's hopes fell as it banked and turned northward.

"Matter transmitter." Manco Fernández had stood aloof from the conversation, thinking furiously. "Do you realize, Blanco, what this means?"

"No, what?" By this time Carter was convinced that the slightly larger Fernández twin operated on two fewer cylinders than his older brother. "Money?"

"Yes, yes. Scientists will pay much to study such a device. But more important than that, much more." His eyes gleamed. "Think what it could mean for crowd flow control at Incaworld!"

"Questions of origin aside," Fewick protested, "you are speaking of one of the great scientific discoveries of the century. Surely you cannot be thinking of exploiting it for crass commercial motives?"

Manco eyed him as if he was crazy. "What else would anybody exploit anything for?"

"I wonder what the power source is," Igor murmured to no one in particular. "I wonder *where* it is?"

"*Sí!*" Blanco fed on his brother's excitement. "Disneyland have nothing like this. We could put one in Cuzco, or even in Lima."

"You have no idea of its range," Fewick pointed out.

The brothers ignored him. Manco waxed rhapsodic. "People would not have to fly into the selva or take the road through Paucartambo."

"The Incas did this," announced Da Rimini with

sudden conviction. "The stonework inside the caves is theirs. The goldwork is theirs. I don' know how, but they were responsible." She kept repeating "they were responsible" as if it was some kind of sanity-preserving mantra.

The evening breeze chilled Carter, still clad in his jungle gear. He gazed longingly toward the curl of smoke and the plowed fields. Even with his hands bound behind him he thought he could outrun the Fernández brothers. He might run into a farmer with a truck, or tourists in a four-by-four.

Da Rimini did not share her partners' ecstasy. "I read your mind through your eyes, Jason Carter. Don' try it. You cannot outrun a bullet." The wildness had returned to her expression.

With a sudden move she jerked Fewick's pistol from its holster. He was a second too late with his hand.

"Madam, you are a witch. We had a bargain."

She grinned nastily. "So complain to your ambassador." She started backing toward the entrance to the cave. "Come on, everybody. We goin' back to Paititi."

"Now, wait a minute," Fewick began. Da Rimini glared at him.

"You say yourself you think it work both directions."

"Yes, but . . ."

"*Vámonos!* Now." She gestured meaningfully with the pistol.

The Fernández brothers eyed one another. Looking resigned, they raised their rifles and gestured for the prisoners to move.

"Oh, good," said Trang Ho delightedly as they

started back the way they'd come. "Another journey. This time I can take notes."

"Ain't you maybe just a little concerned this crazy gadget might not work right this time?" Ashwood asked her.

"*Vang*, yes. Of course it will," the reporter said confidently. "It worked the last time, didn't it?"

Da Rimini used the mini-egg to close the entrance behind them. On the way back to the central cavern one of the two flashlights gave out. Everyone walked a little faster.

"Everybody stand where they were standing before." The reckless way she waved the automatic pistol around as she spoke made Carter more than a little nervous. "I wouldn' want to leave anybody behind." Ashwood reluctantly assumed her position near the egg as best she remembered it.

"Now what?" Manco asked her.

She hesitated. "Run your fingers over the top of the thing, where the cat was standing."

A dubious Fernández complied. Carter tensed reflexively, but nothing happened.

"Keep trying," she ordered her associate. Fernández did so until his arms grew tired and he was forced to stop.

"Tough luck," Ashwood sneered. Da Rimini glared furiously at her.

"The cat made it work before," observed Blanco Fernández with childish logic. Before Fewick could protest, the younger brother bent and scooped Moe off the floor, depositing him atop the ovoid.

"Coincidence." There was pity in Fewick's voice. It lasted until the egg began to hum. Da Rimini looked smug.

"Get ready, everybody." Carter tensed, but Da Rimini was staring straight at him, the pistol leveled at his chest. He tried to decide whether to risk it anyway. If he timed it right she might only wing him, and his chances were bound to be better here than back in the jungle.

He was preparing to run for it when the white light filled his eyes.

As he fought to clear his vision he could hear Fewick commenting thoughtfully, "I was afraid of this."

X

THE roofless circular stone chamber had vanished. There was more than enough light present to make their flashlights and lantern redundant.

They no longer stood in the cave at Nazca, however. Nor had they returned to Paititi. For one thing, the ceiling was much farther away and composed of something smooth and shiny instead of unhewn stone.

On the far side of a wide black and silver walkway strange objects and shapes were arraigned equidistant from one another. Some were enclosed in transparent cases while others stood exposed to the air, which, Carter noted, was now pleasantly cool and dry. Both the fetid humidity of the selva and the desiccated chill of Nazca had been banished.

"Look at this." Like everyone else, he turned at Fewick's call. With an effort, the archaeologist had knelt to inspect one of the ovoid's four legs.

"What about it?" an uneasy Da Rimini asked, unable to take her eyes from the astonishing chamber in which they now found themselves.

"See the color? It's different. More of a greenish blue." He struggled erect, touched the egg. "I think this is different too."

"Impossible!"

Ashwood was studying their silent, softly lit surroundings. "So is this, but I don't think I'm dream-in'."

Manco Fernández let out a cry. Like the egg, they found themselves standing on a platform fashioned of green and yellow ceramic hexagons joined seamlessly together. The platform seemed to run the length of the chamber and matched the one attached to the far side of the black and silver walkway. Both were less than a foot high.

Now he ran to his right and removed from a perch composed of some transparent material the most spectacular single artifact they had thus far encountered. It was a crown fashioned of solid and hammered gold, lined with the iridescent feathers of jungle birds, emeralds, and other gemstones. The workmanship was breathtaking. Furthermore, it looked brand-new, untouched by the ages.

Carefully he raised it high and placed it atop his head. Despite his quarter-Spanish heritage he looked very much the part of the noble Inca. Even Ashwood was impressed. Blanco Fernández executed a mock bow, grinning at his brother.

Fewick, for once, did not lose himself in contemlation of such artifacts. He was much more interested in their new surroundings.

"We have emerged somewhere else," he commented unnecessarily. "This is a modern structure, fashioned by modern means. It most emphatically was not built by people who did not know the wheel."

Carter took another deep breath. Not only was the air here more agreeable than at Paititi or Nazca, it was lightly perfumed, faintly redolent of frangipani.

Trang Ho snapped a picture of Manco Fernández posing in the glorious crown, then moved to cross the walkway to inspect the objects on the far side. As she went to step off the mosaicked platform she stumbled, caught herself, and retreated a step. Cautiously she advanced again, holding both palms out in front of her.

Carter was watching. "Something wrong?"

The reporter spoke without looking back at him. "I can't get down. There's some kind of barrier here."

Further exploration revealed that while they could move to the left or right, they could not get off the platform. The invisible wall was soft, springy, and impervious.

"Someone's coming," Igor announced tersely. Everyone turned to their left.

The old man was short and dark, with black eyes and a large hooked nose. He wore a silvery tunic decorated with blue spots arranged in random patterns and matching silver slippers. The tunic had short sleeves and stopped at his knees. What looked like aluminum braid decorated his right shoulder. On his head he wore a black and silver cap which bulged to one side, and he carried a metal cylinder or tube about a foot long which was lined with dark indentations.

He came around the corner grumbling to himself, but his muttering ceased abruptly when he caught sight of the staring travelers. He stopped in his tracks and gaped at them.

Not one for protocol, Da Rimini advanced as far as the barrier would permit. "What is this place?" she demanded to know. Trang Ho stood nearby, snapping pictures like crazy.

The oldster reminded Carter of someone, but it took a moment to make the connection. He looked

cousin to the janitor at the hotel he and Ashwood
had stayed at in Cuzco.

Overcoming his surprise, the man approached
them and touched the lower part of the tube he
carried. It must have affected the barrier somehow
because he stepped lightly up onto the platform to
join them, displaying no apprehension at the sight of
the Fernández brothers' weapons. He did, however,
note that three of the visitors had their arms tied
behind them.

Inspecting each of them in turn he chose to address
Manco. His manner was decidedly officious and he
waved the tube around for emphasis. For all that he
could understand none of it, his words still sounded
familiar to Carter.

"Can you tell what he's saying?" he asked Igor.

"It is an odd mixture of Spanish and Quechua,"
the guide replied. "There are words I don't recognize
at all, and the accent is strange. But basically he is
telling Manco to put the headdress back where he
got it, and that we should not be up here. It is a
restricted"—he struggled with the last word—"exhibit."

"Exhibit?" Carter stared at the old man.

"From what he is saying I think we are in some
kind of museum. He also wants to know why some
of us have our wrists tied behind us."

It was Da Rimini who replied, leaving Igor to
translate for his Anglo companions. Carter was more
in the dark than anyone, since both Ashwood and
Fewick spoke fair Spanish. Even Trang Ho knew a
little. He felt very left out.

"We're from Cuzco," she told the oldster. "Manco,
put the crown back. We are getting out of here." She

gestured with the pistol. "Everyone, get back around the egg. Hurry!"

Ignoring the old man's protestations they gathered once again around the transmitter. She picked up Moe and placed him atop the egg . . . where the big tom promptly curled up into his tail and went peacefully to sleep. Anxious urgings failed to rouse him.

Da Rimini feverishly ran her own fingers randomly across the upper third of the ovoid. It remained silent and dark. "It's not working." She glared desperately at Fewick. "Why isn't it working?"

The archaeologist spread his hands in a gesture of helplessness. "I am the wrong person to ask about mechanical matters. I cannot change the oil on a car."

Angrily she turned and aimed the muzzle of her weapon at the old man. Carter tensed, but the oldster merely regarded her as one would a particularly interesting new species of bug.

"I'd watch my step," Ashwood warned their captor. "He may not even know it's a gun. If he does and he ain't afraid of it, that says to me he's got reason not to be afraid of it. Which means maybe you ought to for once stop and think before bargin' on ahead."

An uncertain Da Rimini lowered the pistol and used her voice instead. "We have to go back." She gestured at the ovoid. "You have turned it off somehow. Turn it back on."

"Is this the real Paititi?" Carter wondered aloud.

Igor was shaking his head. "I do not know. How could you hide a place like this? *Where* could you hide a place like this? It could be someone's private museum somewhere outside Lima, but that does not explain this man's peculiar speech, or his clothes, or the invisible barrier. Not to mention the transmitters. I am very confused."

"Man, you aren't alone." He raised his voice. "Hey, grandpa! Don't you understand English?"

The oldster glanced briefly in his direction, resumed listening to Da Rimini. Carter contained his frustration, wishing he'd never found Fewick's disc, wishing he'd never left L.A.

"You think he really did turn the transmitter off?"

"I do not know," said Igor.

"Well, at least he seems friendly enough."

"Everybody seems friendly to you, Jason," said Ashwood. "Sometimes I wonder how you've survived as long as you have in the film business."

Abruptly the oldster turned and left the platform. When Da Rimini tried to follow, she found herself blocked once more by the barrier. Despite her exhortations, he disappeared back the way he'd come, walking fast.

In his absence Da Rimini resumed fingering the top of the ovoid, to no avail. She stopped only when the old man returned. This time he had company.

The group halted on the walkway and began arguing among themselves, ignoring the incensed Da Rimini.

"They do not know who we are." Igor struggled to follow the conversation. "They aren't sure *what* we are. I am certain I must be missing some of their conversation."

"Are they Incas?" Carter asked him.

"I do not know. Certainly they look like pure Indio."

Fed up with being ignored, Da Rimini called the

Fernández brothers over. "Maybe they really don'
know what guns do. So we explain to them. Blanco,
shoot at something across the room."

"Are you sure, Francesca?"

"Do it!" she screamed.

With obvious reluctance, the bigger brother turned
and fired a burst from his AK-47. Carter ducked as
bullets ricocheted wildly around the platform. The
fleeting demonstration was very instructive. People
were not the only thing which couldn't step through
the barrier. Bullets were equally restricted.

It certainly accomplished the task of drawing the
visitors' attention, however. One of them pointed
the tube he carried at the platform. The Fernández
brothers promptly yelped and dropped their weapons, as did Da Rimini. All three began shaking their
hands violently, as if their fingers had been caught
in a hot waffle iron.

Da Rimini cursed and lunged to recover her pistol.
The individual who'd pointed the tube at Blanco
Fernández now turned it toward her, whereupon she
howled and clutched at her stomach, collapsing to
the ground. The Fernández brothers gallantly rushed
to her aid, only to retreat with alacrity as she began
heaving her guts all over the nice shiny six-sided
tiles.

"Oh, they're real friendly, all right," Ashwood told
Carter with delicate Texas sarcasm.

As two of the men, including the wielder of the
tube of unpleasant surprises, stepped up onto the
platform, Carter and his companions retreated. Stepping distastefully over the recumbent Da Rimini,
who had by now nearly exhausted the contents of
her digestive system, the men gathered up the two

AK-47s and the pistol. As they rejoined their curious companions Trang Ho tested the barrier, was not surprised to find it back in place.

"That's better," said Ashwood. "Much better." She was greatly enjoying Da Rimini's discomfort. Fewick strolled over and began to untie Carter. The Fernández brothers eyed one another, shrugged in unison. Without their weapons there was no point in provoking hostilities. Da Rimini might have argued otherwise, but she was in no condition to give orders.

"Not only do they know what guns are, they have some interesting variants of their own." Fewick undid the last of the actor's bonds. Carter stretched gratefully, then set to freeing Igor.

"Why'd you do that?" he asked the archaeologist.

Fewick smiled pleasantly at him. "We find ourselves in an awkward and unprecedented situation from which satisfactory extrication shall doubtless require the maximum of mutual cooperation."

"In other words," said Ashwood, "when scared shitless, first priority is to cover your own ass."

"Precisely," said Fewick.

"Excuse me." Trang Ho was pressing against the barrier, camera in hand. "Could you hold that tube thing up so I can get a better shot?"

Whether it was her mix of English and Spanish or her appearance that attracted their attention, they all turned as she snapped her picture. "Thanks."

Carter was listening intently to the babble on the walkway, wishing he'd paid more attention to the limited Spanish instruction he'd received in school.

"Are we under arrest or something?"

"No," Igor told him. "They are more puzzled by us than anything else. Especially you."

"Me?"

"Yes. Also Trang Ho and Mr. Fewick. The rest of us, including Ms. Ashwood, they do not find as intriguing. It has to do with your physical differences. Trang Ho is Vietnamese, while you and Mr. Fewick are blond and blue-eyed. Their confusion over this suggests that their knowledge of the world is very limited and that they have long been isolated from the rest of mankind."

"Are you telling me that these people are Incas, real Incas?" Carter murmured.

"Their descendants, certainly."

"I would venture to guess that these people learned of firearms and writing, Spanish, and perhaps much else from the conquistadores." Fewick studied the high curved ceiling thoughtfully. "I wonder where we really are."

"I'm more concerned with what they're gonna do with us," said Ashwood.

Moe meowed softly. Fewick promptly lifted the cat from the top of the ovoid and placed him on his right shoulder. "Have you ever noticed how cats make much more sensible companions than human beings?"

It made Carter think of Macha, but he did not wish for her presence. She was probably better off back at Paititi.

Four more well-dressed Incas arrived in a small pale yellow cart that traveled silently across the floor on plastic wheels. Carter's imagination was beginning to work overtime.

The new arrivals extracted packages from the rear of the vehicle and approached the platform. After a momentary pause they entered and set their burdens down on the floor. As each container was opened, a new aroma filled the air. Steam vented from two of the smooth-sided cartons. Another contained recognizable utensils.

As the delivery team retreated, the prisoners cautiously inspected what they had brought.

"At least they don't mean to starve us." Ashwood helped herself to a knife and fork while contemplating a potbellied tumbler of amber liquid.

A tall Inca joined them. Carter guessed him to be close to Ashwood's age. His tunic was yellow with bold red stripes and there was a red sun symbol on the tube he carried.

"Of course we are not going to starve you. Think you that we are uncivilized?" Carter's eyes widened.

"You speak English?"

"We can speak many languages. We secretly took the knowledge of it, as we did of other things, from the viracochas. My name, to you, is Apu Tupa."

"Viracocha is what the ancient Incas called the first Spaniards they encountered," Igor whispered to Carter. "Apu Tupa means 'Master Tupa' in Quechua. This is an important personage."

"Where are we?" Fewick inquired politely. "What is this place? Who are you people?"

"And how soon can we leave?" Manco Fernández added.

The man turned to him. "You look much like us. These others do not. Some resemble viracochas. Others are clearly the English or something else the viracocha books speak of." A hand indicated Trang Ho. "That woman resembles no people we know." He looked back at Manco. "You carried weapons." Perhaps wisely, Fernández said nothing.

Apu Tupa continued to study them. "As to your questions: perhaps you know of Vilcabamba?"

Fewick spoke up. "The Inca state that survived in the jungle long after Pizarro and his men crushed the empire."

Apu Tupa nodded. "It was not the only such place. Eventually the viracochas conquered it as well, but they never found *our* city."

"Paititi!" said Igor suddenly.

"Yes. We lived there in safety, stealing up into our conquered lands to learn from the viracochas, killing those who rarely ventured down into our territory. Such killings were always blamed on the jungle peoples and so our existence remained a secret.

"Much time passed. Then we found the true inti-huatana, which allows us to travel along the intiran. The road of the sun."

"The transmitter at what we called Paititi," Igor said.

Tupa nodded. "It carried our people and many who came down from the mountains to join us to this place, where we have lived and learned undisturbed since that time. More than two hundred years ago the intiran suddenly ceased to function, and not all our acquired skills were able to make it work again. So we moved it to this place, where we view and venerate the works of our ancestors. But it is clear that it *is* now working again, because it has brought you to us."

"Then you didn't build the transmitters?" Fewick asked.

"No. Like much that we have since discovered here, they were constructed by Those-Who-Came-Before."

"Aliens," Trang Ho murmured, eyes shining.

"Who or what are Those-Who-Came-Before?" Fe-wick wondered.

"We do not know. We do not even know what they looked like. They left behind no record of their physical appearance. But they did leave much." He straightened. "What they left has made us great. Greater than ever was the empire of our ancestors. Greater than the viracochas.

"I have been appointed to deal with you because I am a student of the ancient world and its languages. In addition to Quechua, Spanish, and English I am also fluent in French, Dutch, and the Teutonic dialects." He looked at the ovoid.

"At first we thought the intiran let people travel along beams of sunlight. Now we know it is a matter of physics, not magic."

In spite of what they'd already seen, Fewick was startled. "You know physics?"

"We know a great deal. Among the devices Those-Who-Came-Before left here is a machine which teaches. Not by voice, but by sending knowledge directly into a person's mind. It frightened us at first, but the machine understood our fright and was patient with us. It studied us and explained the world in terms we could understand. Soon we became comfortable with it. Then we began to learn.

"It was Those-Who-Came-Before who placed the transmitters on Earth. They were observing human-ity long before Pachacuti founded the empire in 1438. Then, insofar as we know, they simply departed, leaving behind their devices both here and on Earth."

"Are we prisoners?" Ashwood wanted to know.

Apu Tupa regarded her thoughtfully. "You are being . . . looked after. We have much to discuss. For example, we would like to know what English people were doing in our homeland."

"We're not English," Carter told him. "We're Americans."

Apu Tupa frowned. "What are Americans?"

"A people who broke away from the English king," Fewick informed him. "They settled the lands to the north of your old empire."

The oldster nodded. "I see." His voice darkened unexpectedly as he pointed his tube at Da Rimini, who flinched. "We know what *she* is. One of the conquerors."

"Just a minute," she protested. "I ain' conquer nobody. You talkin' about things that happen hundreds of years ago."

Carter tried to change the subject. "Did Those-Who-Came-Before build this place too?"

"No. We built this, and much else besides, with the aid of their devices. It is our home now." He looked ceilingward and waved his tube in a great arc. "It is another world, another place. The stars here are different from those of Earth. Two *kilya* reside in our night sky. Though we have learned much astronomy we do not know what place in the heavens Earth occupies, nor how distant it lies from this place.

"We call it Contisuyu. Contisuyu was the southwest quarter of Tahuantinsuya, the four corners of our ancestors' empire." He looked anxiously at his guests. "We would very much like to know what has happened to our homeland in our absence."

Fewick's belly had deferred to his brain as long as possible. Now he chose utensils and a container and sat down, eating ravenously while passing choice morsels to the expectant Moe.

"Well, there's no more viceroyalty of Peru. Your empire's been broken up into parts of half a dozen different independent countries. Spain's no longer a great power, nor is England. The great powers in the world today are America and Russia."

Apu Tupa nodded. "Spanish texts mention the Russia of the czars."

"That's changed, too."

"I see. I have much to discuss with the council. Meanwhile I am afraid you must remain here. Your personal needs will be attended to. You will also discover that the *pirca* which restrains you has been extended to separate you from the transmitter. We cannot risk you using it again."

"You don't have to worry about that," Carter informed him easily. "It doesn't work anymore."

"*You* cannot make it function." Apu Tupa pursed his lips thoughtfully. "That does not mean it no longer works. I am causing to have made small devices for each of you which will enable you to speak with any of us in our own language, and you to understand us. The learning machines make this possible. It will greatly simplify communication between us.

"Meanwhile you will be made as comfortable as possible. You must realize that your appearance here has been a great shock to us."

"Ain't done us much good neither," Ashwood told him.

Apu Tupa blinked as Trang Ho's flash went off in his face. "You who keep making lights: you are not

English, not Spanish. You look somewhat like us, but are different."

"I'm Viet-American. My parents are from a land I guess your people never knew." She sidled up close to Tupa and he drew back reflexively. "Listen, if you guys play your cards right I can get you more buzz than you ever dreamed of."

"Buzz?"

"Sure. Publicity, press, PR. Don't you realize that when you show up in L.A. you people are going to be celebrities? Lost civilizations don't turn up every day. You're going to need guidance, introductions to the right people, contacts, someone to put the proper spin on your arrival. That transmitter system of yours is worth big bucks . . . if it's relatively pollution-free, of course. And your outfits . . . I can set up a lunch for you with a major designer. A few color changes here, the right accessories, and, I mean, you'd be the rage.

"All I want in return is an exclusive on your story." She waited expectantly, beaming.

Apu Tupa stared distastefully at the woman who was standing too close to him. "Of what does this person babble?"

"She is something of a free-lance *quipu* maker," Fewick told him. "One who is not overly concerned with the accuracy of the knots she ties."

"We have not used the knotted rope of the *quipu* for information-recording for hundreds of years," Tupa replied. "Not since we stole the secret of writing from the Spaniards." With great dignity he turned and stepped off the platform. "I go now."

"Hey, at least give me an interview! Just a couple

of questions." Trang Ho tried to pursue, only to be halted by the *pirca* barrier.

"Don't you realize what's going on here?" There was pity in Carter's voice. "What's happened to us? We may never get home. You may never see the inside of a newsroom again."

"Nonsense," Ho said brightly. "These are people just like you and me, not bug-eyed aliens. I don't know anything about the Incas, but I bet they had and still have loves and hates, jealousies and desires. Inevitably there are stories here to be told, and somebody will have to tell them. That's my job."

Ashwood was shaking her head. "Wish I had your optimism, sister."

O'lal had been a Monitor for a long time, but now she did not know what to do or how to proceed. Things had gotten out of hand.

She had successfully tracked and confronted the Renegade, only to have him escape at the last possible instant. When she attempted to pursue he made use of a totally unanticipated method of escape. Only then did it occur to her that it was all part and parcel of his disruptive plans and that once more she had been duped.

Now the means by which he had fled was closed to her. She did not even know whence he had gone. As near as she could tell, the pattern of normal societal evolution on the world whose well-being she had been charged with protecting was still intact.

It might be that the Renegade, having nearly been trapped by her, had simply abandoned his ablative intentions and bolted to safety. In debate with herself she was ultimately unable to convince herself that this was so. His escape was too pat, too smooth, to have been an act of desperate accident. Though she had many other developments to supervise, none were so vital as ensuring that the Renegade was rendered harmless.

Therefore she remained, contemplating his means of flight and wondering if it might be possible, or even wise, to follow. She did not waste time chiding herself for failing to finish him when she'd had the chance. The Renegade was powerful and dangerous. Putting herself at grave physical risk would have done neither herself nor her charges any good.

She could not halt the flow of events the Renegade had set in motion. All she could do was try to channel them into acceptable evolutionary parameters. In order to do this she had to outanticipate, outthink, the Renegade. This she had thus far failed to do, opting instead to exercise damage control until the right opportunity again presented itself.

She suspected his ultimate goal, if not his methodology, and had no intention of allowing him to do any further damage to her charges. She had grown quite fond of humanity, not to mention the primitive Shihararaneth with whom they shared this world. For a non-Shihar species the frail humans showed great promise. It was her task to see that both intelligent races which occupied this world were given the opportunity to develop normally, and this she would continue to do at the risk of her own safety.

Prior to the appearance of the Renegade both humans and primitive Shihar had done well, though humankind required constant supervision. A little nudge here, a push there, was required to keep them from disintegration. Under her supervision they continued to advance. She had no intention of allowing the Renegade to put that progress at risk.

She desperately desired the advice of her peers, but the distances involved were too great, the mature Shihararaneth spread too thin. She had managed to get off a couple of fleeting communications when the elements had momentarily spun into perfect alignment and a nice long string had presented itself, but she could not chance that help would be forthcoming. On herself alone she would have to continue to rely.

Naturally she could not go to the humans for assistance. Revealing her true nature to them would do more permanent damage to their society than anything the Renegade could concoct except revealing *his* own nature. That she doubted he would do, because it could result in an appropriate and probably lethal response from her. No, he would bide his time and play out his game, knowing that as long as he did so she would not risk exposing herself with a direct attack.

But it was hard to remain circumspect when the natural development of the species which had been entrusted to her care was threatened by a lunatic like the Renegade. Not to mention the health of the several blissfully ignorant humans presently functioning under his direct manipulation.

The brethren she had managed to contact briefly had counseled patience. Renegades usually overestimated their abilities and made fatal mistakes, the inimical edifices of their plans invariably imploding from the weight of their own complexity. The difficulty lay in containing the damage they did before this took place.

She drew strength from the knowledge that in order to interfere in human affairs, the Renegade was compelled to rely upon human agencies to carry out his intentions. Given their inherent unpredictability, which they had already demonstrated, this allowed for the possibility that the Renegade might lose control of his carefully crafted disruption without the Monitor even having to act.

So she did not panic, but rather remained where last she had confronted him, waiting to see what would happen next.

XI

THEY did not see Apu Tupa for several days, during which time they were presented with telephone-style headset translators which transformed Contisuyun Spanish-Quechua into modern Spanish or passable English, as the wearer preferred.

When the Inca finally did reappear it was to gesture imperiously at the Fernándezes. "You two will come with me."

The brothers exchanged a glance, then gingerly stepped off the platform. When Ashwood and Da Rimini tried to follow, they found that the *pirca* had been restored.

"Wait a minute." Ashwood leaned both hands against the barrier. "Why just the two of them?"

Apu Tupa looked back at her. "They are our kind. We wish their input."

"You want input? I can give y'all plenty of input."

"Yeah," Da Rimini added. "What about us?"

"You have the look of the conquistadores, the conquerors," Tupa told them.

Carter objected. "I'm no conqueror. I'm an American. My country was hardly started when you had your last contact with your homeland."

"You are European. More important, you are not Inca. We know that the Spaniards had many allies, and we determined long ago not to repeat the mistakes of our ancestors. So we exercise caution." He turned and walked away with the Fernández brothers in tow.

"Wait!" Da Rimini shouted. "What this all about? Damn!"

Igor sat munching on a piece of something like green potato. The Incas had been very big on potatoes. "I do not know, but I don't like the idea of them breaking up the group."

"It may be of no great significance." Fewick was feeding Moe. "As the Fernández brothers are largely of Inca stock, our hosts may simply wish to question them about their lives."

"Well, I don' like it." Da Rimini edgily paced their enclosure. "If we could jus' get to the transmitter and make it work we'd get out of this place."

"We can't," Carter reminded her. "We don't even know how this *pirca* barrier thing works."

Da Rimini glared at him. "I thought you were pretty much an empty-head when I met you, an' I haven' seen nothing to make me change my mind."

Carter smiled sweetly. "I love you too."

"If you children can spare the time maybe we can think of somethin' constructive to do," Ashwood snapped.

"I already have," Fewick announced. "To wit, sampling the native cuisine, which is hearty and flavorful if not particularly subtle."

"How can you think about food?" Igor asked him.

"I am am somewhat kin to the stegosaurus, my bucolic Peruvian friend, in that I have two brains. The one in my head deals with such as you while the one in my belly joyfully occupies itself in the unending pursuit of gourmandish analysis. I see no reason to alter this division of labor so long as we are trapped here." He gazed through the barrier.

"Meanwhile it might be well to contemplate the possibility that the manner of our hosts' inquiry may be other than balsamic. The Incas were known to have done unpleasant things to reluctant prisoners. Making flutes out of their bones, for example. Do not be so hasty to envy our absent associates."

The elected nobles and scientific representatives who had gathered in the conference chamber were arguing heatedly among themselves while the bemused Fernández brothers sat off to one side, trying to follow as much of the babble as they could. The translators they had been given were not perfect and these descendants of their forefathers utilized terms neither man understood.

One did not have to be a linguist, however, to recognize rampant disagreement.

One older noble rose, his remarkable iridescent gray tunic glistening like an Irish beach beneath the overhead lights.

"I think this proposal is a waste of time and resources, and I will vote against it. In the centuries since we fled Earth we have raised here a greater civilization than ever our ancestors dreamed of, peaceful and prosperous." He looked around the table.

"Let the past lie. If we embark upon this course some of you favor, who can guarantee that we will not open ourselves to reconquest by the viracochas? Our population is sophisticated and well defended but not that large." He gestured in the direction of the Fernández brothers. "You have heard the testimony of these two. The Earth is overpopulated, bursting at its seams. We have much empty fertile, temperate land and other humans a hunger for empty places. Is it worth risking everything we have achieved to gain revenge for injustices perpetrated so long ago?"

"There is no risk." The speaker who rose wore a red uniform. "Only we understand the operation of the transmitters. If these two tell the truth, we have now under our control the only viracochas who are aware of its existence. We can attack in secret and if necessary retreat by the same means. The danger is minimal. It will be less so once we have occupied and fortified the ancient base at Nazca."

"Base?" blurted a startled Manco Fernández. "There's nothing at Nazca but treasure and caves."

The man in the red uniform turned to look at him. "Did you explore all the caverns, all the passageways?"

"Well, no. We found a lot of other tunnels leading off in different directions that we didn't have the time to inspect."

The man nodded. "Below the upper rooms are the vast caverns utilized by our ancestors. Or did you think that we moved tens of thousands of people through the single small transmitter by which you arrived? There is at Nazca another transmitter constructed by Those-Who-Came-Before, one much bigger than that which transported you here. We believe it was built to move large cargoes. We made good use of it before it too stopped working. If it is also functioning again we will make better use of it still." He regarded his colleagues.

"Once the ancient Nazca base is secured our assault force will be impregnable. Then we can dictate whatever terms of revenge we desire."

"Just one thing," said Manco. "Those people who accompanied us? The viracochas? I wouldn't trust anything they say. You know how viracochas are."

Another noble eyed him suspiciously. "You were the ones holding the guns."

"Someone had to take charge. It's a long story." Manco hurried on. "My brother and I have made it our life's work to try and restore something of our Inca heritage. It has been a long time since any of your people were on Earth. You are going to need guides, advice, assistance."

"You were brought here," the noble said sternly, "to answer questions. Not to offer unsolicited help."

"Of course," agreed Manco hastily, backing off. "I didn't mean to offend. Did we, Blanco?" His brother shook his head violently. "I was just thinking that if you go ahead with these plans, well, my brother and I are Inca, and you're Inca, and maybe we could help one another achieve our respective desires. I was wondering about one thing, though. Where is the emperor?"

The nobles relaxed and a few smiled tolerantly. "We have not been governed by an emperor for more than a hundred years," the first speaker informed them. "Emperors lost us our empire, our land, and our freedom. When we came here and listened to the advice of the learning machines, we did away with such anachronisms." He gestured around the table. "This is the government of Contisuyu, contentious as it may appear. You see that we have not only progressed in matters scientific."

"You really think you can impose your will and take revenge on the descendants of your conquerors?" the soft-drink bottler inquired.

The red-clad noble whom Manco had come to think of as a military officer replied. "Among the devices and designs left to us by Those-Who-Came-Before are many which, while not intended to be used as weapons, can certainly be adapted for use as such. We do not know how far military science has advanced on Earth in our absence, but I believe we can construct weaponry which the descendants of our conquerors cannot defend against. Our attack will be many-faceted and well conceived."

"That's very interesting," Manco agreed. "What are you thinking of doing? Taking back control of the lands our ancestors lost to the Spaniards? Restoring the empire?"

"That might be an eventual aim," one of the nobles agreed.

"But the Spanish don't run any part of South America anymore," said Blanco Fernández.

"Nothing at all?" The military noble frowned. "Another of your party said as much."

"He was telling the truth. It's all independent."

"How many countries?"

Manco responded when his brother hesitated. "Thirteen. They've fought against each other ever since the Spanish left, and they'd be a lot better off if a greater power forcibly unified them." Eager opportunism lent strength to his suggestion. "Someone like you people, for example.

"They all still share the common Spanish heritage . . . except for the Brazilians, of course."

"Ah yes," murmured another noble. "That ridiculous Treaty of Tordesillas. It would be appropriate for us to put that to right."

"What then of those who destroyed our lands and enslaved our ancestors?" asked the man in red.

"Spain is still a strong European country," Manco informed them.

"It does not matter." The noble looked satisfied. "We will crush them." He narrowed his gaze. "Do not think to enhance your own position with lies. We still do not trust any of you."

Manco was not intimidated. He knew how to handle himself in such confrontations. After all, business was business. "Trust comes with confirmation, and with time."

Murmurs of approval came from several of the assembled.

"We'll help you all we can," Manco added. "If you decide to unify South America and you need somebody local to help you run things, my brother and I would reluctantly sacrifice our own careers to assist in that difficult task." Blanco nodded eagerly.

"In fact, we have some plans of our own which might dovetail exactly with what you have in mind. We'd planned to expand our own interests eventually, of course, but with your help we could do so a lot sooner."

"You have not been brought here to discuss *your* plans." Manco immediately subsided.

The military noble regarded his colleagues. "It is our destiny. Our ancestral dead cry out for vengeance. First we will subjugate the Spain of our conquerors, then return just rule to the lands of our ancestors."

"It may not be as easy as you think," Manco said hesitantly. "Political allegiances have changed a lot in the two hundred years since you've been away. Spain is allied with the rest of Europe in an organization called the European Economic Community. It includes the French, the English, all the rest."

"But not these Americans and the Russians?"

"No, not really, but—"

The noble cut him off. "Then we will conquer Europe. If these other lands are foolish enough to ally themselves with the hated Spanish, they too will suffer."

"Hold on a moment," said an anxious Manco. Things were getting out of hand. "Unifying South America is one thing, conquering Europe another. Taking control of Germany is a tougher proposition than imposing your will on Paraguay."

The noble was not to be moved. "We will do what is necessary. If we agree to make use of your advice, what reward would you expect?"

Manco glanced at his brother, looked back at the expectant nobles. "Well, it's always been a dream of my brother and me to develop entertainment facilities to promote the culture of our people. If you granted us control of that kind of business we'd be quite content."

"Everyone would have to go to *our* parks, ride our rides, eat our fast food," Blanco said.

"Watch our television and our movies. Listen to our radio. Drink Inca Cola. Even," Manco concluded in the hushed tones one usually reserved for speaking in church, "Disney!" He retreated from his dreams long enough to ask an awkward question. "Of course, if there's going to be a long war in which millions of potential customers are killed . . ."

"There will be no long war," Apu Tupa assured him. "Do you still think us as uncivilized as our ancestors? Everything will be done quickly, before the Europeans realize what has happened to them. In addition to employing our own weapons, we can render theirs inoperative. They will have no choice but to submit."

"This proposal is still under debate," another noble reminded everyone. "We must decide."

"Yes," said another sharply. "In the traditional manner."

Apu Tupa looked thoughtful. "It has been a while since that was required."

Manco Fernández was suddenly uneasy. "How do you decide things 'in the traditional manner'?"

"It is a formality," Apu Tupa told him. "Nothing of any great concern. We merely reenact our ancestors' decision-making procedures. That involves discussion among learned nobles, ongoing debate, and human sacrifice." He smiled paternally. "As self-proclaimed defenders of the ancient culture I should think you would be aware of this."

Manco swallowed. "Actually it wasn't something we were thinking of including in the project we've been working on. Can't you substitute something else? Loud argument, maybe?"

"No. Tradition must be upheld. Sacrifices were usually taken from among prisoners of war. Now, who among your party would you propose as a good candidate? Much honor accrues to the chosen one."

"I'm afraid my brother and I can't help you in this," said Manco hastily. "I don't think we're properly equipped to make this kind of decision."

Apu Tupa nodded sagely. "Then I will choose. It shall be the tall female viracocha. Not only is she a descendant of the conquerors, she is by far the most attractive member of your group. Tradition instructs us that where possible, sacrifices should be female and attractive, though it would be nice if she were a bit younger."

"This sacrifice," Manco mumbled. "What exactly does it involve?"

"It is all very clearly explained in the traditions which have come down to us," Apu Tupa explained affably. "In order to divine which course of action to pursue, our ancestors would open the belly of a prisoner and read his or her entrails."

"Somehow I don't think our companion is going to feel honored," Manco replied dismally.

"Nonsense! It will make her very popular among the people of Contisuyu."

"I still don't believe she'll be impressed. Look, you people have come a long way, you've achieved a high level of civilization. You really don't do this sort of thing anymore, do you?"

"It is necessary," Apu Tupa insisted. "You will see."

The Fernández brothers continued to protest on behalf of their former partner, all to no avail.

When the situation was explained to the other travelers, they were appropriately appalled.

"Hey, I don't like the pushy bitch," Ashwood was saying, "but you don't go around slicing folks open to gape at their guts in this day and age."

"You misinterpret our intent," said Apu Tupa soothingly. "We merely wish to examine her entrails." He turned to the stunned Da Rimini. "You will be famous across Contisuyu. Your face will be known to everyone."

"I'm not interested in my face becoming known to anyone! I want it and the rest of me kept private." Looking around wildly she backed away from him until stopped by the exhibit wall. The trio of armed guards who had accompanied Apu Tupa began to advance.

"Keep away from me!" she screamed. "I'm warning you, my hands are lethal weapons!" She extended her fingers threateningly.

The nearest guard aimed an all-too-familiar silvery tube and nudged something on its side. Da Rimini's eyes rolled back in her head and she crumpled like a crepe paper construction. Ashwood sucked in her breath and Carter winced.

"She is only tranquilized," Apu Tupa reassured them.

"What difference does it make if you're gonna sacrifice her anyway?" Ashwood growled.

"The subject should be in perfect physical condition. We would not wish her to damage herself beforehand." The three soldiers were carrying Da Rimini's limp form off the platform. "Don't worry. The events will be widely televised and a viewer provided to you so that you will not miss anything." He grew contemplative.

"It should be most popular. We have not performed a sacrifice with an outsider in two hundred years, much less a Spaniard."

"She's not a Spaniard," Blanco insisted. "She's a Peruvian."

"Whatever that is," said Apu Tupa. "It does not matter. She will be promoted as a Spaniard, a viracocha."

"Promoted?" said Carter.

"Naturally, since the idea is to get as much of the population to watch as possible."

"Right!" said Trang Ho suddenly. "This is great! Human sacrifice stories sell more papers than anything except Elvis sightings and UFOs. I can see the banner now: 'Aliens Kidnap Earth Women for Human Sacrifices on Other World!' " She peered intently at Apu Tupa. "You *sure* you haven't got Elvis around here somewhere?"

The Inca master looked puzzled. "What is an Elvis?"

"That's it, you've gone too far." Carter glared at Trang Ho. "How can you talk like this? They're going to *sacrifice* her, read her insides."

"Am I from Hollywood or what?" Ho protested. "You expect me to express outrage? One lousy human sacrifice wouldn't make the front section of the *L.A. Times* on a slow news day. What are you so exercised about anyway? She was ready enough to kill you."

Ashwood looked thoughtful as she tapped a finger against her lips. "Interesting point."

Carter shot her a look, turned back to Trang Ho. "Suppose the 'reading' doesn't come off well? Suppose they decide they need to have a look at a second subject? Their choice of reading material seems to run to young women. Guess who they'll come for next?"

Trang Ho was not impressed. "Hey, life's a bitch, you know? I just want everyone to be aware that I retain posthumous copyright to all my stories and if you want to use any of my tapes or photos you're morally obligated to pay royalties to my heirs."

"What a coincidence," Fewick observed dryly. "That is precisely what was uppermost in my mind when they came to take one of us away."

A disgusted Carter turned his back on Ho. "You are crazy. You ought to do an article on yourself. 'Insane Reporter Divorces Self from Reality—Takes Pictures of Same.' "

"If I thought it'd sell, I would," Trang Ho replied cheerfully. "Anyway, I have confidence that our hosts will find la Da Rimini's intestines as satisfactorily attractive as the rest of her. She should be pleased. Back on Earth she was a Peruvian nobody. When we get home I'm gonna make her famous there too."

"If we get home," Igor murmured softly.

"Her corpse'll appear in tabloids all over the world," the reporter continued grandly.

"Somehow I do not see that mitigating her displeasure at her present circumstances." Fewick sat on the floor, stroking Moe.

"I thought these people were civilized," Carter muttered.

"Tradition is important in any culture," Fewick declared knowingly.

As Apu Tupa had promised, a viewer was placed on the platform for them. It consisted of a flat gray sheet of soft rigid material supported by a single narrow pole that widened into a circular supportive base. There were no visible controls, no antenna, no cable or cords.

Carter had determined not to watch, but when images finally appeared on the screen he found he could not keep himself from staring along with the rest of his companions.

The view was of an expansive hospital room gaily decorated in ancient Inca colors and designs, a surgery become operating theater in more ways than one. Clad in slick, brightly colored gowns, several men and women waited expectantly. They wore garish makeup and no masks.

Carter ignored the running, upbeat commentary of the unseen announcer. Two attendants dressed like refugees from a bad Broadway play entered, supporting an obviously sedated Da Rimini between them. He could clearly hear her moan. She had been attired in a skimpy yet tasteful costume which Fewick professorially described as a variant on the traditional costume of the Inca "Chosen Women."

"This makes no sense." No one paid any attention to him, their eyes glued to the drama taking place on the screen. "It can't go any further. It's got to stop."

The attendants lifted Da Rimini and placed her gently atop the lavishly decorated operating table, then bound her wrists and ankles at her sides. The costume she wore left her midriff completely exposed and little else to the imagination.

Trang Ho kept up a running commentary of her own, which involved much critiquing of the camerawork.

As the two attendants stepped out of the picture the other occupants of the room moved forward to

arraign themselves around the table. The one standing near Da Rimini's head raised his arms and began
to chant. Carter felt sweat running down his back
and sides as the liturgy rose in volume. Music from
unseen sources accompanied the chanters, an off-
putting mix of traditional Inca harmonics and modern electronics. He recalled Fewick describing how
the ancient Incas used to fashion musical instruments from the bones of their victims.

The song leader lowered his hands and his
voice. A much younger man approached the table
and snapped his fingers importantly, in response
to which a complex, ominous mechanical device
descended from the ceiling to hang suspended above
the table and its helpless occupant. Da Rimini's
glazed eyes focused on the device and despite the
sedation she managed to utter a quite respectable
scream.

The younger man pointed a narrow metal tube
at the sacrifice's body while the background music
soared to new dramatic heights. Though the instrument had a blunt tip and he could make out no sharp
edges, Carter found himself looking away. Trang Ho
adjusted her camera with ghoulish anticipation.

"Well, would you look at that," Ashwood murmured.

"I would not have expected it," Fewick added.

Carter forced himself to turn back to the screen.

There was no sign of blood, no picture of coiled,
pulsing intestines exposed to the air. Instead he saw
that a second image had been superimposed in the
upper right-hand corner of the screen. In exquisite detail and full color it displayed the inside of
Francesca da Rimini's lower torso. Organs glistened

and rippled, blood raced within veins and arteries.

Carter exhaled slowly. The critical "sacrifice" was symbolic. It had not occurred to him that the Contisuyuns might be able to "read" Da Rimini's guts perfectly well without having to cut her open. Like those of his companions, his expectations had been preconditioned by ancestral memories and bad movies.

The interior scan drifted and floated, examining first one part of her body, then another. It changed focus effortlessly, moving with equal ease in and out as well as up and down and from side to side. The traditionally clad professionals clustered around the table engaged in a lively ongoing discussion as the scanner technician continuously readjusted his probe in response to their requests.

"You will recall," Fewick was saying, "that Apu Tupa never said they were going to kill. Only 'sacrifice' her. It is an interesting modern interpretation of an ancient rite."

"Surely they're not going to make the decision whether or not to attack Earth based on a recreational survey of the bitch's insides?" Carter murmured.

"Probably not," the archaeologist agreed. "Like the sacrifice itself, I suspect the purpose of this ritual is largely symbolic." He shrugged. "Or maybe they are. What do you think, Moe?"

The tom sleepily raised his head only long enough to yawn expansively.

As the ritual continued the watchers one by one grew bored and turned away. Trang Ho was visibly disappointed.

"Waste of time," she muttered. "Looks like standard medical college instruction. It'll never sell." She brightened. "Unless I alter things a little bit."

"Maybe you'd better discuss any journalistic inventions with Da Rimini," Igor suggested, "since it looks like she'll be rejoining us after all."

XII

WHEN she was finally allowed to rejoin her companions, Da Rimini proved decidedly uninterested in discussing the print and film rights to her experience, or much of anything else for that matter. Though she responded at first to the Fernández brothers' offer of assistance with an impressive string of curses in both Spanish and Quechua, she eventually allowed them to seat her on one of the beds with which they had been provided.

She sat there trembling slightly, though whether from fear or the lingering aftereffects of the sedative she'd been dosed with no one could tell.

"I thought they goin' to kill me," she muttered. "I was sure they goin' to kill me." She looked up. "What they do, anyway? I don' remember nothin'."

Ashwood smiled contentedly. "Well, for one thing you screamed. Quite loudly."

"They didn't cut you," Fewick told her. "They ran some kind of advanced CAT scanner or X-ray machine over your abdomen and used it to take a look inside your body."

"I see." Suddenly she gazed sharply at the plump archaeologist. Her intensity was beginning to return. "What *parts* of my body?" she asked dangerously.

Bearing in mind a previously demonstrated proclivity toward violence on the part of the attractive

young woman confronting him, Fewick considered
carefully before replying.

"Your stomach. Your kidneys and liver. Your intestines."

Her gaze didn't waver. "That's all?"

Fewick nodded tersely, found a reason to begin
grooming Moe's neck.

"That's okay, then." She leaned back against the
wall, glared angrily around the enclosure. "An' nobody tried to stop them from takin' me."

"Why should we risk ourselves for you?" Ashwood
shot back. "Besides, what did you expect us to do?
Take on armed men with our bare hands? If they'd
taken me instead what would you have done?"

Da Rimini nodded slowly. "Prob'ly the same thing.
Did it help them make their damn decision?"

"They have not said anything to us yet," Igor told
her. He looked over at the Fernández brothers. "You
were gone a long time with them. Do you think they
can do what they say?"

"We don't know what they can do," Manco replied. "They talk a lot but they didn't show us anything. No bombs or nothing." He paused. "They
asked us to help them."

"Y'all ain't goin' to?" Ashwood said.

"Of course not," Manco replied dutifully. "We are
not interested in conquering Europe."

"I wish I could have done something," Trang Ho
murmured.

Da Rimini looked over at her. "To help me?"

"No." The reporter eyed her camera. "I don't know
how those pictures I took off the viewer will come
out. It would've been better if I'd been there in
person."

Da Rimini started for her but soon had to return to the bed. She was still too shaky to engage in any kind of active pursuit.

"All my life I hear of the gold of Paititi," she muttered. "All my life I have searched for it. If I found it I knew I would defend it against anyone who tried to take it from me. But I did not expect to have to fight for it with the original owners."

Carter was studying the exhibits on the platform opposite theirs. "I wonder if maybe we haven't overlooked some important bit of science. Maybe there *is* a lot to be learned from studying somebody else's entrails."

Ashwood made a derisive sound. "Economists have been doing it for years."

Apu Tupa did not return for several days. When he finally did put in an appearance he was accompanied by a woman in a green uniform who proceeded to prod and poke the reluctant Da Rimini.

"What was that all about?" she asked when the woman had departed.

"Postsacrificial checkup." The old man looked apologetic. "We have no wish to harm you."

"You might've tol' me," Da Rimini said bitterly.

"I thought it was implied. Let me say as one who has witnessed several sacrifices that you have very beautiful parts."

Da Rimini's brows drew together. "My parts are none of your business."

"Furthermore, the portents were good. Public support for the invasion is confirmed. We will have our revenge upon the murderers of our ancestors and those who have foolishly allied themselves with them!" He held up a clenched fist. "We will take control of this EEC of yours by such means as the viracochas cannot imagine."

"All right!" Trang Ho exclaimed. "An invasion! Real UFOs!"

Apu Tupa frowned at her. "What is a UFO?"

"You know. Spaceships?"

"We do not have any spaceships. The assault force will travel by means of transmitter."

"Oh, that's right." Ho looked disappointed.

"Our forces will assemble at the Nazca base. There the actual attack will be planned while technicians assemble aircraft and large weapons."

"I don't care what kind of weapons y'all got," Ashwood told him. "Y'all ain't gonna be able to take over all of Europe with what little you can send through one transmitter."

Apu Tupa regarded her haughtily. "Why not? Pizarro conquered the empire with barely a hundred fighters. We do not regard ourselves as any less capable. You will see the power of our weapons when they are brought into play. The learning machines have shown us how to build devices which your people cannot imagine." He turned to leave.

Ashwood advanced to the limits of the *pirca* field. "What about us? What happens to us?"

The old man looked back. "You shall accompany us. Your advice may prove useful. By helping, you may save lives on both sides." He continued up the walkway.

"You'll never bring it off!" she shouted after him. There was less than complete conviction in her voice.

What if they could conquer all of Europe with their

mysterious weapons? Would they be satisfied with that? Or would they move on to other lands? Why, if they could defeat the forces of a whole continent, they might even stand an outside chance of taking Texas!

How would the U.S. and the Soviet Union react to an invasion of Europe? Ashwood gazed at Francesca da Rimini's belly. Did it bulge with the secrets of Armageddon, or only gas?

The Fernández brothers stood off to one side, whispering between themselves. They were about as trustworthy as Da Rimini, Ashwood decided, determining to keep an eye on them. As for Bruton Fewick, his intentions and loyalties were as inscrutable as ever.

That left Carter, their guide Igor, and herself to try and do something about the proposed invasion. Did she really care? What did the fate of Spain, or for that matter all of Europe, matter to her? She'd never even been there. So what if the Contisuyuns conquered the place? They might impose some common sense on the Italians and a little humility on the French. Nor was it likely to hurt her business.

She took an uncertain slug of some yellowish fruit drink, wondering why she should feel so uneasy.

U'chak was grateful to the Monitor for their encounter. It had shaken his self-confidence and made him much more alert. He would make no more such foolish mistakes.

Everything was once more proceeding satisfactorily, if not precisely according to his original plan. That no longer troubled him. He was nothing if not adaptable.

Soon he would engender developmental disruption on a vast scale, undermining the work of the Monitors and leaving delicious discord in his wake. Eventually he would move on to another world to concoct fresh chaos there. It was the destiny he had chosen for himself. The galaxy was becoming far too civilized and settled a place. It was left to him alone to inculcate properly disruptive motive stimuli in the too-satisfied primitive species. A grandly destructive war, for example, would be most stimulating.

No, he would not allow the Monitor that close again. He bathed in the memory of how he had eluded her, in how his escape must be disturbing her and disrupting her work. He was quite pleased with himself. She could not stop him now, he was convinced. Not even if she revealed herself.

There was nothing for the prisoners to do but eat, sleep, and ponder their eventual fates. Carter wondered if his agent had been calling, while Fewick lamented his inability to maintain his regular correspondence. The Fernández brothers worried aloud about how their business was functioning in their continued absence.

By contrast Igor was not concerned, knowing that anyone who had been absent this long in the selva would be presumed missing until he or his corpse came floating downriver.

Apu Tupa still made occasional visits, though most of his time was taken up with assisting in preparations for the invasion. Several times the Fernández brothers were taken away for long periods. Upon their return they invariably offered perfunctory explanations of what had taken place. Carter and Ashwood listened and nodded but thought both men looked guilty as hell.

One day Apu Tupa appeared in the company of an impressive-looking, stocky Inca named Pucahuaman, whose name according to Igor translated as "Red Hawk." His brown tunic-uniform was decorated with red piping and sprays of gold woven into the material. He looked to be about forty, with close-cropped hair and a fullback's build, and if he knew how to smile it was a talent he kept firmly in check during his brief visit.

Apu Tupa treated him with considerable respect without actually deferring to him. For his part Pucahuaman let the older man do most of the talking, interrupting only when he felt uncomfortable with what his translator told him. At such times he didn't hesitate to seek clarification from Tupa. Only after he left did they learn that he was the general in charge of the invasion.

"It is good that you have been so cooperative," Tupa told them. "It means we have not had to make use of other methods of extracting the information we require." Carter felt a slight chill at the admission. Apu Tupa might be old, but there was nothing frail about him.

"Since we have been so helpful," Fewick said, "perhaps you could answer a question for me?" Tupa nodded condescendingly. "Some people have postulated that the long lines at Nazca, where the second transmitter is located, were landing strips for alien spacecraft. Do the Contisuyuns have an opinion on this matter?"

"To the best of our knowledge, Those-Who-Came-Before employed only the transmitters to travel between worlds. Why would they use vessels to cross the same distances far more slowly? Such a theory makes no sense. We believe that the Nazca peoples made those lines and drawings for their own edification."

Fewick looked gratified. "My colleagues and I believe the same."

"Never mind about a bunch of dead folks." Ashwood confronted the master. "What happens to us when your invasion gets under way?"

"As previously mentioned, you are to accompany us to provide information as required," Tupa told her. "It will not be long. Prepare yourselves." With that he turned and grandly exited the room.

"At least we're going home," Carter observed.

"Yeah. Plumb straight into the middle of a war," Ashwood said glumly.

XIII

MONTHS passed, marked by increasing boredom and frustration on the part of the prisoners. Carter was convinced that his agent had long since dropped him. When the day finally came that they were escorted off the platform and out of the museum everyone was grateful despite what their departure portended.

They were whisked out of the building and via air suspension vehicle through an extensive cityscape which was anything but primitive. Tall, shimmering towers rose above gleaming blocks of offices and apartments. There was little in any of them to suggest their architectural origins except for the presence in several buildings of the traditional trapezoidal Inca windows.

Once outside the city their vehicle accelerated markedly, traveling at high speed and in comparative silence through strange forests and grasslands. Several hours later they turned off the main highway onto a side road which eventually led down into a smooth-sided tunnel.

The tunnel opened into a series of vast caverns which had been artificially enlarged and reinforced. Men and women busied themselves at inexplicable tasks. There was no mistaking the air of expectation and excitement which filled the chambers.

Their craft came to a halt in the largest cavern of all. Carter and his companions emerged and found themselves surrounded by uniformed troops and technicians. The troops carried long silver tubes and wore red helmets with translucent face shields. Conversation filled the air, machines moved back and forth according to unknown patterns.

Ranked next to each other and filling most of the cavern were twelve cargo transports the size of wingless 747s, squared off at the stern and rounded near the bow. The drab plastic and ceramic shapes were feathered with mysterious antennae. Carter saw no sign of engines.

That was because motive power was clearly supplied by the gigantic ovoid located at the far end of the chamber. The towering white egg-shape rested on massive golden supports and looked big enough to transmit an oil tanker. Those-Who-Came-Before, Carter decided, had not always thought small.

Workers loaded huge containers and alien machines into the transports through heavy cargo doors located in the stern of each vessel. Troops filed aboard via side entrances.

Pucahuaman was visible off to their right, conversing with members of his general staff.

"Which one is ours?" Manco Fernández noticed Carter watching him, added too quickly, "I mean, on which are the prisoners to be transported?"

Apu Tupa led them past Pucahuaman's group. "We have the honor of traveling with the general staff, so our vehicle will be much smaller."

A short walk brought them to an overlook. Below stood another transmitter. It was the same size as the ones they'd previously encountered at Paititi and Nazca. Sitting next to it was a transport vessel the size of two large trucks.

"The main force will transmit first," their guide explained, "so that by the time the general staff follows, the immediate area will already be secured. According to what we know of the Nazca caverns this should not take much time." Again Carter looked at Manco Fernández. The soft-drink bottler studiously avoided his gaze.

"Once our large weapons and defensive systems are in place we will be able to proceed in a more leisurely fashion." He checked his tube. "Departure should begin shortly. It should be a grand sight. Our transmitters have been inoperative for two hundred years. I look forward to witnessing in person a phenomenon I know only from descriptions in ancient writings."

They watched and waited while the loading of the transports continued. When the last soldier had boarded and the last weapon had safely been stowed the technicians and workers retreated to the upper end of the cavern.

Desperate as he was to see Earth again, Carter found himself hoping the transmitter would not work.

The hum that filled the chamber set his bones to trembling. It was much deeper and more pervasive than anything they had previously experienced. The floor vibrated noticeably. The sound rose steadily in volume and intensity, until the colossal ovoid began to pulse with a prodigal inner glow. Though everyone had been provided with eyeshades, they still turned away when the blast of pure intense light exploded to fill the cavern. Past his ears echoed a scream of displaced air.

A cheer rose from the crowd of workers. When he could see again Carter saw that the first transport in line had vanished. The next was already being moved into position proximate to the transmitter.

It took only two hours to transmit all twelve of the huge transports. There followed a period of rejoicing and congratulations in which the prisoners did not share. Several prominent nobles and military people made speeches.

It was evening before the general staff finally boarded its own transport.

The vessel's interior was incredibly basic, Carter saw. There were no controls of any kind, and minimal instrumentation. Only comfortable seats and couches. Twenty elite soldiers and as many technicians accompanied the prisoners and the general staff.

"We shall emerge in the upper portion of the base," Apu Tupa informed them, "ready to assume preassigned stations immediately. No time will be wasted."

Sealed within the transport they had no way of knowing whether the transmitter would activate. They could not see the flash because there were no windows. But soon after the general staff ceased conversing Carter thought he felt a slight, subtle disorientation. His suspicion was confirmed when two technicians rose to open the single starboard-side door. As it slid aside, a pair of tube-wielding soldiers moved to flank the portal. Others rushed to take up positions outside the transport.

Only then did the technicians and members of the

general staff begin to exit, accompanied by the eight prisoners (Fewick childishly insisted on including Moe as an official member of their group).

The Contisuyuns set up powerful portable lights. In their glow Carter could see that everything was as they had left it. The transmitter rested in its ceremonial stone alcove. The avalanche of gold that Blanco Fernández had brought forth from a nearby vault lay undisturbed where it had spilled. Only one thing was not as expected.

There was no sign of the hundreds of troops who were supposed to have preceded them.

As the general staff's bodyguard spread out to check the main tunnel and side corridors Carter thought longingly of the hillside entrance located not far from where he was standing. This time his arms and legs were not bound. He was a good runner, though stiff from lack of exercise. If he could make it to the exit he might be able to lose himself in the scrub which covered the hills around Nazca. His chances of escaping would be improved if it was night outside.

And what then? What would he tell the local authorities? That above the famed Nazca lines lay a vast cavern presently packed with soldiers descended from the ancient Incas, all of them armed to the teeth with weapons derived from an alien technology? That they had stepped across a gulf of light-years with the sole intention of exacting revenge for injuries they had suffered hundreds of years ago?

He might be better off hitching a ride back to Lima, flying home, seeing if his agent had any work for him, and following any subsequent developments on the evening news. That meant living out the remainder of his days knowing he had abdicated all personal responsibility for whatever happened from then on.

On the other hand, he thought blithely, he didn't much care for the French either.

The general staff was puzzled but not overly concerned. Something had prevented the main force's technicians from setting up battle control here in the upper cavern. They would arrive in due course, perhaps any minute now. Although careful preliminary calculations had allowed for sufficient room in the main chamber below, it was not inconceivable that the arrival of the twelve massive transports had resulted in a cave-in of unknown dimensions. The transports had been sturdily constructed with such possibilities in mind, and provided with equipment for digging out.

In addition to the fact that Apu Tupa was watching them closely there were half a dozen fully alert soldiers poised between him and the tunnel leading to the entrance. Reluctantly Carter controlled his itching feet.

Technicians continued to unload equipment and supplies from the command transport until a soldier came racing down the tunnel to jabber frantically at Apu Tupa. He was out of breath, his face showing a mix of bafflement and terror. The old man listened, occasionally glancing in the captives' direction.

"Can you tell what they're saying?" Carter asked Ashwood as he fiddled with his translator.

She shook her head. Igor had been paying closer attention. "There seems to be some kind of problem."

"I can see that much." He tensed as Tupa came

toward them with two soldiers in tow.

"There is some difficulty. You will come with us. It may be that you can offer information." The two soldiers moved into position to flank the reluctant prisoners.

"Where are we going?" Fewick inquired.

"Down to the central chamber." Tupa's manner was brusque yet cautious. "The general desires your presence."

They were led into a side tunnel which soon sloped downward. It expanded rapidly in size. Light became visible up ahead.

The corridor opened onto the largest enclosed space they'd encountered since leaving Contisuyu. Like some long-forgotten sports arena it stretched off into the distance, a vast cavity hewn from the solid rock beneath the Nazca plains, lit by lights hastily emplaced by Contisuyun technicians.

Off in the distance Carter could just make out a twin to the huge transmitter they'd seen in action on Continsuyu. Squatting serenely on the floor of the cavern were the twelve huge military transports whose spectacular departure had preceded their own. They approached the nearest.

Pucahuaman and his closest aides stood by the transport's door, dwarfed by its size as they argued heatedly with several technicians. The general looked up as the prisoners and their escort arrived.

"We have prodded the interior," he told Apu Tupa. "There is no response." He gestured at the paved area which lay between the transport and the upward-leading tunnel. "This place should be full of technicians and soldiers busily assembling the instruments of invasion. Instead it is quiet. As quiet as a tomb."

Despite impressive threats, the captives were unable to shed any light on the mystery. The general's anger and frustration compelled Apu Tupa to come to their indirect defense.

"It is clear they know nothing of what has happened. It is not even necessary to ask them. Their ignorance shines unblemished from their faces. It coats their very words."

Pucahuaman whirled to glare at the transport. "Why don't they come out? Surely all the doors of all twelve cannot be jammed or disabled? If they are being overly cautious they should at least respond to our presence." He took a couple of steps and kicked hard at the side of the transport, as if the puny gesture might be capable of rousing someone on the other side of the thick plastic wall. It provoked no more response than had anything else.

"Open it," he ordered the nearest technician curtly.

There was some confusion among the techs, who had prepared themselves thoroughly to deal with a multitude of complex possibilities but no simple ones. It was decided to begin near the bow of the transport, with a smaller door located near where the officers should be seated.

Instructions were muttered to a runner who promptly took off for the upper level. He returned shortly with a plastic case in each hand. The techs rummaged through the contents until one rose clutching a triple-tube arrangement. Everyone watched expectantly as he approached the towering wall of the transport and used the device to trace a clearly visible vertical seam. Telltales on the unit glowed silently.

A whirring noise sounded from inside and the technician stepped back. There was a soft click as the door began to slide aside.

As it did so a blast of emerging warm salt water caught the unfortunate technician smack in the face and knocked him off his feet. The flood intensified as the door continued to open, drenching the general, his staff, soldiers, and prisoners with equally damp equanimity and forcing a mad scramble for safety. Yells and screams in English, Spanish, and Quechua were barely audible above the roar of escaping water.

Carter reached out and grabbed Ashwood by the belt of her pants as she threatened to go floating past. She came up sputtering and choking. He held her steady until the deluge began to subside.

The volume of water had been considerable, but it dissipated quickly as it drained out of the transport and spread through the vast reaches of the cavern. A few pools collected in low spots on the pavement.

Along with the escaping water came living creatures. Not the soldiers of Contisuyu, armed and ready for battle, but fish and glistening collapsed coelenterates.

Pucahuaman, Apu Tupa, and the rest of the general staff looked rather less impressive in their saturated soggy uniforms. The general was too startled and groggy to curse.

The water had half drowned captors and prisoners alike. Carter watched Blanco Fernández help his brother to his feet. A waterlogged soldier had the presence of mind to keep between them and the tunnel. Nearby, Bruton Fewick struggled erect and with great dignity waddled over to recover his cat.

The big tom had washed up against a slope and was so drenched he apparently didn't know where to start cleaning himself. He looked like a rejected floor mop in Fewick's hands.

People stumbled dazedly about, trying to wring out their clothes and thoughts. Carter was glad there was no breeze to chill them.

One by one the Contisuyun staff reassembled. The officers were angry, the technicians confused, and the soldiers shifting from foot to foot nearby more than a little frightened. What had happened to their brethren?

Though it struck Carter as anticlimactic, Pucahuaman had a thorough search made of the transport. As expected, no sign was found of the hundreds of soldiers and technicians who had transmitted from Contisuyu. Not a single body, not so much as a lost shoe.

"I wonder what the hell happened," Ashwood murmured. "Not that I'm brokenhearted about it, mind."

"They do not know." Igor was listening intently to the arguments of the would-be invaders. "We came through without any difficulty."

"Via a different transmitter," Fewick pointed out as he stroked his armful of sulking sodden fur. "Remember, neither had been used in hundreds of years."

When a door on the next transport was breached it too proved to be occupied by assorted finned and gelatinous sea creatures instead of eager Contisuyun troops. The apoplectic Pucahuaman raised his eyes skyward.

"*Where are my soldiers!*" he demanded to know. When the heavens declined to respond, Pucahuaman had no choice but to lead his much reduced and extremely damp invasion force back toward the upper chamber. Comical as the sight of the raging, waterlogged general was, Carter was careful not to laugh.

Behind them, the cavern was already beginning to stink.

"What happened to your people?" Carter asked Apu Tupa.

The old man fished an errant minnow from a pocket of his no-longer-elegant uniform and discarded it with obvious distaste. "The technicians have no idea. All they know is that during the process of transmission our forces switched places with a large volume of salt water and its inhabitants. This happened to one transport after another. We doubtless only escaped a similar fate because we traveled via a different transmitter."

A middle-aged Contisuyun joined them, fumbling with his unfamiliar translator. Apu Tupa identified him as the expedition's chief technician.

"Can any of you shed any light on this great tragedy?"

" 'Fraid not," Ashwood told him. "Looks like y'all won't be takin' over Europe after all."

The technician's brows drew together. "Do not be so sure. We still have access to resources you cannot imagine. The nucleus of my staff traveled with me and remains intact, if temporarily dispirited. We may need to downgrade our approach but it is far too soon to admit defeat."

"Well, y'all got balls, anyway." They emerged into the much smaller upper chamber. "I didn't think you were gonna conquer Europe with a few thousand soldiers. I sure as hell don't see y'all doin' it with half a hundred."

Pucahuaman was still loudly lamenting his missing troops. "All those lives lost."

"We do not know that for a fact, my General," the chief technician told him.

Pucahuaman eyed him uncertainly. "Explain yourself."

"We know only that their place was taken aboard the transports by salt water and sea creatures. They may still be alive somewhere on this world, or on Contisuyu."

"That is so. We do not know for certain that they have perished." The general drew strength from the notion. "In any event, we have the memory of their eagerness and dedication to inspire us and lead us onward."

"Have you ever run into anything like this before?" Carter asked curiously.

The chief technician looked embarrassed. "Actually this is not the first time a machine made by Those-Who-Came-Before has malfunctioned. They were tremendously advanced, having achieved a level of technology quite beyond belief. As our ancestors learned to their dismay, however, some of the devices which Those-Who-Came-Before left behind were something less than miracles of perfection. In fact, when activated for the first time several of them fell apart, executed functions seemingly unrelated to their design, or blew up. As a result, those of my distinguished predecessors who survived acquired a degree of caution as well as knowledge.

"The life of an operating technician tends to be a short one."

"Perhaps this incident explains why Those-Who-Came-Before have never returned to your world, or to ours," Fewick suggested.

The chief technician nodded thoughtfully. "While their inventive abilities were unsurpassed, some of their construction appears to us now to have been downright sloppy. I am reminded of the learning machine which we thought was designed to instruct its users in advanced materials techniques but instead convinced those first four who made use of it that they were small, flightless birds."

"How terrible," Ashwood said. "Were you able to cure them?"

"No, but tragedy was averted. They formed a whistling musical quartet whose recordings are still quite popular among our people. Sadly they were unable to perform in public because of a distressing tendency to peck members of the audience while begging for food.

"Another device was clearly designed to process raw logs into sophisticated wood products. Three technicians were splintered to death before their colleagues finally managed to turn it off. So you see that the development of our Contisuyun civilization has not been without its difficulties."

"Why don't you give up on this?" Carter urged him. "Go home. Forget about what happened to your ancestors five hundred years ago."

The chief technician stiffened slightly. "No, never! We will press on until none of us are left to uphold the honor of the Inca. We shall devise a new plan of attack. Somehow we will finish what we have begun here. It is our destiny."

"Among other men that word is sometimes a synonym for madness," Igor said quietly.

"Dedication also," the chief technician argued. He turned at Apu Tupa's approach. Judging by the look on his face some of the master's confidence had returned.

"It has been decided that several technicians will use the small transmitter to return to Contisuyu tomorrow. It may be that they will learn what has happened to our people. In addition, they will present the problem to our scientific establishment. I am confident it will be solved, whereupon a fresh invasion force will be trained and transported.

"The rest of us will remain here to work on the command post."

The chief technician concurred with the plan of action. "You see? You underestimate our resources as well as our resolve." He left to rejoin his colleagues.

Technicians continued to uncrate and activate equipment all the rest of that day. Under Manco Fernández's guidance, Pucahuaman and several others hiked to the cavern's entrance for a view of the world of their ancestors. They returned more determined than ever to take their revenge against the descendants of those who had driven them from Earth.

The prisoners were allowed to sleep unbound. With all but one light extinguished to conserve power, and that operated by two guards, it was unlikely that anyone would or could make a silent dash for the exit before being discovered.

Carter considered trying to sneak past the guards anyway by feeling his way along the walls in the darkness. Unfortunately the large number of side tunnels rendered the idea impractical. He'd experienced total darkness in a couple of commercially developed caverns in Texas and knew too well how utterly disorienting it could be. Furthermore, they had been assigned sleeping spaces between the rear of the upper chamber and the invaders. Even if he could somehow find his way, it was unlikely he'd get very far before stepping on a sleeping soldier or technician.

Gradually prisoners and captives alike fell asleep, lulled by exhaustion and silence.

There was just barely enough illumination from the single distant light to make out the figure bending over him. Carter rolled over but was unable to identify any features in the near blackness.

"Keep quiet." He recognized Igor's voice. "I thought I heard something."

"So what?" Carter mumbled sleepily.

"I thought you would be interested." Instead of explaining further, he tugged on the actor's arm, indicating he should follow.

Four steps later Carter stumbled over something yielding. "Christ, if you gotta pee, go toward the light. Ain't that what they set it up for?"

"Igor heard something," Carter told Ashwood.

"Big whoopee. Anybody's lived in the jungle as long as he has probably hears stuff all the time."

"That was kind of my reaction, but he's being real insistent."

"Hell," she muttered. "Now you got me awake anyway." She threw back the thin blanket she'd been allotted and followed.

"I can't see a damn thing," Carter mumbled under his breath. "Where are we going?"

"You'll see," Igor whispered back at him. "Careful here. Use your hands to feel your way around the stone."

Carter did so, sensed Ashwood doing likewise. "What stone?" he asked.

"The intihuatana. Watch your footing. Remember to take one step up into the transmitter enclosure."

The actor frowned in the darkness. "What are we doing here?"

"This is where the sound I heard came from."

"I'm too old to be playing follow-the-leader in the dark," Ashwood grumbled tiredly. "I'm going back to my blanket." Carter felt her left hand leave his waist.

In the near perfect silence of the cave there sounded a querulous meow.

"I'll be damned," Carter muttered. "It can't be."

"I thought you would want to find out," Igor told him. "I believe it is your animal. It definitely is not Mr. Fewick's." The meow sounded again, slightly louder this time.

Ashwood resumed trailing her younger companion. "How the devil can you tell cats apart in the dark?"

"Because this one kept us company all the way from Cuzco. I am very attuned to animal odors. It is part of my business. Of course," he added, "I could be wrong."

Gingerly Carter felt his way through the ceremonial stone entrance. "But how could she get here?"

"Remember that it was Mr. Fewick's cat who accidentally activated the Paititi transmitter in the

first place. Perhaps there is something in a cat's
body odor which triggers the transmission pattern.
Or more likely, it has something to do with the way
in which they walk atop the device. Their weight in
combination with their foot patterns, maybe.

"If this is your animal, she may have traced your
smell to the transmitter at Paititi. Or she may have
decided to curl up atop it. I remember the material
of which it is fashioned as being quite cool to the
touch. Cats in hot places seek out cool ones in which
to sleep.

"By whatever means, contact with it seems to
have resulted in her being transmitted here prior to
our arrival. It would have been a frightening experience, as would the later arrival of dozens of noisy
people. It would be hard for an animal to pick out one
human's smell among so many, even if we had not
all recently been soaked to the skin. I suspect that is
why she has not sought you out. Or her experience
may have made her suspicious."

Carter's extended fingers contacted something
hard and smooth: the transmitter. "Macha?" he
murmured softly.

The responding meow was much louder. "Son of
a bitch. It *is* her. I thought she might hang around
Paititi."

"I imagine she waited for you to return," Igor surmised. "Or maybe not. There is plenty of small life
in the jungle for a cat to eat, and the cave offered a
secure, cool place to sleep. If I were a cat, I would
have stayed there.

"And then one day she jumped up on the transmitter, activating it, and was sent here." He paused
to allow the significance of that thought to sink in.

"Fewick's animal managed to activate it twice. Why not yours?"

"Back to Paititi." Ashwood's breathing came fast in the darkness. "Wouldn't that be nice?"

"What about Fewick and the others?" Carter wondered.

"What about them?" Ashwood said sharply. "You trust any of 'em?"

The actor hesitated. "Not actually, no."

"Then screw 'em. Talk to your cat. Let's see what she can do."

"She probably has to retrace a specific pattern," Igor murmured. "Can you induce her to get up and walk?"

"No problem."

Fumbling in the darkness, Carter sifted the air with his right hand until he touched something soft, warm, and furry. Macha meowed again. Running his fingers down between her ears, he began stroking her back. A deep-throated purr filled the air.

"She's doing it," he informed his companions. "She's walking. I'm petting her."

"I can hear that," Ashwood murmured. "Keep it up."

Sooner than any of them dared hope, the transmitter began to emit a sonorous hum. In the darkness, the whorls of intensely colored light that began to coalesce deep within the ovoid's hermetic depths were more pronounced than ever.

"It's working!" Ashwood observed huskily. "It's working!"

Farther up the cavern, sleepily voiced questions were beginning to displace the nighttime silence. They were soon replaced by shouts. Lights blinked to life, silhouetting frantic figures against the smooth stone walls.

"*Hurry up!*" Ashwood yelled, not whispering anymore.

Carter could see several swarthy figures running toward them. The nearest dropped to one knee and aimed something in their direction. Light glinted off a two-foot-long tube.

The increased illumination allowed Carter to see beyond the arched back of the animal he was petting. Igor was staring back at him as the volume of anxious shouts and queries rose.

"You both realize, of course," his guide told them, "that this might send us back to Contisuyu instead of to Paititi . . . or somewhere entirely different."

They were not given time to second-guess. The humming noise was now intense enough to tickle his bones. White light overwhelmed Carter's senses. His stomach turned upside down as somewhere someone cursed in a strange language.

The last thing he heard was Ashwood saying tightly, "I always did hanker to travel an' see the worlds."

XIV _____

HE stumbled, losing contact with the cat, and it took him a moment to recover his balance. It was impossible to take stock of his surroundings because they stood once again in total darkness.

His outraged pupils tried to focus. "What happened? Did they turn out their lights?" At any moment he expected a blast from a guard's tube to send him sprawling on the ancient stonework.

Something hit his chest hard and he almost yelled. Then it curled up in his hands, purring contentedly, and he relaxed. He felt Igor brush past him as he cradled Macha against his right arm.

"D'you think they'll come after us?" Ashwood wondered.

"They do not know where we have gone. They may think we're dead. Or they may decide it is not worth trying to pursue us. We are only three." The guide was picking his way forward. "We should make use of every minute of freedom before they make up their minds what they want to do."

"Makes sense." Carter took a step, hit something bulky, and went sprawling. Macha yowled and leaped clear.

"What was that?" Ashwood asked. "You okay, cuddles?"

"I'm fine. I just fell over something." In the darkness he felt the object which had tripped him. "It's a pack. Feels like mine. If it is . . ."

He dug at the fabric-covered lump. The pull-tights and straps were all as he remembered them. So were the wonderfully familiar contents: cans of fruit juice, a big box of waterproof matches, a small 35mm camera. He shoved them all aside until his fingers closed around a hard plastic tube.

The beam from the small but powerful flashlight lit their surroundings. He located Ashwood, then Igor. They were still in a cavern, but the walls were close, the ceiling low. They were no longer at Nazca.

Igor was beckoning. "Over here."

While Carter held the light the guide recovered his own pack. It lay next to those belonging to their captors.

"We're back," he declared unnecessarily, his companions having already reached the same conclusion independently. "We will make our way downriver to Puerto Maldonado, where I intend to buy your cat the biggest fish to be had in the central marketplace."

"Do you guys hear something?" Ashwood whirled.

A familiar but now ominous hum was rising from the ovoid.

"Dammit!" Carter turned his light to his left. A few whorls of color were beginning to amalgamate within the transmitter's depths. "They're coming after us!"

"Well, do something!" she yelled.

"What? I don't know how to turn it off!" He and Igor surrounded the device, both men hesitating helplessly before its inscribed but otherwise featureless surface.

"Get your cat."

Carter looked around. There was no sign of Macha. "She must've run outside!"

Any second now swirling colors would engulf the ovoid, there would be a flash of intense whiteness, and a dozen or so armed and angry Contisuyuns would appear to confront them. He did not think they would be given another chance to escape.

Ashwood was screaming. "Do something! Knock it over, break it!" She picked up a fist-sized rock, ran toward the transmitter, and heaved her missile. It bounced off the polished material without affecting it noticeably.

Maybe a bigger one, Carter thought. There were several large stones lying on the floor of the cave near their packs. He took a step toward them.

Macha, it developed, had not run outside. Instead, she had stayed close by. Too close.

He stepped on her tail.

Emitting a jaguar-sized yowl, she sprang as far away from him as she could, to land atop the pulsing ovoid. There she turned, bristling, her claws digging at the surface of the transmitter as if it were some primordial ancestral scratching post.

As she did so light brighter than the sun filled their eyes. It was accompanied by even a louder yowl. The last thing Carter saw was a large ball of fur flying across the cave as the transmitter shattered.

He did not lose consciousness. An acrid smell filled his nostrils as the force of the explosion knocked him down. Rolling over to aim his flashlight, he saw that the transmitter had burst like an egg struck by a slug from a .44. Smoke curled from its exposed innards. Further inspection revealed that what had once been ancient, complex instrumentation had been fused into a mass of runny, silver-hued slag.

Igor had hit the ground hard. Now the guide was sitting up and holding his head. There was a lot of blood, but as Carter knew from his work with special-effects people, head wounds always bled a lot.

"I will be all right," Igor mumbled. "It is not deep."

Ashwood had found her own pack and extracted a second flashlight. Now she played the beam over the ruins of the ovoid.

"This sucker's not gonna be sendin' nobody nowhere for a long time. We're safe."

"I stepped on Macha's tail," Carter told her. "You saw what happened after that. She jumped on top of the transmitter and started pawing around. Crossed some circuits somehow . . . I don't know." He helped Igor bind his undershirt around his forehead. "You're okay?"

She nodded. "I was farther away than you guys when it blew. Notice the silence?"

With a start Carter realized that the explosion had been soundless. It seemed to him that like the build of a certain actress he knew, such a thing defied various natural laws, but then so did the transmitter itself.

They found Macha lying stunned but apparently otherwise intact at the base of the far wall, her fur smoking slightly. The cat responded to Carter's presence with a couple of uncertain meows. She offered no resistance when he picked her up. Slowly she began to preen herself.

"Our packs are intact, as are those our captors left

behind." Igor knelt and began rummaging through his own. "We should have enough supplies to get us back to the Pinipini. If no one is waiting for us there we can build a raft and float back down to the Alto Madre de Dios. Once there we can make our way to Shintuya."

"What then?" Carter wondered aloud. "We've been invaded. Sure it's a small invasion, but that doesn't seem to bother Pucahuaman and his people. We don't know what kind of surprises they can spring on the rest of the world."

"We'll notify the authorities when we get to Cuzco," Igor replied.

"Yeah, that'll take care of it," Ashwood commented derisively.

The guide looked back at her. "I am not stupid enough to think they would listen to us for a moment if we told them the truth. What I will tell them is that we discovered an important archaeological site at Nazca and that it is being looted by armed foreigners." He looked confident. "*That* will get a reaction faster than anything else."

They took what they wanted from their captors' packs and stuffed them into their own. Only then did they pick their way back outside.

The jungle humidity dampened Carter's skin but not his spirits as he and his companions emerged into the sunlight. Their surroundings were achingly familiar: the line of sun-dappled trees which marked the edge of the selva, the overgrown paving stones under their feet, the ancient wall of Paititi with its still indecipherable petroglyphs stark against the gray stonework. Nothing had changed in their absence. He remembered what

Igor had told them about how the local Indians feared the site. As recent events had proven, such ancestral terrors had more than a little basis in fact.

"Let's get movin'," Ashwood said briskly. "It ain't gonna get any cooler standin' here, an' the sooner we make it back to civilization, the sooner we can see to it that our friendly visitors from Contisuyu don't do any serious damage." She struck out in the lead, toward the path that led back to the river.

They had traveled a good ten yards when something enormous came screaming out of the sky to land with a colossal *whump* in the jungle less than a quarter mile away.

When the dirt and leaves and branches and dismembered insects had begun to settle, they rose cautiously. Macha peeped uncertainly out from beneath the ragged shell of a mistreated pandanus leaf.

"Maybe," observed Ashwood shakily, "the Contisuyuns are even more resourceful than we thought."

"If they can react this fast," Igor added fatalistically, "there's not much point in our trying to run."

A short walk brought them to the edge of a gully. Below, water from a newly diverted stream ran around the lower edge of a large, fluffy white cloud. It lay amidst shattered trees and other vegetation, looking exactly like something plucked bodily from the sky above and dumped intact into the jungle. It was not what they expected to see.

As they stared, the outlines of the cloud grew hazy. Carter blinked, but it was the cloud and not his eyes that were playing tricks on him. Slowly it transformed itself, until they found themselves gazing down at a verdant hummock covered with a dense growth of small trees, ferns, and other succulents.

A single palm poked its head out of the hummock and swiveled to inspect its surroundings.

Minutes passed during which nothing happened. Then an opening appeared in the side of the hummock, revealing a dark interior. Something not unlike a large blotchy beige carrot standing on its thick end emerged. Instead of arms, thin root-like tendrils extended from the mid to upper portion of the creature's corpus. Locomotion was provided by a dense pad of six-inch-long cilia beneath the base. Scattered seemingly at random around the upper third of the conical frame were a number of flat glassy discs varying from quarter to silver dollar size. If they were eyes they had no pupils. Several lumpy green straps crisscrossed the wrinkled body like rayon bandoleers.

As the incredible apparition scuttled to the edge of the opening a second creature appeared behind it. It was identical to the first save for being slightly larger and possessed of a few more roots, or tentacles, or whatever the squid-like appendages were. This second nightmare nudged up against its predecessor, promptly knocking it over the edge to land with a discordant *splat* in the mud below.

Carter could not be certain, but instinct led him to suspect that this did not constitute the creatures' normal mode of disembarkation.

A third materialized and bumped up against the second, which overbalanced for a moment but did not follow its unfortunate companion into the muck.

It turned, or rather pivoted, to confront the one behind.

Carter squinted in discomfort and grabbed at his ears. It felt as if a tropical bumblebee had chosen that moment to commence construction of a hive inside his head. The sensation was more disconcerting than painful. A glance revealed that his companions were suffering equally.

"I do not know what they are," Igor commented through clenched teeth, "but they are not Contisuyuns."

"Well, I've seen something like them before," Ashwood said.

Carter turned to her in surprise. "You have? Where?"

"Just last year, at a particularly good restaurant in Colorado, in the house salad."

"That's right," he snapped. "Get set to ingratiate yourself with them." He returned his attention to the fantastic scene below. "Actually they kind of remind me of some of the petroglyphs at Pusharo and Paititi. What are they, and where did they come from?"

"That must be some kind of camouflaged ship," Igor decided. "Since they do not travel by transmitter, it may be that they are not friends of the Contisuyuns."

"You hope," muttered Ashwood tersely.

The rugose cone which had landed in the mud picked itself up and began using its root-tentacles to flick muck from its flanks. It was about six feet tall, Carter estimated, though without knowing what it was made of he had no way of guessing its weight.

The creature standing in the opening suddenly

pointed two tentacles in their direction. Both its companion and the one on the ground pivoted to gaze up the slope.

The irritating buzzing in Carter's head gave way to a crackling, popping noise as the bee in his brain abruptly switched from hive building to grub frying. Just as he was about to start pounding his skull against the nearest tree to try and mute the internal cacophony, the crackling faded and he heard quite clearly.

"Hullo there, chaps."

Carter blinked, lowered his hands. Peering into the gully he waved hesitantly by way of reply. "Hello yourselves, whoever you are."

"Whatever you are," Ashwood murmured under her breath.

"All that matters to me is that they're not Contisuyuns." Igor held on to the branch of a nearby tree as he leaned over into the gully for a better look. "What are you doing here?"

"What are *you* doing here?" the creature standing in the aperture replied. How he knew it was the one in the opening doing the talking Carter didn't know. It had no visible mouth. But he was certain nonetheless. "You don't look much like Contisuyuns, what?"

"We're not Contisuyuns," Igor informed it. "We're locals, natives of this world. But you know about the Contisuyuns?"

"We know a bit of them, yes. They don't know much about us. Now I'm afraid that may have to change. Pity, that. They refer to us as 'Those-Who-Came-Before.' "

Carter swallowed hard. "You mean, you're the

people who built the transmitters and the learning machines?"

"All these centuries to develop and they're still slow-witted." The creature standing farther back in the opening gestured with several of its tentacles. "Of course we are," it replied.

"Quite so, quite." The one on the ground was still brushing at itself.

A hidden ramp silently extended itself from the lip of the portal to the ground, allowing the second pair of creatures to join their brethren below. It was an uncertain but fascinated trio of humans who descended to greet them. Macha remained on the rim of the gully, observing the encounter with detached feline interest.

"I'm sorry," Ashwood announced upon concluding a preliminary up-close inspection of the visitors, "but you don't look like no superrace to me."

"Did we say we were super anything?" replied the most diminutive of the aliens, whom she immediately dubbed Shorty. Its companions she labeled Crease, for a particularly deep groove along its "front," and Tree, for being the tallest. They proffered no objections to the unrequested appellations, nor did they counter with names of their own.

Displaying unexpected flexibility, Shorty twisted slightly to regard its companions. "She thinks we're representatives of a superrace." Mental laughter tickled Carter's brain.

"What twaddle. We are no such thing." Crease seemed to be the most serious member of the trio. "We are simply very intelligent."

"Then why'd you go away and leave all that stuff on Contisuyu?" Ashwood asked it.

Root-tentacles rippled. "Groups of us like to establish ourselves on new worlds and then move on. We are easily bored, you see. Also, we harbor an intense dislike of packing. It's most enjoyable to begin anew with each new settlement, build new infrastructures and all that as we go along. Keeps us fresh, don't you know?"

"Not that we don't like to revisit old haunts every hundred years or so," Tree added. "When some of us went back to check on Contisuyu we found that the old homestead had been appropriated by humans. Obviously some of them had stumbled over the old links we'd left behind here and made use of them. They seemed to be having such a sprightly time of it that we decided to step back and leave them alone, to see what they'd make of it.

"After a while we de-energized the link with this world so that they could develop on their own. Then a few months ago the agency on Booj, our home-world, which keeps an eye on all registered transmitters, reported that several in this vicinity had unexpectedly been reactivated. So it was decided to send a team out this way to check on things."

"Why should you care?" Ashwood asked.

Tree inclined toward her. "Primitive locally developed technology does not impact upon our existence. Transmitters fall into another category entirely."

"Unfortunately," said Shorty, "some of the navigational aids we left here have been altered over the past millennia. As we never expected to have to return to this place, they were not maintained. In addition, our ship's tolerance for error was greatly reduced by our desire to utilize a high-speed approach in order to avoid detection. I am afraid our landing was rather less than perfect, the result of which is that our vessel has sustained some damage."

"It was all your fault," said Tree.

"Whose fault? Who was at navigation control during final approach?"

"Don't try to put the blame on me." Tree's root-tentacles were waving around. "Who mismanaged a simple visual interpretation of the final coordination sequence as we came in over the major ocean?"

Carter hesitated. "You're not talking about the lines in the ground at Nazca, are you? Those don't really designate landing patterns."

All three aliens inclined toward him. "Well, of course they do, old chap. What on Booj did you think they were for? Don't you trust the evidence of your own eyes?"

"The drawings on the plains." Igor was confused. "What about the big drawings that can only be viewed properly from high overhead? The eagle, the puma, and the rest? Surely those aren't navigational aids as well?"

"Blimey, of course not." Crease sounded amused. "Those were executed by the humans who lived in the area at the time the patterns were installed, for the amusement of their visitors. Us. The designs are quite pleasant in a primitive sort of way, don't you think?"

"Obviously we're communicatin' by some kind of telepathy or mental projection," Ashwood noted. "But if you don't mind my pointin' it out, your English sounds kind of funny to us."

"As does yours to us," Shorty replied. "Doubtless

this is due to our having learned it during our last visit to your world, which was somewhat over a hundred of your years ago. As I am sure you are quite aware, your verbalizations vary considerably with time as well as geography."

"During such occasional revisits to worlds where we have once dwelled," Crease went on, "we enjoy engaging isolated and exceptional representatives of the local species in conversation. The last human we had the opportunity to converse with was a most fascinating individual, a mathematician of extraordinary gifts and vision. The four of us spent many enjoyable hours together debating both the nature of your species and reality."

"Einstein!" Ashwood blurted excitedly.

Crease flexed upper tentacles. "Sorry. Don't know the fellow. Our gentleman was a chap named Charles Dodgson. A teacher and a bit of all right. Turned to your primitive photography for a hobby after we convinced him there was more of a future to it than the simple line drawing he'd been doing at the time. More than once he spoke of utilizing snippets of our conversations in stories which could be related in human terms. It would have been a supreme accomplishment on his part if he had been able to do so. I fear much of our terminology was quite beyond him, as was our math."

"Lewis Carroll," Igor exclaimed. Ashwood gaped at him. He ignored her. "You said your homeworld was called Booj? You would not by any chance refer to yourselves as Boojums?"

"That transliterates rather well, old chap."

Igor was smiling, reminiscing from childhood. "You might be interested to know that your human acquaintance Mr. Dodgson eventually did make a pretty good attempt at humanizing some of your terminology."

"Look," Carter interrupted, "this is lots of fun, but we've got a real problem here. The Contisuyuns have been harboring a five-hundred-year-old grudge against the people who drove their ancestors off this world and now they've returned seeking revenge."

"You humans." Crease sounded disgusted. "I for one don't think you'll ever develop a real civilization. That's not for us to decide, of course. All that concerns us is the possible misuse of any technology which could conceivably affect the worlds on which we presently dwell."

"What exactly is going on here?" Shorty inquired.

Carter and Igor, punctuated by Ashwood's occasional pithy interruptions, proceeded to detail what they knew of the Contisuyuns' intentions.

"Dear me." Tree was distressed. "The transmitter system was designed to facilitate commuting, not foment aboriginal conflict."

"That's the problem with mass transit," Shorty added sagely. "If one isn't careful, any sort of riffraff can make use of it. We cannot allow the transmitter system to be used for aggressive purposes."

"Quite," Crease agreed. "It would set a bad precedent."

"Then you'll help us put a stop to whatever the Contisuyuns have in mind?" Ashwood asked them.

"From what you have told us it does not sound like they have a great deal to work with." Tree hummed thoughtfully. "Like their technicians, I do wonder what caused the old cargo transmitter to malfunction so."

"Are you sure you weren't the one who pro-
grammed it?" Shorty suggested archly.

"You couldn't program a route to a defecatory,"
the taller alien replied.

"Actually," Crease said apologetically, "the transmitter complex, like our navigational system, has
never quite been perfected." As Carter recalled the
number of times he'd already traveled by transmitter
he discovered that he was sweating. "Occasionally
we lose something, or someone. They usually turn
up somewhere else, safe and sound but more than a
little cross with the engineering. I fear we are often
as impatient in execution as we are brilliant in theory and design.

"For example, immediately prior to our arrival it
was noted that the local transmitter had once again
become inoperative."

"I'm afraid that's our fault," an embarrassed Carter informed the alien. "My pet must've interfered
with the field or whatever it is at a critical moment
and the damn thing just blew."

"Actually, old chap, this part of the network was
supposed to have been cut out of the system centuries ago, when your people began to develop mid-
level technology. That it became operative again
was doubtless due to some bureaucratic mix-up at
Central Control which we're still trying to trace.

"Since you have conveniently removed this transmitter from service, however, we have only the two
remaining at Nazca to concern ourselves with, and
your destructive interaction may well have rendered
them equally inactive."

"Then the Contisuyuns might be trapped there,
unable to get back to their homeworld. They might

be desperate. If that's the case, will you help us take care of them?" Ashwood asked. "If you think they can still do any damage with most of their invasion force disappeared, that is."

"Oh, there are other methods they can employ," Crease observed thoughtfully. "Being considerably reduced in number, I should think their next step would be to try to make use of learning machine technology."

Carter frowned. "I guess I don't understand. What harm can they do with something like that?"

"The learning machines are designed to implant information directly into a subject's mind. Very useful for educating the reluctant student." Crease paused for impact. "Such implants need not be benign."

"You mean they could influence politicians' minds or something?"

"You don't need high technology for that," Ashwood noted dryly. "Can you keep them from doing that?"

"No, but the effects can be neutralized if we can get close to their equipment, which can then be destroyed. After all, we are the inventive geniuses, not the Contisuyuns." He lapsed into a contemplative silence before commenting further.

"It will take the self-repairing instrumentation of our ship a while to restructure itself. Meanwhile we will aid you in seeing to it that the Contisuyuns do not misuse our technology. We will help if such help is in order, so that those marooned on your world do not act with hostile intent."

A soft hiss sounded from the vicinity of Carter's boots. Looking down, he saw that Macha had decided to vacate her perch and rejoin them. Now she was confronting something whose arrival none of the humans had noticed. The two animals circled each other slowly, curious and unaggressive.

The new arrival was slightly larger than Macha. While neither ocelot nor margay it was as indubitably feline as its presence was puzzling.

"Where'd this little guy come from?" he wondered aloud.

Quite unexpectedly, Shorty tilted forward to stroke the cat's spine with the tip of a root-tentacle. "This is"—the mental projection sounded vaguely like "Grinsaw"—"our companion."

"Oh, I get it." Ashwood smiled. "You guys picked up some cats on your earlier visits."

"Not at all," said Crease. "Cats have always been among us, from our earliest days on Booj. They are quite charming company. In fact, every civilized society we have encountered coexists with cats. Their presence among your kind bodes well for your future."

"But cats evolved here," Igor insisted. "They are native to this world."

"Can you be certain of that?" Crease pressed him.

"Well, no. I mean, I have not been around for the entire duration of vertebrate evolution. It is simply what I was taught in school."

The Boojum was understanding. "And I'll bet you wouldn't recognize a mimsy borogove if it displaced right on your head. You people have much to learn, what?"

"They seem to be hitting it off," Carter commented. He was far more interested in Macha's immediate well-being than in possibly conflicting histories of her ancestors. The two cats were darting hither and yon now, cavorting about rocks and bushes with all the comportment of a couple of old friends.

"Are there any other transmitters hidden on Earth?" he asked as the thought suddenly occurred to him.

"No. Only the one here and the two at Nazca. Transmitters are intended for mass transit. Isolated visitations are always carried out by ship."

"If you will convey us to Nazca by domestic means," Tree informed them, "we will see to it that any technology of ours which the Contisuyuns intend to pervert to inimical ends is rendered permanently dysfunctional."

"I'm afraid it's not going to be that easy," Carter replied.

"What complications do you foresee?" the Boojum asked him.

"Well, for one thing, we can't just stroll into Cuzco in the company of three giant ambulatory vegetables."

"Ah, quite," said Crease. "It is noted that we resemble your flora somewhat more than your fauna, and that this disparity could engender some comment."

Igor had been devoting some thought to the obvious problem. "Why don't we turn that to our advantage?"

"Kid, you been out in the heat too long," Ashwood said.

The guide was quite serious. "Many times have I helped scientists take their precious specimens down the river to Puerto Maldonado for shipment back to Europe or the U.S. If our friends can remain motionless when necessary we can simply tell the curious that we are carrying three large and important botanical specimens to Cuzco for shipment to America." He eyed the aliens.

"You can act like plants for a little while, can't you?"

Carter quickly warmed to the idea. "We can say that their devices are scientific instruments. I can pass myself off as a botanist. I played a microbiologist in *Red Plague from Orion*."

"There is no plague in Orion," Shorty insisted. "Only antisocial agitators."

"What about the park rangers?" Ashwood wondered.

"I will deal with them in the unlikely event we encounter any," Igor assured her.

"This will be jolly amusing." Crease was pleased. "We are agreed."

"Good. Now I got a question." Ashwood stood quite close to the bulky Boojum. "If you ain't got no mouths, how do you eat?"

"Infrequently," Crease informed her. "Except for our minds, our metabolisms are quite slow. That is why we live to what you would consider a great age." The leading edge of his base curled up slightly to reveal the cilia beneath. "There is a mouth in the center of our locomotive digits."

"So you sit in your food. Great. Remind me not to invite you to my next fancy dinner party."

"There is one small related problem which I might as well mention now. While we do not need to eat often, our continued good health requires the regular ingestion of certain important trace elements.

Due to our awkward landing, our total supply was destroyed on impact."

"That's terrible," Carter said.

"Not to fear. Our records indicate that a vast natural source of the necessary nutrients is present in this part of your world, so we anticipate no difficulty in obtaining them as necessary."

"What about leaving your ship here?"

"As you can see, it is quite effective at altering its appearance to match its surroundings. It does this automatically. Once sealed, I do not think it will be noticed."

Igor nodded approvingly. "How much equipment are you going to need to take care of any Contisuyuns who still want to fight?"

"Very little," Crease told him.

Ashwood grunted approval. "That's good,'cause if we make it out of this stinkin' sauna, the only place this woman's gonna backpack to from now on is the nearest market."

While unable to move as fast as the humans, the Boojums did not tire as easily in the heat. Furthermore, one of the devices they had insisted on bringing along turned a couple of beached logs into excellent dugout canoes within an hour of reaching the river. There was no need to waste time laboriously building Igor's proposed raft.

Soon they were paddling their way downriver, the Boojums going rigid on the rare occasions when the travelers passed a house along the southern bank. Out in the center of the current they were blissfully free of insects, and Carter had time to wonder if the Contisuyuns had been able to call in the reinforcements Pucahuaman had spoken of. If not, they might have only the general and his staff to deal with.

Though he had confidence in the Boojums, he fervently hoped the latter would prove to be the case when they eventually arrived at Nazca.

XV

CONTISUYUN soldiers searched every inch of the cavern, even checking the vast main chamber below where the twelve huge cargo transports held fast to their secrets . . . not to mention tons of rapidly decaying fish. They did not linger long there, however, because the salty stench threatened to overcome them.

"No sign of the three escaped prisoners," the officer in charge of the search finally had to report to Pucahuaman.

The general looked tired. "Then they must have transmitted, as we suspected. They surely did not slip away past us."

"Can' you go after them?"

He looked back at the viracocha Da Rimini. Another time, another place, he would have courted so attractive a woman. Now he was wholly occupied with professional concerns.

"My technicians inform me that the transmitter is no longer functioning. That means that not only can we not pursue the escapees, we cannot return to Contisuyu for help until it is repaired. If it can be repaired," he added disconsolately.

"Then what are you going to do?" Manco Fernández asked.

Pucahuaman glanced at the "Peruvian," as he

called himself. "Some of my staff will try to effect repairs on the transmitter. The rest of us will work to devise still another plan of attack."

"What? Just this handful of you?"

"I will not wait to see if the transmitter can be repaired. Soldiers grow stale if they are required to sit in one place and do nothing. Meanwhile we have much science at our disposal, technology such as the hated Pizarro never imagined. There are ways of conquering people without using guns." He was grim and determined. "We came prepared for many eventualities. You will see."

"I admire your boldness," said Bruton Fewick. "You should not let the three who got away worry you. They are either dead or back at Paititi, from which they will be some time extricating themselves. The three of them combined would not constitute a single dangerous human being, and they will have a difficult time convincing the authorities that a threat to all Europe has materialized at Nazca, of all places."

"That's for sure," Trang Ho added. "I write invasion-from-out-of-this-world stories all the time, and nobody ever believes them."

Pucahuaman listened to his translator and found himself nodding in agreement. "Hesitation and uncertainty are what doomed our ancestors, a mistake I do not intend to repeat. We will move quickly." An expression of distaste crossed his face as he observed the cat cradled contentedly in the archaeologist's arms. "Do you carry that animal everywhere?"

Fewick smiled down at his pet. "Moe is my constant companion. He goes every place with me."

"It is unnatural."

"What can you possibly do?" Da Rimini wanted to know. "You can' get no reinforcements, you can' even tell your people that you in trouble."

"You will see." The chief technician was beckoning anxiously and the general left to confer with him.

"What do you think?" Da Rimini wondered aloud. "Have these people got anything?"

"They remain confident." Manco Fernández continued to watch the general. "You have seen what they are capable of."

"They don' know what's wrong with the transmitter."

"That does not mean it is beyond repair," Fewick told her. "Ah. Apu Tupa comes."

The old man's step was jaunty. "There is a way. Among the instrumentation we brought with us in the command transport is a device which when correctly tuned and suitably amplified affects human perception. A derivative of the original learning machines, it was to be used to help in pacifying the conquered civilian population after their military forces were defeated, and to assist in disarming recalcitrant soldiers."

"You mean it's some kind of mind-control machine," said Fewick.

"Its application is not nearly so broad. But over a period of time it can persuade subjects to change their minds about specific matters. If included as part of an otherwise harmless broadcast and repeated at regular intervals, the subliminal suggestions it makes will not be noticed, but instead will be unconsciously absorbed and acted upon by the general population."

"There's no such thing as subliminal suggestion,"

Trang Ho argued. "It's an unfounded belief."

"Our knowledge of human physiology is greater than yours." Apu Tupa drew himself up. "The device *will* work. All that is required is an effective delivery system. In order to achieve the requisite results we must be able to reach a minimum of fifty percent of the target adult population." He frowned slightly.

"Our only problem is that we do not have with us the resources to effect appropriate delivery." His gaze narrowed as he regarded the five. "Any form of electronic mass visual communication would be adequate for our purposes. Does your world now possess such a system?"

Bruton Fewick pursed his lips thoughtfully, which gave him the aspect of a lewd Buddha as he exchanged a knowing smile with the ebullient Trang Ho.

"I believe we can be of assistance. You must trust us to do a little groundwork for you first."

Apu Tupa was wary. "Why should we trust you?"

It was Trang Ho who replied. "Because each of us has ambitions as great as yours. Besides, you can send armed men to accompany us every step of the way."

"I will speak to the general."

Pucahuaman was reluctant but in the end agreed to accept their help.

The owner of the pickup truck they flagged down out on the plain was more than a little reluctant to take so many strangers all the way into Nazca, but the Fernández brothers managed to convince him with promises of payment in dollars instead of intis.

The first thing the brothers did upon reaching

Nazca was to check in with their office. They were pleased to find that the soft-drink business had run smoothly in their absence. Trang Ho located a fax phone and filed her accumulated tapes and pictures with her agent in New York, knowing that while none of it would be believed, all of it would find a ready market.

Then they and their fascinated Contisuyun escort went shopping.

Even with an antenna set up in the bushes outside the entrance, the set could only pull in a few local channels. Fortunately, for a third-world country Peru boasted a surprisingly robust domestic television industry. There was more than enough available programming to be representational.

"You say that this 'television' is everywhere watched?" An amused Apu Tupa considered the cartoon which currently filled the screen.

"Not yet everywhere," Fewick informed him. "But you'll have saturation coverage in Spain, the rest of Europe, and America. That's what you want."

"It won' work," said Da Rimini. "How you gonna get people in England to watch the same program as people in Spain?"

Fewick smiled. "Europe now has widespread satellite television coverage. A transmission from one country can be viewed simultaneously everywhere else. If a sufficiently popular live broadcast can be developed it will be watched unaltered in every country at the same time."

"Sure, but how you gonna get local TV stations to carry it?"

"By offering financial incentives they cannot refuse. You forget that the Contisuyuns' Inca ancestors

filled this cavern with considerable wealth. I think
that if we offer to pay independent European channels to carry the broadcasts, instead of asking them
to pay the producers, as is the usual arrangement,
they will be eager to accept. Even if the broadcast is
not to their liking they will be unable to bring themselves to decline the opportunity to reap enormous
profits at little personal risk. Stations in America
have been doing exactly that with religious programming for many years."

Da Rimini was still skeptical. "Jus' because we
put somethin' on the air don' mean people are gonna
watch it."

"No indeed. We must therefore develop a car-
rier, a means of infection if you will, that is at
least minimally attractive to a widely based audience. Something people in many different countries will *enjoy* watching. Something with univer-
sal appeal."

"A comedy show," Blanco Fernández suggested.

"*Khong,* no." Everyone looked at Trang Ho. "You
gotta have something that'll make people want to
tune in regularly. Something that'll grip 'em without
letting go. Real, vital television that can profoundly
affect people's daily lives. Something like *Dallas* or
Dynasty. A soap opera."

"Ah!" Manco Fernández's eyes lit up. "*La telenovela.*"

"Exactly," said the reporter.

"What makes you think we can get something of
our own on the air?" Da Rimini wondered.

"Mr. Fewick already said. Getting something on
TV isn't a matter of being good, it's a matter of money and who you know. It'll be harder to translate all

this treasure into real money than it will be to put on a broadcast."

"We can help there," Manco said eagerly. "We ship our own money and that of our friends out of the country all the time. We know art dealers and goldsmiths. It can be done. But that is not the most wonderful thing about this."

Fewick's brows drew together. "It's not?"

"No. If we have a big show that we are paying for, it will look peculiar if we do not use it to sell something. The show must have a sponsor, if only as a cover for our real intentions." He paused for emphasis. "What better than Inca Cola? When we have finished, it will be the most popular soft drink in all Europe!"

Trang Ho shrugged. "Why not?"

"You are all crazy," Da Rimini decided suddenly. "So I mus' be crazy too. Where do we start all this?"

"Assuming the Contisuyuns concur," said Trang Ho, "we start where everybody starts in television: with a pilot episode. But we can't do that here." She tapped her chin with an index finger. "Let's try New York. L.A. would be better, but I know more people in New York and there's better access to Europe.

"I can serve as producer. I've done enough stories about them to know how to act. But nobody in the business will take me seriously unless I look like I have a heavyweight backing me." She glanced meaningfully at Fewick.

"I hope your intent is to be more than merely amusing."

"Absolutely. You're well spoken, you look the

part, you even have East Coast connections because of your family."

"My 'family,' " Fewick replied impassively, "does not watch television. In their opinion PBS barely scrapes the fringes of cultural respectability. Their idea of a light evening is to apply Freud to the plot of the last opera they saw."

"So much the better," said Trang Ho. "Nobody in television will know what you're talking about but they'll be afraid to admit their ignorance. That's always a good approach. Now, I know people who can put us in touch with writers. We'll do some lunches, start putting things together creatively while the Fernández brothers handle the finances and the Contisuyuns refine their instrumentation. This is going to be great! We're going to throw Europe into turmoil and I'll have an exclusive on the whole process from beginning to end."

Fewick was shaking his head. "I suppose your idea of an ideal assignment would be to interview God and the Devil prior to the Final Conflict."

"Only if they'd let me have an exclusive on the pictures," the reporter replied.

"How are we going to get all this in place?" Manco asked.

"Charter . . . no, we'll *buy* ourselves a plane," Trang Ho announced. "That way we can go wherever we have to and transport any necessary equipment in complete secrecy." She looked up at Apu Tupa, who had been listening intently. "How about it?"

"Your suggestions please me. Some of our number will remain here: soldiers to guard the base, technicians to try to repair the transmitter. If those who escaped return, it will be to an unfriendly reception.

The rest of us will accompany you to fulfill our grand design. This will not be revenge as we conceived of it, but satisfactory it will be." He gestured at the set.

"I know we will succeed. Yesterday I saw one of the things you call commercials. It was for something called Perrier. If this television is so powerful that it can persuade people to pay money for water, then we will have no trouble using it to implant our message in the easily malleable minds of its viewers."

When all was in readiness, even to dressing the Contisuyun soldiers and technicians in contemporary clothes, the invasion force flew in the 727 purchased in the name of the Fernándezes' company from Lima to Bogotá and then on to New York. Though he found the attire constraining, Pucahuaman looked particularly natty in his gray silk suit. While red was the color of Inca and therefore Contisuyun nobility, Trang Ho managed to convince him that a crimson suit would be a bit too conspicuous for the Big Apple, even for someone involved in TV.

They did not marvel at the steel and glass towers of Manhattan, having dwelled among more aesthetic structures on their own world. The ethnic olla podrida which swarmed through the streets, however, did impress them, since their ancestors had known only themselves and the viracochas. It had the additional benefit of allowing them all to blend in easily.

The Fernández brothers were more awed by their surroundings than the Contisuyuns, while Da Rimini was in seventh heaven. Finally she herself was in New York instead of just talking to people who had been there.

Fewick booked half a floor in a mid-range midtown hotel while Trang Ho confirmed the meeting which was to take place the next day with the writers her friend had contacted earlier. Fewick would accompany her, as would Apu Tupa and Pucahuaman. Both Contisuyuns had been studying their English and intended to participate without the aid of their conspicuous translators. Suspicious as always, Da Rimini insisted on being included.

"Just let me do most of the talking," Trang Ho said as she relaxed in the spacious suite they'd chosen for the meeting.

"I dislike the notion," Pucahuaman told her.

"Well, you aren't commanding troops here. If you want to bring this off you'd better leave the details to me."

Apu Tupa sipped at his drink, the taste of which he found most congenial, and attempted to reassure his commander. "All has gone well thus far. Allow the woman to proceed." Pucahuaman grumbled but said nothing further.

The bell rang and Trang Ho rose to answer the door. "Just sit back and relax. Compared to the people you've met so far, these guys are going to seem strange to you. They just flew in from the Coast."

"How should we act?" Apu Tupa was feeling slightly light-headed and very relaxed indeed.

"Confident, wealthy, and not too bright. Just like any other executive producers." She opened the door.

The two men who entered were dressed in short-sleeved shirts and open jackets. One wore slacks and loafers, the other jeans, sneakers, and dark sunglasses. Apu Tupa whispered to Fewick.

"Why does the short one cover his eyes? The sun is not harsh in here."

"It's part of his tribal costume," the archaeologist explained. Apu Tupa nodded understandingly.

Brief introductions identified the pair as Danny and Sid. The former unholstered a microcassette recorder while his partner placed a laptop computer on the dining table, plugged it in, and booted it up.

Danny was lean, blond, and possessed of incredible energy. Though he addressed himself to Trang Ho, he kept glancing in the Contisuyuns' direction as he spoke.

"All right: what kind of show are we talking about here?" As his partner spoke, Sid waited with fingers poised over the laptop's keys. Straight black hair fell to his shoulders and his expression almost as far. More than anything else he looked like a mortician preparing to record the vital statistics of the recently deceased.

"Come on, gimme some help here," Danny urged his hosts. He had an irritating habit of snapping his fingers as he talked. "I mean, are we talking comedy, drama, what? We're running on your time but I'm not one of those schmucks who get off on wasting other people's money. Of course, if you're not sure what you want to do," he said eagerly, "we have some interesting original concepts of our own that—"

"Dramatic," Trang Ho told him, interrupting. "And we want to do it live."

"*High* concept." A facile faux fey whistle of appreciation emerged from Danny's lips as his partner tap-tapped on the laptop. "Feed me specifics, sugar." He hesitated. "I mean, not that we don't like doing originals, but to tell the truth we're actually better at reworking and adapting than at coming up with new stuff. It's a special talent, you know?"

The general had sat quietly for about as long as he was able. Ignoring Trang Ho's warning look, he launched into the conversation with his heavily accented English.

"I am Pucahuaman. This is my advisor, Apu Tupa."

"Right," said Danny attentively.

"We come from another world to which our ancestors fled to escape death and torture."

Trang Ho shut her eyes while Fewick inhaled sharply. As for the two writers, neither blinked.

"Death and torture, right. Good stuff." The blond didn't miss a beat. "You getting all this, Sid?"

"Yo." The cadaver's fingers flew in eerie silence over the laptop's keyboard.

Encouraged, the general continued. "We have returned to take our revenge upon our ancient enemies, the Spaniards. All who try to stand in our way will suffer."

"Good, good, go with it, you're on a roll, man!" The blond's enthusiasm was boundless. Though concentrating on Pucahuaman's laborious speech, he still managed to notice the tension building in the room.

"Hey, why's everybody looking so uptight? Relax! We can work with this. Can't we, Sid?"

"Yo."

"High concept, yeah. C'mon, don't stop now." Danny rose and began pacing like a hyperthyroidal rat. "What else you got?" He started to sit on the coffee table only to find that it was already occupied.

Moe meowed warningly and the blond resumed his pacing, keeping his distance from the ticklish aroma of residual tuna fish which enveloped the table and its single four-legged occupant in a contented feline halo.

Pucahuaman straightened on the couch, ignoring Trang Ho's frantic semaphoring. "There is a device which if properly utilized can influence entire populations. It will be used to turn Spain's allies against her."

"Fantastic," Danny insisted. "A sci-fi soap opera! We can do wonders with this stuff. You must've been sitting on the treatment for years."

"No. We have been forced to improvise," the general told him.

"I'm impressed." The writer's face contorted as he focused on a vision beyond the range of mere mortals. "I see sort of a cross between the Bond flicks and *Days of Our Lives*, with maybe a touch of Monty Python. You got anybody in mind for the principal roles?"

"No," said Trang Ho before Pucahuaman could further complicate matters.

"Just as well. Sid and I can handle the casting. With your approval, of course." The way he paused showed that he expected objections. Upon hearing none he rushed onward, lest they surface.

"And we can set one of the primary roles right now." With a flourish he whirled and pointed at the startled Da Rimini, who almost reached reflexively for the gun she didn't have. "You'll be the perfect love interest, sweetheart. We'll pit the two main protagonists against each other for your favors."

"*Qué!*" was all Da Rimini could mumble, more than a little lost.

"Oh yeah. A tall new face like yourself, put you in some tight uniforms or something. You'll knock 'em dead, especially the Hispanic audience. I mean, the demographics are *now*, baby. Your people are *happening.*"

Slightly dazed, Da Rimini looked to her companions for assistance.

"Why not?" said Apu Tupa, astute observer of human nature that he was.

"Indubitably, my dear," Fewick murmured. "Go with the flow."

"Then it's settled. Man, this is gonna be great! We'll play it absolutely straight, I mean, like it's really happening. Putting it out live'll make it a sensation. This has Emmy written all over it. We're talking primetime breakthrough here." He poured himself a drink.

"Okay, now: time. What are we talking here? Half hour, hour, miniseries? Give me some parameters."

"Whatever you think would persuade the largest number of people to watch," said Apu Tupa in measured tones.

"Hey, I like the way you think, sir." He glanced over his shoulder. "Let's try for an hour, Sid. Open with a two-hour made-for-TV movie, set up the basic situation, describe the invasion, intro the main characters . . . the usual. Not neglecting your input, of course," he added hastily to his attentive audience.

"We can furnish many details," Pucahuaman assured him.

"Details, yeah. Those are always nice."

"And all the time we can be broadcasting our message."

Trang Ho sucked in her breath and Fewick twitched slightly. Danny was staring at the general, and even his monosyllabic companion had turned to look.

"Hey, nothing personal, sir, but Sid and I, we're like artists, you know? We have kind of a problem with this message thing." For the first time since the meeting had begun an uncomfortable silence filled the room.

Apu Tupa put a hand on the general's shoulder. Pucahuaman met his gaze, then smiled somberly at the writer.

"I understand. I did not mean to suggest that we would in any way interfere with your work."

"Okay." Danny's enthusiasm returned immediately. "Don't worry. Leave it to us and we'll deliver the audience you want." Avarice glistened on his face like an Italian cosmetic as he glanced at Trang Ho. "Did I understand you to say that the show's already fully underwritten for a whole season?" She nodded. "Yes, just leave it to Sid and me and we'll take you where you want to go."

"There's something else," she said. "We don't want to break in the U.S. We want to open in the European market, build a rep there, then sell through here."

"Interesting marketing strategy. Isn't it, Sid?"

"Yo." Fingers hovered above keys.

"Better suited to films, but if that's the way you want to do it . . ."

"It is," she insisted.

He shrugged. "It's your sponsor's money. Got a production team in mind?"

"We plan on setting up our own."

"Good, good. Keep complete control, hold on to all the ancillary rights. We can go through Granada or one of the other British independents for English distribution, RAI Italy, maybe Monde in France. Sid and I'll handle it."

Trang Ho shook her head. "We're going out live so we want the show receivable live. That means Sky Channel."

"More money," the blond warned her.

"Let us worry about that. You tend to the writing."

"Deal. This is gonna be a groundbreaker. We'll call it"—he paused for emphasis—"*Day Becomes Tomorrow*!" Fewick winced. "It's all coming together now. We'll have a scientific advisor . . ."

"We will be your advisors," said Apu Tupa.

"Yeah, sure. I didn't mean one who'd actually *do* anything. But it's always nice to have a big name tacked on the credits at the end of the show. Sagan, maybe, or Asimov, or Nancy Reagan's astrologer . . . what the hell was that broad's name? Squiggly? Oh well, no matter. You get the idea. Strictly for snob appeal."

"Yo," said Sid enlighteningly.

"The shows must be broadcast exactly as written," said Pucahuaman portentously, "or else the subliminal messages they will carry will not be effective."

"Subliminal messages?" Danny frowned. "Like, from the invaders? Hey, *super* gimmick! The PR people will eat it up." His voice was full of wonder. "You people have so many great ideas I hardly know which ones to incorporate into the story line first. But don't worry. You just keep throwing concepts at Sid and me and we'll see that all the good stuff gets worked in."

Which is precisely what they all spent the rest of that afternoon doing.

U'chak could not keep from smiling. This world was almost as amusing as the Monitor's futile attempts to prevent him from implementing his design.

True, he had not foreseen the extent to which the Monitors would risk breaking their own rules to contain him, but it did not matter. Not since a succession of unexpected developments had actually worked to his advantage. No, he was moving much too fast for them, delightedly riding the disruption he had initiated while they struggled comically to catch up. All that was needed now was to keep it channeled and events would progress of their own accord until social critical mass was reached. Then he would happily reap the resulting whirlwind.

He could imagine the Monitors' frustration. They had taken a considerable risk, only to find themselves once more outmaneuvered. They did not have his foresight, his incisive talent for planning far ahead for multiple eventualities. They would always be several jumps behind.

So pleased was he with himself that he let down his guard enough to execute an ecstatic spring through a slippery gap in reality, returning to land perfectly on his feet, as always. As expected, his gesture of delight went unremarked upon. Though fun to manipulate, these creatures were woefully deficient in the higher perceptions.

He would miss them when they destroyed themselves.

THEY had no trouble when it finally came time to leave Manú. Igor knew every ranger by name. They did not question where he had obtained his peculiar botanical specimens nor whether he had official authorization to remove them from the park.

In Cuzco the sale of a small golden amulet from Paititi brought in more than enough money to charter a plane to take them to Nazca, where for the first time the Boojums began to complain of weakness due to the lack of the vital trace elements they had alluded to earlier.

"Tell us what y'all need and we'll go into town and buy the stuff," Ashwood told them.

The aliens had assembled in the sunny private courtyard that backed onto their hotel suite. Completely enclosed, it offered them a place where they could move about freely without being seen from the dusty main street. The hotel staff had been apprised on arrival of the gringos' "specimens," so not even the maid lingered over her cleaning duties to study the three strange plants.

Wandering through the courtyard and rooms, the Boojums picked and prodded at various artifacts of human civilization, commenting on the progress that had been made since their last visit more than a hundred years earlier. Macha and Grinsaw played hide-and-seek among the potted plants and wrought-iron patio furniture.

"What kind of vitamins should we buy?" Carter asked.

"Not vitamins, old chap." With multiple root-tentacles Shorty poked at the black and white TV. "According to the old records, everything we require is present in the proper proportions in a small fish which is found in abundance off this coast. I shall describe the fish to you."

It meant nothing to Carter or Ashwood, but Igor knew instantly what the Boojum was talking about, as would have any Peruvian schoolchild.

"Anchovies. They were nearly wiped out many years ago."

"How could you wipe out such a substantial natural resource in so short a period of time?" Shorty wanted to know.

"You would be surprised to what extent humans will go to service their own stupidity," the guide replied.

Ashwood rose from the couch. "Igor and I'll head on into town and fix y'all up. Jason, you stick around and keep our guests company."

Carter looked down at her. "Who appointed you captain of this ship, Marjorie?"

She stood close to him, whispering. "Lemme go with Igor, cuddles. I don't like admittin' to it, but frankly, sometimes these elegant vegetables get on my nerves, know what I mean?"

He sighed. "Go ahead, then."

Carter watched his companions depart, then relaxed as best he could while the trio of aliens resumed their inspection of the suite. Everything fascinated them, right down to the plumbing and wiring.

"There has definitely been material progress." As Tree held up the room deodorizer Carter found himself wondering whether the Boojum had eyes in the back of his head or a head in back of his eyes. "Social progress is another matter entirely."

"Quite," Crease agreed. "You persist in engaging in petty conflicts, to the great detriment of your development. Not that that's any of our business, but when our own technology threatens to become involved it is time for us to intervene. Irrational conflagrations have an uncomfortable way of spreading out of control, beyond even the worlds on which they begin."

"There's something I've been wondering." Carter sipped at a glass of purified water. "When you guys abandoned Contisuyu, why'd you leave all that equipment behind? Surely not just because you get a kick out of 'starting over' elsewhere?"

Crease managed the difficult task of conveying embarrassment telepathically. "Actually, old boy, we kind of lost track of Contisuyu."

Carter blinked. "You mean you forgot where it was?"

"Afraid so. As a species, we tend to be a trifle absent-minded at times. Things get overlooked, lost in the files. You know how it is."

"A whole world?"

"If a transmitter isn't used for a long time and the records of its location are misplaced, well, there are plenty of other things to keep one's attention. The galaxy's a big place. It's not like we left any of our own people there.

"As a matter of fact, I believe we've lost track all

told of some twenty or so worlds. Bit of a disappointment, what?"

"For supposed superbeings you guys are kind of a letdown," Carter murmured.

"We don't claim to be perfect, old chap. Possessing a high level of technology doesn't make one a god. Our old human friend Mr. Dodgson had some interesting views on the subject."

Someone was knocking at the door. Carter paused long enough for the aliens to retire to the courtyard, where they resumed their rigid, plant-like postures.

Igor followed Ashwood in. Both carried large, flattened boxes.

"Would you believe," said Igor as he set his burden on the table in the center of the room, "that the Peruvian fisheries have been so devastated by overfishing that you can't find canned anchovies even in a tourist town like Nazca? Now, if we were in Lima . . ."

"So what's this?" Carter gestured at the boxes.

Ashwood wiped sweat from her forehead. "The only solution we could come up with. 'Cui' and anchovy pizza. We nibble on the pizza while our friends suck up the anchovies. I hope four larges'll be enough."

It was interesting to watch the Boojums carefully pluck the tiny fish fillets from the top of each pizza, delicately strip them of cheese and tomato, and then slip them underfoot, where they vanished silently into respective anterior mouths. Meanwhile the humans feasted on the pungent remnants that the aliens ignored. What anchovies the aliens did not consume the two cats gratefully scavenged.

Carter managed to consume the contents of two

boxes all by himself. It wasn't like an order from Spago, but despite their somewhat peculiar ingredients he still enjoyed them. After all, a pizza was a pizza.

"Not bad," he commented, licking his fingers when he finished.

"Glad you liked it," said Ashwood. She was eyeing him strangely.

"I didn't recognize some of the toppings."

"Some of it was tropical fruits," she told him. "They're real big on fruit here. Then there's the meat, the *cui*."

"Some kind of pork, right?"

Ashwood was grinning in a way he didn't like. "Not exactly. Igor told me that *cui*'s a traditional Incan food that's still popular in this part of the world. It's guinea pig."

Carter sat up straight. "Guinea pig? You mean, like the little furry . . . ?"

" . . . critters you find in pet stores, right. Also called *conejo de las Indias*. Rabbit of the Indies. The people here serve 'em all sorts of ways. Ground, like on the pizza. Split and broiled. Fried and . . ."

What little Carter remembered of the remainder of the litany he heard from the vicinity of the bathroom, wholly absorbed in a violent physiological reaction to Ashwood's disclosure which the Boojums found intriguing but distinctly counterproductive. Igor chided Ashwood, declaring that were he so inclined he could as easily nauseate her with descriptions of meals scrounged from the depths of the selva.

"Not me, cutes." She was unimpressed. "I'm from Texas."

They rented a pickup truck, the Boojums riding in back in the open bed. Looking as much like small trees as they did, their presence did not attract undue attention from the townsfolk.

Once out on the open plain, they withdrew their strange green bandoleers from a box and snugged them onto their conical frames.

It took quite a bit of driving around before they located what they thought was the hillside which concealed the cavern in which they'd been held prisoner by the Contisuyuns. At sunset they parked and locked the truck before proceeding on foot, taking a roundabout route to avoid discovery. The plan was to approach the entrance to the cave from above.

"Surely they have guards posted," Ashwood declared as they fumbled their way through the brush.

"What do we do when we reach the entrance?" Igor wanted to know.

"Leave these problems to us, old boy." Shorty gripped several devices in his tentacles. "The chaps and I will handle things, hopefully without bloodshed. Even if these Contisuyuns have made preparations for dealing with intruders, they will not be prepared for us. While they may have studied and mastered some of our technology, they have no idea what we look like because we do not leave reproductions of our physical selves scattered about. We consider that an archaic vanity."

"Also," Tree added, "we're rather shy, what?"

"You really think y'all can take control without hurtin' anybody?" Ashwood stepped over a dead log.

"If we cannot, then we do not deserve to regard ourselves as the highest known form of intelligence," Crease declaimed portentously. "Much less as the guardians of true civilization."

Carter lengthened his stride until he and Igor were out in front of the others. "You think they can bring this off?" he asked the guide.

"I have no idea. We still know very little about them, except that they are polite, forgetful, and very intelligent. We do not even know what their real motives may be."

Carter frowned. "You think they're lying to us?"

The guide looked up at him, his face unreadable in the moonlight. "We have no way of knowing. When you live and work all your life in the selva, where the people as well as the animals are masters of camouflage and deception, you learn to question everything. However, we must trust them because we *do* know what the Contisuyuns intend." He held a branch aside to let Carter pass unscathed.

"As to whether they can do what they claim, *quién sabe?* But I think it is better to try this than come storming in with a truckload of soldiers and police, which was my original idea."

Having spent months sequestered in the dreary, dry underground base, the guard was tiring of his companions as rapidly as he was of his surroundings. Like the rest of the team he looked forward to night duty because it offered the only real break in the otherwise screamingly dull daily routine. At least while posted on guard outside one could enjoy the fresh air and occasional strange nocturnal sights of one's ancestral home.

Along with everyone else he wondered what kind of progress the great general, Master Apu, and the others were making. Much time had passed without any contact. Had they been discovered and imprisoned or worse, or were their plans proceeding smoothly? He took heart in the knowledge that no viracochas had come looking for the base.

Frustrated technicians continued to pore over the transmitter, unable to determine what had caused it to fail. Should their efforts continue to be thwarted, the soldier knew he and his companions would have to live out their lives without ever seeing Contisuyu again. He banished the unpleasant thought. Did not the histories declare that the hated conquistadores had sailed for the old empire awash in similar fears? As a descendant of the great Incas, could he do no less?

What had happened to the hundreds who had transmitted from the homeworld aboard the twelve transports? That was another thought never far from his mind or those of his friends. He had known many of those vanished fighters personally. The technicians said they might not be dead. Simply elsewhere. He hoped it was so.

During the day small local aircraft sometimes flew directly overhead. They took no notice of the carefully concealed entrance. Nor did those who came on foot to gaze at the ancient lines of Nazca come near the steep, unspectacular hillside. At night the barren plain was deserted, but the officers insisted on maintaining a watch. The soldier and his companions were glad of the chance to get outside for a few hours.

Hands clasped behind his back, stun tube holstered at his side, he walked over to a shrub half again as tall as himself and snapped off one of the thin green branches, inhaling of the sharp fragrance his action released. Though Contisuyu boasted an intriguing and varied ecology of its own, this world was full of smells at once ancient and new.

Intending to repeat the procedure with the next bush in line, he grasped its nearest branch and was more than a little startled when it jerked free of his fingers. While he gaped at it the shrub immediately behind him pressed a small device against a certain place on his neck. Stiffening, he collapsed against it, his eyes rolling back in his head.

Gently Crease lowered the unconscious guard to the ground. Pivoting on his cilia, he ambled toward the entrance, his colleagues following immediately behind.

Carter was half asleep by the time Tree returned to the waiting humans.

"It's over," the Boojum informed them. "A bit of all right, it was."

"I didn't hear any shots." Ashwood strained to see down the slope.

"There was no need for fighting. Nearly everyone inside was asleep. By taking our time we were able to eventually incapacitate the lot without anyone being alerted to our presence. Your nervous systems are easily manipulated and located conveniently near the outside of your bodies. Until we choose to awaken them, they will continue to sleep the soundest sleeps of their lives." Tree paused thoughtfully. "It would be more accurate to say they have been placed in a state of enforced estivation.

"There is a possible problem, however. Utilizing your descriptions we searched carefully for those of your own kind whom you say are aiding the intruders. We did not find any of them. Furthermore, there are fewer Contisuyuns than you told us to expect."

"Damn," Ashwood muttered, as surprised by the revelation as the Boojum. "I suppose we shouldn't have expected 'em to sit still. You can bet they're off makin' mischief somewheres."

"I will bring the truck up." Igor started back down the slope while Carter and Ashwood followed Tree toward the entrance.

It was strange to be back inside the upper cave, stranger still to see the bodies of Contisuyun soldiers and technicians lying motionless on pallets on the floor. Farther down, the twelve huge transports sat as before, the nearest two with their ports gaping wide and still stinking powerfully of dead fish.

There was no sign of the Fernández brothers, Francesca da Rimini, Bruton Fewick, or Trang Ho. Nor were General Pucahuaman or Apu Tupa present. Tree was correct: the invaders were significantly diminished in number.

Where had they gone?

Not back through the transmitter: the Boojums confirmed that.

"They spoke of using alternate technologies against Europe," Carter said. "There aren't many of them. How much trouble can they cause?"

"That depends on their resourcefulness." Shorty waved a pair of root-tentacles for emphasis. "We will know when we find them."

The other Boojums looked on while Shorty revived one of the estivating officers. That brave and dedicated warrior took one look at the creatures bending over him and promptly fainted. The second man they brought around was possessed of greater intestinal fortitude.

At first he refused absolutely to talk, but when

informed that he was in the actual presence of Those-
Who-Came-Before he grew positively voluble.

"New York." Carter sounded dubious. "Why
would they go to New York?"

"I do not know." The officer was understandably
unable to take his eyes off the Boojums. "There
was talk of utilizing learning machine technology
to influence the minds of the viracochas, but how
this was to be implemented I do not know."

"If they have gone to New York," said Crease,
"then we must follow and find them."

"Do y'all have any idea how big New York is?"
Ashwood kicked at the ground and the revived officer flinched. "We don't know where to start looking.
They can disappear among millions of people and
if that Trang Ho's still working with them you can
bet she's got Apu Tupa and the rest lookin' halfway
normal. Not that it would matter in New York."

Carter addressed the officer. "You must have some
idea of what they planned to do."

The officer hesitated. Tree leaned close and the
man drew back, a mixture of awe and terror on
his face. "I remember that the viracochas spoke of
broadcasting messages by means of their television
network."

The Boojum straightened. "There is your answer.
Such a simple delivery system would not work on
us, but a primitive people like yourselves might easily fall under its sway."

"We're already under its sway," Ashwood replied.

"Given limited resources it would be the most
effective way to control large numbers of individ-
uals."

Carter was thinking aloud. "There are only so

many ways to get a broadcast on the air. I know a few people in the business." He looked up hopefully. "I can make inquiries. If they've gone through the usual channels we can trace them."

"Then we waste time here," said Crease.

Shorty gently but firmly returned the helpful officer to the arms of Morpheus. By the time Igor had brought the truck as far up the slope as he could manage, they were waiting to join him.

A large portion of the treasure they had discovered earlier had vanished. Ashwood correctly surmised that it had been converted into cash, but more than enough had been left behind to facilitate their own departure. A chartered executive jet conveyed them all to New York.

An unexpected problem arose at Kennedy International when a cantankerous customs official insisted they produce official documentation allowing the export from Peru of exotic "tropical plants." When a carved lapis idol with emerald eyes turned up in place of the requested paperwork they were permitted to pass without having to answer any additional awkward questions.

Carter ensconced them in a small hotel that was so eclectic and so exclusive that the management didn't bat an eye at guests who insisted on traveling with their own decor. For the rate they were paying they could have housed a herd of armadillos in the bathroom.

Even in New York the three Boojums would have attracted attention if they'd gone ambling down the avenues, so Igor and Ashwood were left to attend to their needs: answering questions, discussing television, and ordering out for the occasional anchovy pizza, while Carter busied himself with inquiries and visits to agencies and production companies.

Weeks passed before he returned to their suite with a photo supplied by a small public relations firm.

"That's Da Rimini." Ashwood took the picture from Carter's fingers. "I'd recognize the batty bitch anywhere. But she looks different somehow."

"Professional makeup." Carter sat down on the couch, glad to be back in the hotel. It was hot and sticky outside, standard Manhattan summer weather. It reminded him of the Manu. "She's actually performing in their broadcasts. I didn't know she had any acting ability."

Ashwood sniffed. "The kind of ability she needs is all up front, and that she's got. Besides, if the Contisuyuns can make whoever's watchin' their drivel believe what they want 'em to believe, convincin' their audience that Da Rimini's an actress must be a cinch." She crumpled the photo. "Where're they taping?"

"They're not," Carter told her. "They're broadcasting live via satellite, and not from here. In Europe."

Ashwood was only slightly surprised. "Makes sense, I suppose, since it's the Spaniards they want to take revenge against."

"Not only the Spaniards. Their transponder's footprint covers most of Europe, and they send out simultaneous translations in a dozen languages. They're not taking any chances." Something warm brushed against his ankles and he looked down to see Macha and Grinsaw peering out from beneath the couch. The sight made him smile.

It was still a mystery to him how two such simi-

lar animals had managed to evolve on two entirely different worlds. The notion of convergent evolution was not one that often cropped up at the parties
he attended and so he was largely ignorant of the
concept. He'd intended to discuss it further with the
Boojums, but somehow never got around to bringing
the subject up.

Besides, there were more pressing matters to attend to.

"I would've come across that sooner," he said,
indicating the photo, "if I'd started with stills from
European operations."

"So where are they working out of?" Ashwood
asked him. "Madrid? London?"

"You won't believe it. Obviously they wanted to
stay as far out of the public eye as possible while
still having access to trained technical support. They
couldn't do that at someplace like Cinecitta or the
BBC." The odor of anchovies hung powerfully in the
air.

"So how do we stop 'em? Go in with guns blaz-
ing?"

"We prefer to avoid that sort of thing," said
Crease. "It would be much more efficacious if
we could accompany their established program
with some countervailing subliminals of our own
design, thereby counteracting the effects of their
work. All that we need is temporary control of
the instrumentation they are using. Regardless of
how they have adapted our technology I doubt it is
beyond our understanding. It should not be difficult
to make the necessary adjustments."

Carter frowned. "I don't see how we can do that.
If we go busting into their facilities the first thing

that'll happen is they'll go off the air. We wouldn't have a signal to make use of."

"Piffle." Shorty shuffled over to a window. "We shall manage. We will deal with the technical difficulties if you can handle your fellow humans."

"You may not think so," Ashwood said evenly, "but y'all have the easier end of it."

"We must not dally," Crease warned them. "The more often they broadcast, the more ingrained becomes whatever message they are transmitting and the more difficult its effects will be to counter."

XVII———

IT was easier to charter a jet out of Manhattan than it had been from Lima, but more difficult to get into Scotland than it had been New York. Nor did Igor, who was the specialist in such matters, think it would be a good idea to try and bribe the phlegmatic customs official who barred their exit from the airport. They could not afford to waste valuable time trying to explain their situation to a magistrate.

So they had to remain close to the airport while their botanical specimens were placed in quarantine and properly fumigated. Meanwhile Carter's worst suspicions were confirmed when Igor discovered Inca Cola for sale at the airport snack shop. The Fernández brothers had wasted no time.

An anxious week passed, but the Boojums appeared to have survived their experience undetected and unharmed.

"Bit of a peculiar sensation," Tree was saying. "It made us itch a little, but caused no damage. We have the ability to seal our pores against chemical intrusion."

"Personally I found it rather refreshing," Shorty said. "I have no more love for the local parasites than did the officials who sprayed us."

"And they didn't suspect you were anything other than mindless vegetables?" Ashwood asked.

"Not in the slightest," said Crease. "They went about their tasks with considerable indifference."

They were resting comfortably in the walled backyard of the rustic farmhouse Carter had rented, one of many such facilities available to visitors to the Edinburgh area. In the distance ancient stone walls crisscrossed gently rounded heather-swathed hills, keeping cattle and neighbors from coming to blows just as they had for hundreds of years.

In the industrial suburbs of the city fifteen miles to the south lay the private production and broadcast facilities of Atahualpa Ltd. The Contisuyuns had named their company after the Inca emperor who had been treacherously slain by Pizarro's men.

"Cheeky of them," was Shorty's observation.

The first thing they did after moving into the cottage was to watch the next primetime episode of *Day Becomes Tomorrow*. Carter found it excessively maudlin but competently directed and acted, as would inevitably be the case with any professionally produced British show. Because he had been alerted to watch out for it he was also aware of the subtle manipulation of his thoughts and emotions the show engendered. Anyone ignorant of what the Contisuyuns were up to would simply think they had been powerfully affected by a well-made program. As the Boojums pointed out, the effect was subtle and difficult to detect.

"Folks are used to being manipulated by TV." Ashwood turned from the set as the closing commercial came on. "They'll soak up the Contisuyuns' message without realizing what's being done to them." She shuddered. "If it's been goin' on like this for weeks then the whole European audience ought to be well and truly primed for whatever the Contisuyuns have in mind."

"I tried to resist," Igor added, "but even in English the story drew me in and held me. A good telenovela will always do that, but there was more to this. One could sense what was happening, but only if one had been forewarned." He gazed at his companions. "Suddenly I have this vague dislike of anything Spanish."

Ashwood nodded. "It works, all right."

"You know," Carter said wistfully, "I thought Da Rimini was pretty good."

"Why shouldn't she be?" Ashwood snapped. "She sure as hell acted up a storm for you back in Cuzco."

Except for Da Rimini, the show's cast was made up of professional British performers. Neither of the Fernández brothers, Fewick, or Trang Ho had put in an appearance, but there was ample evidence of their complicity. The latter two were listed in the closing credits as executive producers, while the brothers were named as principal sponsors.

Everywhere they went they were assaulted by signs advertising the new taste sensation, Inca Cola. Out of curiosity, Carter bought a six-pack and brought it back to the cottage. Everyone tried it, including the Boojums, and declared it to be astoundingly ordinary. Its success in Britain in the absence of any distinguishing taste therefore constituted further proof of the effectiveness of the Contisuyuns' subtle transmissions.

"It helps, you know," Tree said, "that your kind is so susceptible to this type of suggestion."

Carter nodded. "When I was shopping I asked several people how they felt about Spain and the Spaniards. Not a subject likely to come up in casual, everyday conversation. You wouldn't believe how hostile some of the responses were. Yet when I asked them why they felt that way not one could tell me. It puzzled them to have it pointed out."

"There's more to it than that," Ashwood muttered. "They've got somethin' besides stirrin' up anti-Spanish sentiment in mind."

"We should proceed carefully," Igor warned his companions, "lest we alarm them and they react by moving their operations somewhere less accessible."

The revelation arrived, conveniently enough, with the morning *Daily Express*. It was Igor who noticed the item, which his American friends had passed over.

"Here it is. This coming Saturday. How could I have forgotten, even with everything that has happened to us? *Madre de Dios*, today is already Tuesday! We have very little time in which to act."

Carter and Ashwood crowded around the guide, who held up the back section of the newspaper so all could see. Even the two cats seemed intrigued.

"I read the whole damn rag from front to back." Ashwood leaned over his shoulder. "Nothin' I saw set off any mental alarms."

"Did you read the sports section?"

She gave him a funny look. "Why would I bother with the sports pages?"

Igor tapped the article which had caught his attention. Carter glanced at it and nodded sagely.

"I still don't get it," Ashwood said.

"Liverpool and Barcelona are playing Saturday in Barcelona for the European soccer championship," the guide explained. "British football fans have a reputation for violence. In addition to them the stadium will be packed with fans from all over the Continent. With *Day Becomes Tomorrow* having primed an anti-Spanish fuse from here to Greece, the slightest spark could set off a major riot."

"Which could escalate beyond the bounds of sport," Carter added, for once being a step ahead of her. "And it says in the local TV guide that the show is running a one-hour special this Thursday night. Obviously the Contisuyuns have been pointing toward this."

"Don't give us a lot of time to do anything." Ashwood was watching Tree, who stood swaying next to an open window. "Well? Do our resident veggies have any brilliant suggestions? Have you been listening to any of this?"

"We hear everything, madam," said Tree.

"Quite." Crease was examining the remnants of the human's breakfast. "Somehow we must gain control of the broadcast facilities. Our aim should be not to cancel the proposed transmission but to reprogram it to suit our own ends. We must counteract the Contisuyuns' litany of bellicosity with counterveiling subliminal reassurances. This should not take long; a few minutes of broadcast time accompanied by an appropriately reinforcing delivery would be sufficient."

"Might as well ask for a couple of hours," Ashwood grumbled. "They ain't gonna let us or anybody else rewrite their script."

"First we have to get inside." Carter looked thoughtful. "We ought to be able to manage that as long as we can avoid Da Rimini, Fewick, and the

others. The local technicians won't know us from
Adam."

"What about the rhubarbs-who-came-before?" She
jerked a finger in the Boojums' direction.

"We can arrive at the last minute concealed in the
delivery vehicle you have rented," Shorty replied,
"and remain motionless and out of sight until it
is time to reprogram the instrumentation. We will
deal with those humans who are in control of the
transmission in the same manner as we dealt with
the Contisuyuns at Nazca. No one will be injured."
The Boojum pivoted toward Carter. "It is imperative
that while the altered suggestiveness is being broadcast it be supported by appropriate verbal accompa-
niment."

"In other words, the story line that's going out has
to be altered to match your subliminals?"

"Quite. Otherwise the contrast between what the
human audience feels and what it sees and hears
will negate our efforts. It would be as if the visual
portion of one of your commercials were broadcast in
tandem with the sound track from an advertisement
for an entirely different product. No harm will result,
but neither will we have succeeded in repairing the
emotional damage or counteracting the prejudice the
Contisuyuns have engendered. Should we attempt
this and fail we may temporarily frustrate their quest
for revenge, but we will have sacrificed the element
of surprise. They could resume their assault elsewhere, possibly with a different approach.

"No, we must succeed the first time."

Carter straightened proudly. "Improvisation's
always been one of my strong points. You take care
of the electronics and I'll handle the story line."

"Jolly good," said Crease.

"You're out of the mind they'll blow away," Ashwood insisted.

He put a hand on her shoulder. "Marjorie, I can
do this. Remember, they broadcast live. By the time
anyone important enough gives the order to cut the
satellite link the Boojums will have done their job.
And I'll have done mine."

"What about the rest of the cast, the other actors?
Won't they just stop dead in their tracks when
another performer shows up unannounced and starts
spouting lines that aren't in the script?"

"Not if I can come up with viable dialogue. If
they're competent actors they'll adapt. They won't
have any choice because they're live. Until somebody says cut or wrap they'll keep going, just like
the technicians and the people up in the booth.

"Everyone will be looking at everyone else. The
director will think my appearance is a producer's
gimmick, the actors will think it's a ploy of the
director, and rather than blow the show they'll all
wing it rather than go to black. I'm figuring they'll
hang with it at least until the next commercial. I
only have to stay on for a few minutes."

"You're goin' to get your fool self shot."

"I don't think so, Marjorie. They may have guards
posted at the entrance, but there shouldn't be any on
the set."

She was still reluctant. "You're all crazy. Suppose
when you drive up to the gate somebody wants to
take a look in the van?"

Carter had already considered that. "Igor can tell
them that the Boojums are props for the show. The
guards will believe him. What else could they be?"

They spent the next morning reconnoitering the studio. From the outside the old film complex looked little different from the other commercial buildings that filled half the industrial park south of Edinburgh. Vacant fields alternated with sprawling, usually windowless single-story distribution facilities and assembly plants.

A large satellite dish peered heavenward from atop the main structure. Chain link fencing topped with concertina wire enclosed the grounds. While Carter had been correct in his assumption that the Contisuyuns would not have armed men conspicuously on patrol, it was also clear they had no intention of allowing casual visitors to roam freely about the studio.

The Boojums were possessed of several acute senses, but vision was not one of them. So it was left to Carter and Igor to sit in the front of the van and swap a pair of hastily purchased binoculars back and forth as they studied the grounds.

"I see one guard station," Igor murmured as he stared through the glasses. "One man inside."

"That rambling structure would be administration," Carter decided, peering past the shorter man. "The broadcast facilities are probably located behind it. Technical should be next door, under the big dish. That's where you need to take our friends."

Igor lowered the binoculars. "What about you? How will you get onto the set?"

Carter chewed his lower lip. "I don't know. It'll be a lot tougher to slip in there unchallenged than into Technical. The longer I can delay my 'entrance,' the greater the surprise and the better chance I'll have of pulling this off. Ideally I need to keep out of sight until right before I step in front of the cameras."

"Then we need to find a way in, where you won't be noticed," Ashwood opined from her seat next to the door.

Carter turned. "There is no other way in."

She smiled and gave him a playful jab in the ribs. "How do you know if you don't have a look? Let's take a drive around back."

After circumnavigating the studio they parked in the lot of the plastics factory next door, whose busy workers ignored the unmarked delivery vehicle in their midst.

Ashwood squinted through the binoculars. "There's an old dirt road crossin' the empty field between the studio and here. It ends at a gate." She gripped the field glasses tighter. "I see a big chain and a heavy padlock. No problem."

"I thought you told me that you had nothing to do personally with those robberies your boyfriend was involved in years ago?"

She lowered the binoculars. "What I said was that I never killed nobody. I didn't say nothin' about a little recreational breakin' and enterin'."

He made a face. "So when do we go in?"

"Early in the morning, before the crew arrives to start settin' up. Guards'll be changin' shifts and less alert. We'll take some sandwiches or somethin' and find a place where we can hide until evening."

Carter frowned at her. "Who said you were coming with me?"

"Why not?" she shot back. "I'd look out of place in the van with Igor and I'm damned if I'm gonna squat back at the cottage and wait for the menfolk to come ridin' in to tell me how their evening went.

Besides, if somebody stumbles into us maybe I can distract 'em. Tell 'em I need their help in wardrobe. I can make *that* believable enough." Twisting in her seat, she glanced back at the Boojums. "They start sending at seven P.M. How soon after they're on the air should he make his 'entrance'?"

"It does not matter once we are in control of the technical facilities," Shorty told her. "We will of course be able to see him on your boxy little visual monitors once he enters the field of view. At that time we will begin to broadcast our altered suggestiveness in conjunction with his improvised dialogue."

"Let's wait 'til at least the second half of the show," Carter suggested. "That way they won't have time to put a countervailing message on the air if they somehow manage to retake the transmission room."

"Ripping good notion, old boy."

Ashwood peered around Carter's bulk at Igor. "Head for the gate just before airtime. That way you won't be parked where you might attract the attention of some bored road cop. Also, you can say that you got caught in rush-hour traffic . . . I guess they got rush-hour traffic hereabouts . . . and that the 'props' you're deliverin' are needed right away for the show. Rent-a-cops don't like bein' yelled at, and it'll be so close to airtime there won't be time for him to call somebody else to run a check, so he ought to wave you on through. You couldn't bring it off at a studio in L.A., but I'll bet they're more laid-back hereabouts."

"The timing is very close." Igor sounded concerned.

"We will have ample time." A rush of reassurance emanated from the Boojums. Suddenly Carter felt completely confident. "Once we have taken the broadcast facilities we will retain control of them until our work is concluded. The Contisuyuns will not have time to realize what has happened to them. By the time they do it will all be over and their nefarious intentions come to naught."

"I just thought of something." Ashwood regarded her companions solemnly. "Assuming we bring this off, what's to keep them from starting all over again with another show someplace else?"

"We will see to it that the dangerous equipment is obliterated beyond repair," Crease told her. "Learning machinery is very delicate and requires components and manufacturing facilities not present on your world. The Contisuyuns who are marooned here are not capable of reconstructing such facilities, even with paid human assistance. These are technicians, not engineers. Your best auto mechanic could not assemble a car from piles of metal and plastic."

"Then let's go back to the cottage." Ashwood yawned noisily. "If I've got to get up early to save the world, or at least this part of it, I want to get a good night's sleep in before it's time to go to work."

XVIII _____

IGOR and the Boojums wished Carter and Ashwood well as they left for the studio at sunup in the small rented car. The aliens and their anxious Peruvian driver wouldn't abandon the cottage for another ten hours or so. Carter gave Macha a goodbye caress, whereupon Tree assured him they would watch over her as carefully as they did Grinsaw.

For the second time in as many days Carter found himself parked in the plastics company lot gazing through the binoculars at the studio. Arriving workers ignored the couple in the compact, intent only upon checking in.

"The area around back's deserted," he was murmuring. "No guard, no dog, nothing."

"No point in hangin' around here, then." Ashwood opened her door and slipped out.

No one challenged them as they strolled casually across the dirt field that separated the two industrial blocks. When they reached the chained gate Carter kept watch while Ashwood did something to the clunky padlock with a small piece of metal. A distinct *click* was followed by his companion's grunt of satisfaction.

"Like ridin' a bike. Once you've done it, you never forget how." She rapped the lock against a metal pole and it obediently popped open.

273

Carter slipped it free of the chain and eased the gate aside. Once in, he replaced both without closing the lock.

The old film studio was much larger than was needed for the production of a single television show. No doubt it had been chosen for its isolation as much as anything else. The empty buildings offered plenty of cover for the two intruders as they worked their way toward the front of the complex, intending to check out the larger of the two sound stages first.

Sure enough, technicians and performers were arriving at and departing the barn-like structure in a steady stream: actors and wardrobe people, makeup specialists and caterers, gofers and gaffers.

Working their way around back they were gratified to find an unlocked door. There was no reason to secure the sound stage, Carter mused, if you had confidence in your perimeter security. The rear of the cavernous edifice was a sargasso of dusty props and fragments of stagework, unused lights, and half-trimmed lumber. What light there was filtered back from the front of the building where the show was produced.

Carter picked his way carefully forward, Ashwood following close on his heels, until they came across a Victorian couch backed up against a false pub front. It was dark and quiet, a good place to hole up 'til evening.

They waited there, eating their sandwiches in silence as cast and crew began to arrive to prepare the night's broadcast. Eventually curiosity and boredom led them to abandon the comfortable couch. They worked their way toward the bustle until Carter found a crack in a painted backdrop through which they could see a little of what was going on.

Pucahuaman, looking comfortable in a gray business suit, stood by one of the big cameras chatting with Apu Tupa and another Contisuyun Carter didn't recognize. Not far from them the director was blocking moves with two of his performers.

Scottish technicians worked on the cameras and lights. Far from the stage and the intervening twenty rows of empty, raked seats other techs busied themselves within a large, glass-enclosed soundproof control booth.

Another figure appeared on stage to interrupt the director, towering over him and the other two performers. Carter gave a start as he recognized Francesca da Rimini, stunning in an elegant dark blue dress and professional makeup.

"Can you see?" Carter edged aside so Ashwood would have a better view.

"Yeah. The conspiratorial homicidal bitch looks pretty good."

"Pucahuaman and Apu Tupa are there. No sign of Fewick or the Fernández brothers, but I'll bet Trang Ho's around. Patrolling the dressing rooms or something."

"Doesn't matter," said Ashwood. "This is gonna come off before they know what hit 'em. By the time anyone reacts it'll be too late. The Boojums will have done their work."

Carter nodded agreement as he checked his watch. "Our friends ought to have left the cottage by now." He glanced through the backdrop. "Think I'll take a little walk."

Ashwood frowned at him. "Are you crazy, handsome? What if somebody spots you?"

"I'll be careful. I think I saw something out there I'd really like to get my hands on."

"She'll recognize you before you open your mouth."

Carter made a face. "Not her. Something just as wordy, but not as loud. If I can get it, it'll be a big help." Staying in a crouch, he headed off to his left.

Ashwood was left to wait uneasily until he returned, triumphantly clutching a magazine-sized wad of paper in his right hand.

"Somebody left a shooting script on a chair. I can do more than just improvise now. I can do a little mental rewriting. And you can coach me."

Ashwood looked doubtful. "I ain't no script girl."

"Come on, Marjorie. The fate of European civilization is at stake."

She shrugged. "Oh well. I guess it beats pickin' the lint out of the couch."

Igor stood in the grass next to the delivery van's open door, his attention flicking back and forth between the rolling, landmarkless countryside and the map he held in both hands. Ancient, identical stone walls divided up the pastures through which the narrow two-lane road ran. A single farmhouse and barn crowned the hill to his right. It did not look anything like the Contisuyuns' broadcast complex or the plastics manufacturing plant which stood next to it.

He knew that by now they should be at the outskirts of the suburban industrial park where the studio was located, which they manifestly were not. Turning the map sideways gave it more aesthetic appeal but did not in any measure clarify his confusion. It was full of mysterious, crisscrossing black and blue and red lines, cryptic numbers and symbols, and roads whose names changed every other kilometer. Jason Carter had navigated the morass with ease. Certainly he should be able to find his way. Wasn't he a guide by profession?

He had to admit it was simpler in east Peru, where roads were few, intersections an event, and the selva gravid with familiar signs. Perhaps he shouldn't have been so confident, should have put aside his pride and asked for directions. Now there was no one to ask.

That did not mean, however, that his increasing bewilderment went unnoticed.

Since the Boojums' comments were projected directly into his mind it was impossible for Igor to ignore them.

"Silly blighter calls himself a guide," Shorty was thinking. "He finds his way through the jungle but can't navigate a primitive system of roads!"

"Time is becoming important." Crease's thoughts were tinged with understandable impatience. "We must not linger."

"Look, this is more complicated than it seems." Igor spoke without turning toward the van, knowing that the Boojums could pick up his thoughts no matter which way he faced. He tapped the map with an accusatory finger. "Everything runs into everything else, there are name changes that make no sense, the numbers shift according to no pattern that I can understand, and the map is several years old anyway. In my country it is much simpler.

"Take this road here. It is called Angus Lane and supposedly runs into something called the A-8, which turns west to become the M-74, where we get off onto the A-12 to go south." He had the dazed look of a citizen listening to a politician trying to explain the rationale behind a new tax.

"I must have taken the wrong exit out of the Marley Circus on the west side of the city. But it should still have directed us south." His voice dropped. "I knew that last underpass did not look right, and that the name Dreary Road was not promising."

"We should be on the M-14, not the M-74," said Tree firmly.

"Bloody nonsense!" Shorty snapped. "What do you know about it, you who can't even plot a—"

"Shut up." Crease redirected his impatience to their driver. "If you are not certain where we are or which way to proceed, old chap, you must seek advice from a local."

"I am afraid I will have to," Igor confessed, his quiet macho self-assurance utterly devastated by the otherworldly complexities of the Royal Auto Club map.

Another kilometer's drive brought them parallel to a field in which an elderly man rode a wagon being pulled by a pair of heavy horses. Igor climbed out of the van and walked over to the stone fence.

"Excuse me, sir! Hello there!" He waved hopefully, trying to attract the farmer's attention.

The man must have heard because he brought the wagon to a halt, secured the reins, and climbed down. As he approached the fence he kept tugging at the brim of his cap as if fearful it might take advantage of the unexpected interruption in the day's routine to take flight.

He examined his visitor with obvious interest. "Well, now, laddie, where might you be from?"

"Peru." With no time to waste, Igor rushed on. "Can you tell me how to get to the M-14?"

"The M-14?" The man drew back in astonishment. "Laddie, you're nowhere near the M-14."

"I know, I know. That is why I'm asking you how to *get* there." Igor tried to restrain himself.

"Well, now." The man massaged the granitic stubble of his chin as he looked to his right. "One might continue on the way you're goin' until he came to the next intersection. Sad to say, there's no sign there since a couple o' the boys knocked it down last year after consumin' a few too many pints at the Black Dog. You turn to the right. It gets mite bumpy as you go down the hill, where you'll come to the old railroad bridge. I think your machine will fit beneath. Go under an' after another two kilometers you'll come to a bitumen road. No sign there either."

"The boys again?"

"Nay. Bleedin' penurious Conservative government. Turn to your left and you'll be confrontin' the loop access. Take it up an' all the way 'round an' you'll find yourself on the M-14 neat as you please."

"Thank you, sir. Thank you!"

"Aye, you're welcome, laddie. But . . ."

Igor was already behind the wheel, slamming the door shut behind him. The van's tires squealed as they threw gravel, leaving the old farmer to gaze contemplatively after the disappearing vehicle. Eventually he turned and headed back up the rocky slope toward his waiting team.

"O' course, *I* wouldn't go that way." He sighed, shaking his head as he walked. "Young folks these days got no patience in 'em."

Activity among the swarming actors and technicians was rising to a fever pitch as broadcast time approached. Having satisfied himself that he'd memorized as much of the script as was possible in the short time available to him, Carter found himself wondering if the Boojums were already on the grounds preparing to take over the satellite uplink complex. He checked his watch anew. As Crease had pointed out, timing would be of the essence.

So don't waste it worrying about the aliens, he admonished himself. *Concentrate on the script, on what you're going to say.* Even if any unforeseen complications arose, he reminded himself, his allies were beings who had built matter transmitters and starships. Absurd to think they couldn't deal with the unexpected.

A point of character nagged at him and he flipped open the script to page 32.

"Bloody hell. I knew one of us should have ridden up front to navigate," Shorty was thinking. "I just knew it."

Igor stood by the open driver's side door. "Oh yes, that would've been useful, especially if some policeman had seen me driving along with a gesticulating plant in the passenger seat."

"Piffle! What policeman? We have not encountered a living soul since we received instructions from that elderly fraud you questioned."

The three aliens had assembled behind their driver to join him in staring at the underside of the old railroad bridge. As events had just demonstrated, the helpful farmer had been no more accurate in his assessment of spatial relationships than he had been in his directions, the result being that the top of the van had struck a very large, very solid supporting timber dating to 1878 which had peeled back the roof of the rented vehicle like soft cheese, not incidentally pinning it in place.

"Maybe you would like to take over the driving, too?" Igor suggested angrily. Spitting and the sound of claws digging at metal walls sounded from inside the van. Even the cats seemed frustrated, he thought. He'd already let some air out of all four tires in an attempt to lower and free the van, to no avail. It was jammed tight beneath the bridge.

"I wonder if so dense and sarcastic a species is worth saving?" Shorty mused angrily.

"At least we have legs." Igor walked to the front of the van, inspecting the underside of the bridge. "For a supposedly advanced race you certainly are critical of others." Pushing down hard on the van's hood produced only complaining metallic squeaks.

"If both of you would devote as much energy to contemplating methods for freeing our vehicle as to trading insults, we might find a means of departing this wilderness," Crease observed darkly.

Ashwood shifted uncomfortably on the couch. She was used to a firm work chair, and the overstuffed relic was cramping her backside.

"What time is it?"

"Twenty minutes 'til seven." Carter was squinting through the backdrop. "No reason to assume they won't start on time."

"When are you plannin' on making your entrance?"

He checked the purloined script. "There's a halfway logical opening here, just after they return from the mid-break commercials."

She nodded. "You're gonna have to give the performance of your life."

"I know." He returned his attention to the crack in the backdrop. "Actually I'm kind of looking forward to it. At least I'll be doing something serious for a change."

Fewick leaned back in the reclining chair in the control booth, stroking the cat curled in his lap as the director called for quiet, preparatory to beginning the evening broadcast.

"We've come quite a ways, Moe." His fingers scratched beneath the animal's chin and the big orange tom purred approvingly. "Perhaps when we commence stage two of this operation and our Contisuyun friends enable me to take control of the great museums of Europe, Mum and Pater will finally acknowledge my presence. As disdainful as they have been of my field work, I should think they would find a switch to administration most gratifying.

"Think of it! I, Bruton Fewick, in control of the destinies of the world's greatest museums. There will be some changes made, I promise you that. After the emphases in the field of archaeology are appropriately altered to suit my theories, I shall branch out. Into art perhaps, and then science. The world will be a better place for the irresistible intrusions of Bruton Fewick. You think so too, don't you, Moe?"

The tom glanced lazily back up at him, its expression inscrutable as Pucahuaman and Apu Tupa entered the booth. From there they could watch and comment on the show in sound-shielded comfort. The Scottish and English technicians busy at their consoles ignored the three men and concentrated on doing their jobs. Broadcasting live television via satellite was no task for the lazy or indifferent.

In another room in another building nearby, Contisuyun technicians would receive the audio and visual from the studio. After adjusting the levels, they would feed the composite signal through some peculiar and elegantly sinister apparatus of their own devising before shooting it up to the *Eurosat III* for distribution to sets and stations across Great Britain and the Continent. Two armed Contisuyun soldiers flanked the only entry door. Once transmission of the show began, no one would be allowed to leave or enter.

The local technical people did not question the unusual procedure. Their job was to record and transmit the show to a chosen destination, and if that destination happened to be the building next door instead of a recording studio or local station, that was none of their business so long as the Bank of Scotland continued to cash their checks.

Pucahuaman barely glanced up when the director called for action and the opening title of the show appeared on the monitors in the booth.

"This night will live forever in the memories of my people. Tomorrow the great football game between the Spaniards and the English will dissolve into rioting and chaos, the culmination of all our careful work and preparations. As people throughout Europe watch it happen, the anti-Spanish feeling we have instigated will spread, pitting former allies against one another and plunging governments into crisis. There will be calls for punishment and for sanctions. And every week, every Thursday night at seven o'clock, *Day Becomes Tomorrow* will be there to provide subtle suggestions and offer sly advice on what future course of action the citizens of Europe should take."

"After we have revenged our ancestors," Apu Tupa added, "we will move to influence the outcome of elections in specific countries, promoting those candidates whose policies please us and decrying those whose do not. It will be the beginning of the new empire. Eventually we will rule this planet as it should be ruled: from the navel of the world. From Cuzco."

"And everyone will have to drink Inca Cola twice a day, and visit their local Incaworld once a month," Fewick reminded them merrily. "Remember your promise to the Fernández brothers."

"We will not forget." Pucahuaman turned his gaze downward, toward the production that was getting under way. "I would not have thought this possible were it not for the assurances of the small woman Ho that this world of our ancestors can be controlled completely through this television."

"I never cared much for the medium myself," Fewick told him. "And as long as it does not interfere with my work I do not care what you do with the world." He smiled down at his cat. "What do you think, Moe? Should we let our friends take over the world? You don't care as long as they don't interfere with the international flow of cat food, do you? I thought not." Together with Apu Tupa and the general, he leaned back to enjoy the show.

"What is the problem now?" A tired Crease peered out the open rear door of the delivery van. Macha and Grinsaw clustered curiously near his cilia.

Igor had parked by the side of the road and crawled

under the truck. He wiped sweat and dirt from his face. "This vehicle we rented isn't new. I am afraid the rear axle is broken."

"What does this mean?"

"It means," said Igor as he slid back out on his backside, "that it will no longer go."

"How long will it take you to effect repairs?"

The guide stood, brushing at his dirty clothes. Macha seemed to be eyeing him accusingly. "I can't fix this. It would take days and the services of a fully equipped garage." He checked his watch. "It would not matter if I could fix it. We do not need a truck now; we need a much faster means of transportation."

"This is a bit of a mess, what?" Tree sounded discouraged.

Igor strode out into the empty road. "We will have to try and flag someone down, take his car if necessary."

"Is that a form of subliminal influence?"

"You might say that. If I am not stopped for speeding we just *might* get to the studio in time."

The first car to come roaring toward them nearly hit the wildly gesticulating guide, swerving to go around him at the last possible instant. Upon observing this encounter the three Boojums wordlessly climbed out of the van, lowering themselves to the ground with the aid of their powerful root-tentacles. They proceeded to align themselves next to Igor and parallel to the pavement, each extending a tentacle outward in quaint mimicry of the guide's thumbs-up posture.

"What are you doing? You are not supposed to reveal yourselves, remember?"

"We have relied too much on you already," Crease informed him. "The technique does not appear complicated yet you have failed to make it work; therefore we feel compelled to attempt it ourselves."

Igor's lips tightened into a thin line. "Suit yourselves, but I do not think it will obtain transport for us any faster."

He broke off as the whine of an approaching vehicle sounded from behind the next hill. The rugose beings imitating his gesture showed no inclination to return to the interior of the van. With a sigh he turned to face the unwary oncoming motorist, despairing of inducing anyone to stop anytime soon.

XIX

CARTER had chosen an unimportant expository moment near the beginning of the third act to make his entrance. According to the script there would be only two performers on stage at the time and if he was lucky he would be able to take over before they realized what was happening. It seemed the most natural place in the story for a stranger to put in an unexpected appearance and he'd prepared his improvisational dialogue accordingly.

Much depended on whether his startled fellow actors would react professionally or simply panic. He was relying on the immediacy of live TV to keep them in line, but there was no guarantee. Therefore he planned to say as much as he could as quickly as possible.

As the show progressed he saw Pucahuaman, Apu Tupa, and Fewick leave the control booth. Bored, no doubt, or intent on other business. Excitement stirred within him. Without anyone on the set to recognize him he might be able to talk until the next commercial before studio security personnel reacted.

Odd that all his training as an actor had led him finally to a role fraught with far more meaning than any he'd ever envisioned. He was about to give the most important performance of his life and he doubted it would last more than a few minutes.

It might also be his last performance.

"You ready, good-lookin'?" Ashwood was a comforting, maternal presence nearby. Well, not entirely
maternal, he reminded himself. "I just want you to
know that no matter how this turns out, you got
more guts than anybody I ever knew."

"You're just saying that to bolster my nerve."

"It's workin', ain't it?" She grinned at him.

He rose and made his way to the edge of the backdrop, easing it forward just enough to let him slip
past at the critical moment. Their hiding place lay to
the right of the stage and no one was looking in that
direction. No doubt the Boojums had already tak-
en control of the uplink facilities and were patiently
awaiting his appearance.

"Seriously, Jason, it's been my pleasure to have
made your acquaintance. Maybe Security'll just stun
you. I couldn't tell if the guards we saw earlier were
packin' guns or those funny-lookin' tubes. I'd feel a
lot more comfortable if this was a bank you were
fixin' to break into. Then I'd know for sure."

He had to smile. "Getting nostalgic?"

"Only for a .38."

According to the script a quick change of sets was
scheduled for the commercial break between the second and third acts. As technicians swarmed over the
stage positioning scenery and props, he hoped to mix
with them without being noticed, thereby putting
himself in position to step before the cameras right
on cue.

He was surprised how relaxed he was, how prepared he felt. What he was about to attempt wasn't
unlike live theater, one of his enduring loves for

which he was never chosen. Well, this time he'd gone ahead and cast himself, and nobody was going to fire him until he'd delivered his lines.

Of course as Ashwood had so succinctly pointed out, they could still fire *at* him.

"So you see," the young actress not twenty feet from where he was standing was declaiming melodramatically, "how that Spanish corporation has nearly ruined us, despite all we have done for them, despite my father having given his life for the good of the company." She turned away from the matronly woman who was playing opposite her.

"Because of that, because of *them*, now I won't be able to marry Edward." She began to sob.

"I am so sorry, my dear." The older actress walked to her mark behind a writing desk and picked up the letter opener lying there. "If only your brother Jack were here. *He* would know what to do about these lying cowards. But unfortunately he—"

"There's no need to panic, Aunt Dora," insisted the tall, self-possessed actor who strode out onto the stage. He had the presence of, if not an Olivier, at least a Hoffman. "I was able to change my travel plans at the last minute. Now I'm here where I belong, ready to help my family."

Both actresses gaped at him. In the context of the story line, their astonishment and surprise seemed perfectly natural.

The older woman started to turn to the director for an explanation, realized that everything she was doing was going out live, and to her everlasting credit and Carter's undying delight managed to stutter without breaking character, "I . . . I beg your pardon?"

As if he'd rehearsed it all week Carter strode across the set and settled into a chair opposite the two women. "I canceled my flight. Just made it back from the airport." He stared straight into the actress's eyes and said with a grin, "You didn't expect me, did you?"

The two women exchanged a look. Then the younger smiled at the older. They'd been told how important tonight's show was. Obviously this was the old actors' gag of throwing a ringer into the production in an attempt to rattle them. Always good for a few laughs. The expression on this new guy's face as much as confirmed their suspicions. Well, it hadn't quite worked. They were in on it now and they'd play along until the next break.

Which was what Carter had been counting on all along.

He stayed perfectly in character as the girl's older brother, his dialogue based on what he'd been able to divine from his hasty examination of the evening's script. It was laced with plenty of pro-Spanish sentiment, designed to mesh smoothly with the Boojums' manipulation of the Contisuyuns' mind machinery.

"It turns out that the Spanish government corporation wasn't responsible for your father's death after all," Carter declared encouragingly.

"It wasn't?" said the younger actress with becoming sincerity.

"Not at all. It's the fault of those you thought were your friends all along, those strange Contisuyuns. I found out that they've been manipulating you and Aunt Dora and everyone else while trying to blame the Spaniards for nonexistent misdeeds. They're attempting to sow dissent and discord across Europe by stirring up unfounded hatred against the Spanish populace. It's all part of a plot to gain revenge against people long dead."

At any moment he expected to hear the director scream "Cut!" or security men to pile on stage in spite of the running cameras to drag him away, so he was more than a little nonplussed by the continuing calm. Fortunately he had enough presence of mind to keep talking.

From where he was sitting he couldn't see the pandemonium which had engulfed the control booth, nor did any noise reach him from inside the soundproof enclosure. It turned out that having gotten Act III successfully under way, the director had left to take a leak, leaving matters of direction in the hands of his capable but presently very bewildered assistant.

That worthy saw no reason to intervene. Everyone on the set including the unidentified actor seemed to know what they were doing, so who was he to break into a live broadcast? Or to think of it another way, where production was concerned, if it didn't look broke, don't try and fix it.

Obviously there had been a last-minute script change on which he hadn't been consulted. Being distinctly peeved hardly constituted sufficient reason to interfere. What else could you expect on a production where peculiar-looking Indians, imperious fat men, and a peripatetic Vietnamese-American reporter kept wandering freely on and off the set? In a few minutes they would break for a scheduled commercial and no doubt it all would be explained to him then.

Meanwhile he sat back, did his best to look unconcerned, and enjoyed the performance. Those technicians on the set who looked to the assistant director for edification saw a man completely in control of himself and his work. They could do no less. The cameras and microphones continued to record.

Carter rambled on, enjoying himself now and wondering if Ashwood was silently applauding from her hiding place behind the backdrop. No doubt this continent-wide exposure would help his career, if he didn't end up shot. He knew he was delivering a memorable performance.

Once as he was turning he got a good look at the frantically gesticulating technicians up in the control booth. A moment later the booth door burst inward to admit the recently departed Pucahuaman, Apu Tupa, and Bruton Fewick complete with tomcat. While the Contisuyuns ranted wildly at the technical director Fewick turned to stare in disbelief down at the stage. Carter imagined the renegade archaeologist's state of mind and found the vision pleasing.

Meanwhile no one took any action to interrupt the broadcast.

U'chak was just awakening to what was happening. With everything going as planned he had once again allowed himself to relax completely and as a result it seemed that once again he was to be denied. His fury and frustration knew no bounds as he tried to puzzle out what had gone wrong.

He quickly realized that rather than being technical in nature, the problem lay with the human playacters. At the same time he was shocked to sense that a nonhuman, non-Shihararaneth intelligence was at work nearby, with the result that his design was not merely in the process of being altered but shattered, all because he had for a second time allowed overconfidence to gain sway over him.

A hasty evaluation suggested that the damage to his design might be beyond repair. For all his abilities, the one thing U'chak could not manipulate was time, no matter how angrily he scratched and clawed at it in his repeated attempts to get a grip on the slippery concept.

Seeing his intricate and carefully wrought plans being methodically demolished before his very eyes not by some higher intelligence, not by a Monitor, but by a single low-level human was more than he could stand. Nor could he influence the humans around him to repair the damage, as he had in the past. Their reaction times were too slow, their manipulative abilities far too limited.

His rigorous self-control vanished in the realization that if he didn't do something right then, that instant, all he had worked for would be lost.

He leaped.

A circular smooth-edged four-foot- wide hole appeared in the thick glass of the control booth, perfectly delineating the diameter of the vortex generated by the Renegade's passing. The technician nearest the aperture swore as she raised both hands to protect her face from flying glass that did not materialize.

Carter turned as the younger actress playing opposite him screamed and stumbled backward. Pure undiluted hatred in the form of a bulbous silvery teardrop had exploded out of the control booth, expanding as it arced toward him. Claws of fluid stainless steel reached like chrome putty for his face, directed by seething eyes the color of molten sulfur.

Realizing instinctively that if it touched him he would shrivel up and perish as quickly as ash from a cremated newspaper, he tried to duck. He was dimly aware of people around him yelling.

Something hit him in the ribs with the force of a velvet hammer, lifting him completely off the stage and smashing him to his right. He slammed into the false wall of the drawing room set, cracking wood, plaster, and possibly a rib or two. Tumbling to the floor, he rolled over once and lay still, dazedly trying to catch his breath.

At the same time he realized that it was not the hellish teardrop which had struck him.

Revelation!

Even as they exulted, the Monitors sensed the danger. In finally revealing his true self the Renegade had committed a fatal error. Thus exposed he could for the first time be confronted and dealt with on a physical level.

Although the distance involved was slight, there was no time to rejoice in the discovery. Reaching the same conclusion independently and simultaneously, O'lal and her companion chose the shortest slipline through reality and jumped, transforming themselves into two long streams of tightly organized particles able to speed down a short, twisting existential plane between the myriad of friction-inducing molecules which would otherwise have stood in their way. O'lal chose a slightly different path in order to try to save the human whose continued intercession had been so valuable, while her companion moved to deflect the Renegade's attack.

They knew it would be close. Not that it mattered in the scheme of things if one lone human died. Negation of the Renegade and his intentions was what was important. But she respected each sentient in her charge and had grown fond of this one in particular. It was worth the effort to her to try and save him.

In nanoseconds they coalesced inside the studio, O'lal striking Jason Carter and shunting him to one side as gently as she could, her fellow Monitor interspersing himself between the human and the onrushing Renegade.

A tremendous clap of thunder rolled across the set, accompanied by a brilliant flash of light. The concussion shattered what glass remained in the control booth, bent equipment and burst camera lenses, knocked technicians, crew, and performers to the floor, cut the transmission, and momentarily deafened everyone inside the building.

In the air ten feet above the set, two gleaming metallic wraiths twisted and coiled violently about one another. Successive thunderclaps and rings of glowing light emanated from the sizzling, spherical rainbow which enveloped them. Carter alone was in position to see a third stream of silver hover momentarily above his prone form before turning to smash its way into the fiery bubble overhead.

Suddenly the Renegade found himself fighting no longer to destroy but simply to break free. All had happened in an instant: anger, decision, attack. The realization that he'd made a mistake. The Monitors had been waiting patiently for just that. Now they had him and would not let go.

They were strong, but he was stronger. Rage lent

energy to his efforts. He would break free or disbond them in the attempt, then resume his disruptive efforts, even if he had to begin all over again with a different scheme elsewhere.

The Monitors were tenacious. He had never expected to have to do battle with more than one of them at a time and the effort required was physically taxing.

No one had to give the technicians and crew orders to abandon the studio. Hands covering their outraged ears as·they blinked at the bursts of light, they fled the set, running and stumbling toward the exits.

Somehow Marjorie Ashwood got Carter upright and helped the numbed actor stagger through the quivering building. Outside, they spotted Igor and the three aliens milling about in the parking lot and hurried to join them.

"We left when the transmission was cut," announced Shorty silently. "We heard the explosions. What is happening?" Fleeing technicians ignored them, wholly intent on reaching a place of safety. Those who glanced in their direction doubtless thought of actors in costume.

Carter was able now to stand on his own, for which the exhausted Ashwood was more than a little grateful.

"Something came out of the control booth. Something like nothing you've ever seen. I felt sure that it wanted to kill me." He coughed, one hand going to his bruised ribs. "Something a lot like it pushed me aside and then two of whatever they are set to struggling with the first." He looked back at the studio complex, which continued to shudder from the force of escalating internal concussions. "As far as I know they're still in there, fighting."

Crease regarded the trembling structure. "It can be nothing other than a snark. A phenomenon I believe we discussed with Mr. Dodgson but which confused him greatly. I think he thought we were referring to ourselves. Quite absurd. A snark is most definitely *not* a Boojum."

"Then what the hell is it?" Ashwood asked, shuddering slightly. "I saw the damn things, but I don't believe 'em."

"To encounter one is rare and always terrifying," Tree informed them. "Sometimes they are benign, sometimes deadly. They are a life-form, if indeed it is a life-form they are and not a natural force, that is most rare and wondrous. We do not even know if they are fashioned of matter as we understand it.

"The few verified reports of encounters come from different worlds, suggesting that they are either a galactic phenomenon or else able to travel between widely scattered systems by means unimaginable to us. As you see, we know very little about them. According to your description, something has drawn not one but three of them here. Most extraordinary."

"I know one thing." They all looked at Carter, who was gazing back at the building. "One of them just saved my life."

"Their motives are capricious and incomprehensible. We are not even sure if their movements are guided by instinct, sentience, or randomness. Consider yourself privileged to have observed such a phenomenon."

"You observe 'em." Ashwood brushed at her jeans. "Me, I'll wait for the movie."

Sound deafened them (another explosion or a scream? Carter wondered) and everyone turned back toward the building. The roof and walls were collapsing inward, imploding, subsumed in brilliantly colored light pierced through with flailing silver cables. Other flickering hues ran along the cables as if they were giant fiber optics, only to burst from the waving tips as lambent balls of fading flame. Each time one of the lightning-like spheres shot into the air, a miniature sonic boom would roll outward from the disintegrating structure to rattle the spectators assembled in the parking lot. Flames began to lick upward, feeding on the crumbling complex.

A moment later something within blew up with the force of a fully loaded bomber smashing head-on into a mountainside, vomiting the steel roof skyward and showering the dazed onlookers with glass slag and lumps of molten metal. A piece of video camera landed near Carter's feet, the tough housing reduced to a glob of plastic taffy. Ashwood was one of several people knocked off their feet. It was his turn to help her erect.

"What the hell was *that*?" Shakily she joined the others in staring at the remains of the studio. The entire complex had been reduced to unsalvageable rubble, flattened as thoroughly as if by a tactical nuclear weapon.

"So much for the Contisuyuns' mind-manipulating machinery." Carter looked over at the Boojums, who were only slightly less mystified than the humans. "Look, everybody around here is pretty wasted right now, but that won't last forever. Nobody's questioned your presence yet. If you still want to preserve your anonymity you ought to get back in the van."

"Jolly good idea." Crease pivoted on multiple cilia.

Ashwood came up short near the back doors, frowning at the crumpled roof. "What happened to y'all? You run into another snark out there?"

Igor lowered his eyes. "Not exactly. A railroad bridge. You did not know, but we were almost too late. We were stuck out in the countryside somewhere. I was thinking that we could not possibly get here in time when the most amazing thing happened. An industrial lifting copter flying past noticed the accident and stopped to see if they could be of assistance. Inca gold did the rest and, after making temporary repairs to our broken axle, the crew transported us and the van here without ever setting eyes on the Boojums, who remained inside.

"I did not even have to lie to the guard at the entrance to the parking lot. When he saw the copter set us down and the Boojums climb out the back he sensed instinctively that we had something to do with the show. He never questioned me about our means of arrival.

"Once inside the complex our friends dealt easily with any who got too curious. They immobilized the guards and technicians at the uplink facility in the same fashion." He raised his eyes to Carter's face. "By the time we arrived you were already on the set, performing."

Carter gawked at him. "You mean I went out there and exposed myself and you weren't even in control yet?" The guide nodded as the Boojums climbed into the back of the van.

"I could've been killed, for nothing!"

"Ah, these humans." Shorty leaned out to help Tree up beside him. "Their powers of perception never cease to amaze me."

Something in the front seat meowed plaintively and Carter walked around the van to open the door. Macha leaped out into his arms. As he caressed her Grinsaw hopped out, walked with great dignity to the rear of the vehicle, and jumped in the back to rejoin his Boojums.

"Poor thing." Carter spoke soothingly as he stroked her behind the ears. "Bet all this noise and confusion has you scared to death. Well, it's all over now. When we get back to L.A. I'm gonna buy you the biggest scratching post you ever saw and feed you nothing but gourmet cat food from Gelsen's." Gently he placed her on the seat next to him.

Cars continued to screech out the entrance as fleeing cast and crew burned rubber in their haste to escape. One nearly ran smack into a pumper truck coming the other way as the first representatives of Greater Edinburgh's fire department began to arrive, the workers at the nearby plastics plant having sounded the alarm.

"So the only way y'all could've made it here in time to be of any use was by helicopter, an' one just showed up?" Ashwood looked dubious as Igor nodded. "Sounds like a helluva coincidence to me."

"Sometimes it is best not to question all things," Tree pontificated. "To the best of our knowledge, coincidence does not flout natural law."

"What I don't understand," Carter said pensively, "is why this snark thing would want to attack me. And why then? Was it after the same thing as the

Contisuyuns? Or was it just another crazy coincidence?"

"One would have to inquire of the snark." Shorty was staring at the burning building, observing the local fire department in action. "They have been suspected of interfering in sentient affairs, though as in everything else involving them nothing has been proven for certain."

"I wonder if everyone got out," Ashwood was saying. "Not just the locals, but Fewick and Da Rimini and the Contisuyuns."

"I'm sure Trang Ho did," Carter commented. "People like that always survive, so they can make the lives of the less fortunate miserable. That's a natural law."

"It does not matter." Crease emanated assurance. "With their equipment destroyed the Contisuyuns can never again influence large masses of your population, nor can the ones isolated here ever return to their world to mount another attack. You need no longer fear that what little stability and maturity you have managed to achieve will be disturbed by external forces."

O'lal and the Monitor who had arrived to reinforce her were reasonably pleased with their efforts. By revealing his true nature the Renegade had given them no choice but to likewise expose themselves in order to deal with him. Yet conditions had been sufficiently chaotic at the critical moment that she was confident no record of their materialization had been made. Nor were the few frightened humans who had witnessed the climactic confrontation likely to persuade others of their kind of what they had seen. Knowing her human charges as intimately as she did, she was convinced that the brief realization of the Monitors would soon be forgotten.

It had been close. The Renegade had demonstrated incredible, unprecedented strength. She could never have defeated him alone. Even the combined exertions of her colleague and herself had barely been equal to the task. Only their unexpected appearance had enabled them to seize an initial advantage and hold it to the end.

The Renegade still lived. Seeing that he was about to be overwhelmed he had expended a titanic burst of energy in breaking free of the Monitors' grasp and fleeing via the tenuous, difficult-to-negotiate places that curled and tunneled between interstellar mass. Both Monitors had elected not to follow. The Renegade had been defeated in his aims and wounded in his bonding. He should not reemerge to trouble any evolving species for some time to come.

The three humans joined the two cats in the front of the van and Igor eased them out of the parking lot. Those of the cast and crew who'd wanted to had already fled, but there was still a line of arriving, siren-blaring municipal vehicles to avoid. Once clear of the industrial park their guide took the road that led toward the city.

A sliding window gave those in the cab access to the van's cargo bay. Carter spoke hesitantly.

"How did I do? Did we do it?"

"It was a jolly good effort, young human. Jolly good!" He recognized Crease's turn of mind. "Of course we will not know for certain if our efforts were successful until your newspeople broadcast from Spain tomorrow, but I am of the opinion that we had ample time to counteract the effects of the

Contisuyuns' subliminal propaganda. There should
be no riot, and without a dose of regular weekly
reinforcement on the television, what irrational anti-
Spanish feeling persists should fade rapidly from the
collective European consciousness."

Carter allowed himself to relax. "What now?"

"We drive to our current residence to gather your
baggage and erase any traces of our presence here,
whereupon you may convey us to the continent you
refer to as South America. Upon our return to Paititi
we will remove all traces of the transmitter there,
reboard our vessel, and depart your world, leaving
it to evolve naturally, in its own way and its own
time, without any further outside interference.

"Contisuyu will do likewise, memorializing their
lost expedition as a sad but forgettable incident in
their own history."

"What about that snark thing? What if it comes
back?"

"The threat to the stability of your society was
mounted by the Contisuyuns," Tree assured him.
"That has now been dealt with. The snark's presence
we cannot explain, but personally I think you worry
overmuch. There is no point to doing so because one
cannot affect a snark's actions anyway. One might
as well waste time worrying about tripping over a
singularity."

"What about the Contisuyuns like Apu Tupa and
Pucahuaman who are stuck here?" Ashwood wanted
to know. "What happens to them now?"

"I venture to say that they will either integrate
themselves into your society or be locked away as
insane. In any case they no longer constitute a danger."

"They still have the use of the treasure at Nazca and Paititi," she pointed out. "On our world, treasure is power."

Crease thrust a root-tentacle through the opening and waved it about by way of emphasis. "A small matter which we are prepared to deal with. Our ship is equipped with a compact but very powerful device with which we will methodically reduce to dust any evidence of advanced technology such as the inoperative transmitters and the fish-filled transport vessels of the Contisuyns, together with the treasure. We will then utilize it to collapse the caverns, burying them forever beneath tons of solid stone. As that part of your planet is tectonically active, several small, highly localized 'earthquakes' should go unremarked upon.

"Both sites will be rendered useless to Contisuyuns and your people alike." A long-drawn-out mental sigh filled the van. "It will be a great relief to leave this world, which delights in inventing problems where none exist."

"Will you ever come back?" Carter asked as they changed lanes to avoid a slow-moving truck. "Will we ever see you again? You could teach us so much, help us deal with our problems."

Crease was sympathetic but firm. "That would constitute the same kind of interference, albeit on a more benign level, as that intended by the Contisuyuns. No, you must develop in your own way, at your own pace. For us to provide assistance would be . . . unaesthetic. Not to mention psychologically damaging to the majority of your kind. Sorry."

"Perhaps someday," Tree added, "you or the Contisuyuns or some other race will reach a level where we can interact as friends and equals. It would be nice to have someone to play cards with."

"We'll make it," Carter said confidently. "You'll see. We'll get there."

"That would be ripping, old sport. Simply ripping." Crease caressed his shoulder encouragingly. "Of course, you'll first have to do something about this visual fungus you call television or it'll rot your brains. That much is self-evident even to casual visitors such as ourselves."

XX

SPAIN dominated the next day's news, topped by the final score of the European championship game: Barcelona 3, Liverpool 2. According to Igor, who eagerly perused the sports pages, it had been the best championship game in a decade, full of unrelenting action and great plays. Rioting was mentioned only in the context of a small-scale confrontation which had taken place outside the stadium proper and was reported to have involved some bad paella whose inimical influence was of gastrointestinal rather than subliminal origin.

As for any lingering irrational anti-Spanish fervor, it vanished in the euphoria generated by the determined, gutsy performance of the Spanish national team and its injured goalkeeper. The rest of Europe applauded the Spaniards' excellence . . . with the exception of certain parts of England, which had lost.

The primetime evening news also had a piece on the destruction by mysterious explosion and fire of the old McCarie film studio complex south of Edinburgh. There were pictures, reports from still dazed eyewitnesses, reassuring pontificating by the police and fire chiefs, reminiscences by actors who had worked there during the studio's cinematic heyday, and clips from the films and television shows which had been produced at the site.

The report concluded with a somewhat jumbled interview with the studio's owners, the Fernández brothers of Peru. They announced that since the complex had been insured, they expected to suffer no significant financial loss. They were in fact philosophical about the damage and enthusiastic about returning home. Having been bitten by the entertainment bug they intended to build a new studio of their own for film and television production on the outskirts of the city of Miraflores. Based on the success of their telenovela *Day Becomes Tomorrow* they foresaw no difficulty in raising the necessary financing.

Upon conclusion of the brief interview the Scottish commentator ventured a snide aside about novices who enter the entertainment industry with delusions of grandeur. He then segued smoothly into a story about a berserk grandmum who was presently holding her landlord's family at gunpoint in Berkshire, demanding that she be allowed to keep her pedigreed Pekinese in her one-bedroom flat no matter how much he do-dooed on the owner's front stoop.

"Maybe," said Igor with a slight smile, "the Fernández brothers can introduce the Contisuyuns to the delights of the soft-drink business."

Ashwood lounged on the cottage couch. "I think folks like Pucahuaman and Apu Tupa will manage to take care of themselves."

"They're adaptable." Carter was watching Grinsaw and Macha chase each other around the living room. "They've demonstrated that already. If nothing else they can go into the antiquities racket. They

must know where a lot of stuff in Peru is buried."
He turned to the guide.

"If you think you can see our friends safely back
to their ship by yourself, Igor, Marjorie and I would
sure appreciate it. We've had about enough traipsing
around and this saving-the-world stuff is damn tiring. I want to spend a week at La Costa and then get
back to work."

The diminutive Peruvian smiled. "By all means,
go back to the States. I will take care of things and
perhaps someday I will visit you there."

Shorty slid a pair of root-tentacles around Carter's
shoulders. "We have great hopes for you chaps. Left
to yourselves I think you *will* mature, as will the
Contisuyuns on their own world."

They parted at the airport. Carter and Ashwood
headed first-class to Los Angeles while Igor and his
Boojum "cargo" boarded a chartered jet for the long
flight back to Peru. Igor refused to leave until he'd
extracted a promise from his friends to return to
his beloved Manú someday so that he could give
them a proper tour of its unmatched animal and
plant life, his naturalist's commentary undisturbed
by interstellar distractions.

Manaus was fascinating, but the little Spanish that
Carter had picked up during his previous travels did
him no good in the only country in South America
where the official language was Portuguese.

He was relaxing in his cabana, listening to the hyp-
notic hum of the ceiling fans while waiting for the
iced tropical drink he'd ordered from room service to
arrive. They'd just wrapped final location shooting
on *Death Dealers of the Amazon* except for a day of

background shots to be taken around the city, and
he was luxuriating in the completion of a crummy
job well done. Maybe he wasn't doing *Henry IV*, but
he was learning to live with the compensations.

The script had actually been less illiterate than the
majority of its ilk, with a few lines a normal adult
human being wouldn't be embarrassed to be seen
uttering in public. And Marjorie Ashwood had been
there to lend a sympathetic ear to his complaints.
As the nominal star of the tropical opus he'd used
his leverage to get her hired on as head of wardrobe.
Since both the male and female leads were called
upon to perform largely in various states of undress,
the picture was practically a vacation for her.

"You're just gonna have to get used to bein' young,
rich, famous, and handsome," she told him. "And
if you hang in there, maybe by the time you're old
and wrinkled you'll start gettin' some respect from
your peers . . . not to mention all those nice juicy
character roles.

"Just remember that Gable once tried to play the
premier of Ireland, complete with accent, and that
it nearly destroyed his career."

There was a knock and he rose to open the door.
When he saw who was standing in the portal he
almost slammed it shut. Only the sheer overpower-
ing beauty of his visitor prevented him from doing
so.

"Don' look so shocked." Francesca da Rimini's
smile was as wide and beautiful as the Amazon
River itself. There was no hint of hostility in her
tone, no threat in her manner. "It's not like we don'
know each other."

"Yes, do let us come in," said the man standing

next to her. Bruton Fewick wore Carrera sunglasses, white tropical Italian silks, and a mildly outrageous straw fedora. The familiar shape of a big orange tomcat pressed against his left ankle.

Carter ignored him, as any man would, in favor of Da Rimini. The rough-hewn giantess of Cuzco had been transformed into a pillar of feminine magnificence, a cross between a contemporary sex kitten and a Scavullo model. Unable to resist, he stepped aside and followed her with his eyes as she took a seat on the rattan couch, crossing her legs with frictionless precision. Fewick flopped down in a nearby chair while Moe set to exploring the room.

"I've always said that the only drawback to the tropics is the heat." Carter's old nemesis wiped sweat from his forehead. "Well, aren't you going to offer us something to drink?"

"There's a pitcher on the way and I think there're extra glasses in the cupboard." He blinked at Da Rimini. "What are you two doing *here*? I don't understand."

"Then you are in good company, my friend, because there are many things we do not understand ourselves. As for example how you managed to slip into the studio in Edinburgh and successfully undo in a few minutes what the Contisuyuns had been working on for months."

Carter glanced warily toward the door. "Speaking of the Contisuyuns, where are they?"

Fewick's fingers fluttered indifferently in the cabana's cooled air. "In Peru. Most of them went to work for the Fernández brothers."

"I thought that's where you'd be too, digging up every tomb in the country."

Fewick sighed deeply. "Do you really think that after everything that's happened I could be satisfied with a return to a profession as dull and desiccated as archaeology?"

"I thought you loved it."

"Nonsense! It's boring, dirty work. I only went into it because I thought it might make my parents respect me." He made a face. "Though it sometimes still strikes me strange how soon after our failed enterprise in Scotland I lost all desire to pursue my research any further. Be assured that I am much happier now, not to mention more pleasant to be around. I had not realized how single-mindedly I had been driven by an ambition I barely understood."

The drinks arrived. Carter signed the chit, passed out glasses, and poured for his visitors. He was not quite ready yet to think of them as guests.

"So what have you been doing since?" he asked conversationally.

"It was most unexpected." Fewick sipped at his glass, looking content. "After the great, albeit abbreviated commercial success of *Day Becomes Tomorrow* I found myself, as executive producer, inundated with offers to produce other programs."

"But you've got no previous experience in the television business."

"Apparently that is not a necessary qualification." Fewick smiled broadly. "After considering these many onerous proposals, most of which begged us to spend obscene quantities of other people's money at our discretion, dear Francesca and I decided to form a production company to develop projects which she would star in and I would produce." He ran a finger around the rim of his glass.

"I had never considered the advantages of a career in show business. For one thing, I can now act like the bastard I have always been, the difference being that in my new profession I am openly admired for it. Nor is it important that I am overweight and physically unattractive. All that matters is where I park and at what tables I sit in certain restaurants. The parallels with the ancient hierarchical structures I used to study are quite striking. For example, I have found some of the similarities between the social structure in Hollywood and that of ancient Assyria most enlightening."

Carter downed half his glass. "What about pleasing and impressing your parents?"

"Oh, them." Fewick sniffed disdainfully. "Their approval is no longer vital to my self-esteem. As there are more psychotherapists and psychiatrists per square mile in Beverly Hills than anywhere else on the planet, I have been able to avail myself of excellent professional help. I no longer care whether Mum and Pater approve of my life-style or not. They are no longer what is happening.

"Actually they consider Hollywood to be a step down from archaeology. I expect their attitudes to change when they see how much money I am making."

Carter stared at Fewick for a long moment, then turned to Da Rimini. "What about you? What about all the injustices you told me you wanted to right, the embarrassments you've suffered all your life, the anger and frustrations that built up inside you as you matured?"

"Oh, those." She sipped delicately at her drink. "A condo in Los Angeles, a pied-à-terre in Manhattan, and a home in Miraflores have taken away much of the anger. It is so won'erful when so many people on the street recognize me from *Day Becomes Tomorrow*. You should know, *querido*. Besides, I've spent my whole life actin'. Is better to do it for a living than for some cheap revenge thing." She regarded him out of half-lidded eyes.

"You been doin' pretty good from it yourself."

"Which brings us to the reason for our visit." Fewick shifted in his seat, the rattan squeaking beneath his silk-encased bulk. "All of your films have been successful. You are, as the film lingo says, a draw. So we would like for you to work for us."

Carter could no more than gape.

"For a percentage of the net . . . well, gross, if you insist. Points, up-front money, other participatory perks. The usual star treatment. I have taken the time to study your films in detail and as a result I have boundless confidence in your natural ability to appeal to the great indiscriminate ticket-buying public. My people can cobble together a contract . . . provided you feel that you can work with Francesca, here."

Her expression switched to sultry as effortlessly as one would change slides in a projector. "Dear Jason. I do so hope you won' let it threaten a promising working relationship because I once say something about letting some ants eat you alive. I've changed since then, though dear Bruton says I'm still basically the same vacuous maniacal airhead I was when you first meet me. Of course, that only his opinion."

Rising from the couch, she gyrated over to place

her arms on his shoulders, portions of her body several inches closer to him than the rest of her. Fewick looked on with amused insouciance.

"What do you say, *querido*?"

"You'll . . . have to talk to my agent first." Carter found himself drowning in Francesca's eyes . . . or at least slipping into dangerous waters.

"Mahvelous," said Fewick. "When you get back to L.A. we'll all do lunch."

"After all," said Da Rimini huskily, "it not as if we haven' work together before."

"You wanted to *kill* me."

She disengaged herself, pouting. "Why mus' you bring up silly old things? Everything is differen' now. You are differen', I am differen', everybody differen'. Much better."

He considered. From the very first he'd found Da Rimini attractive. If one disregarded her homicidal tendencies, partnering with her on a set could be a lot of fun. It was always hard for him to find an actress he could interact with eye-to-eye.

"This isn't a trick? You're not trying to recruit me into some crazy project to take over the world or unsettle society?"

"Unsettle society?" Fewick looked nonplussed. "My dear fellow, why would I want to do anything as absurd as that? I am making entirely too much money from society as it is presently constituted. The last thing I would want to do is unsettle it. When people are unsettled they don't go to the movies.

"As for taking over the world, nothing could be further from my mind. For one thing, if I were successful I wouldn't have the faintest notion what to do with it. The administrative details alone would be stressful beyond belief. My therapist would have a fit. I don't want to run the world: I merely want to own a substantial portion of the preferred stock. No, no. I am a loyal supporter of the present inequitable status quo."

A bemused smile lit Carter's face. This wasn't exactly how he'd expected things to turn out. On the other hand, it wasn't a bad way for things to turn out, either.

"We'll talk," he said decisively. "I don't suppose you have a script in mind for our first coproduction?"

"Certainly. I commissioned a story from one of the top names in the science-fiction field, which I then naturally had rewritten the instant I got back to Bel Air. A fine, moral, uplifting tale full of insight and human understanding. We're going to call it *Technoslaves of the Ginza*. I am confident it will appeal to you. The toy licensing potential alone is unlimited."

Carter sighed resignedly. "More crap."

"Yes," Fewick admitted, "but wait until you read it. This is *aesthetic* crap. It will make buckets of money and you get to emote like crazy as well as bare your pectorals. Come now. Any role is what a good actor makes of it."

"You don't bear any grudges for what happened?"

"Grudges are bad for business. To this day I do not understand how I allowed myself to become swept up in such foolishness. That is not like me. It is almost as if I was under some kind of external control." Moe hopped up into his lap and he began to stroke the cat reflexively.

"More nonsense, of course. I consider my partici-pation in what happened to have been a temporary aberration, never to be repeated." He smiled. "My therapist says it is all right for me to feel good. You have no idea what a relief that is."

Carter picked up the pitcher. "This is getting watery. How about I call for a fresh one?"

"That would be sweet." Da Rimini pursed her perfect lips and blew him a kiss.

Ashwood, Carter reflected as he reached for the house phone, was going to have a cow.

XXI

THE Renegade's patience was paying off. He had managed to delude the Monitors into thinking he had perished during the confrontation, when in reality he had at the last possible instant slipped away via an unsuspected, almost invisible gap in the spatial continuum.

His mind had been working furiously ever since. They had not found him and, not finding him, could not hurt him. He was nothing if not resourceful. Given time he could, he *would*, construct a new plan of disruption more fiendishly clever than the last. On the ruins of the old he would erect an entirely new game, one he could not help but win.

Already the groundwork had been laid, and neither the Monitors nor the poor simple creatures whose welfare they were charged with protecting were aware of his ongoing ministrations. He was quite pleased with himself.

Moe the cat glanced around to make certain no one was watching him before he jumped lightly from the balcony of the cabana to the ground below. He shook himself, taking stock of his surroundings. The alley behind the hotel was deserted. There was nothing to observe or interfere with his exercise.

Turning to his left, he strolled up the broken pavement. He did not see the other cat perched atop the telephone pole he passed beneath. Its eyes followed his progress.

Then it leaped.

At the last instant he sensed its proximity and jumped. Jumped impossibly far, farther than was physically possible for any member of the genus *Felis*.

Moe did not belong to the genus *Felis*.

Jumped in fact the length of the alley, landing on the curb of the street it intersected. Furious beyond measure, resolving this time to kill or be killed, he prepared to retrace his path with another, far deadlier jump. Orange fur began to ripple tenebrously, giving way to streaks of gray like shot silver.

His incredible senses detected a distinctive curve in the continuum, one that if athletically accessed should bring him up and around behind his tormentor and put him in position to strike a lethal blow. He smiled to himself. No more hiding, no more stalking. It was time to make an end of it. He would finish the travesty . . . now!

He jumped.

Simultaneously a fourteen-year-old boy balancing on his shoulder a radio-cassette player the size of a small armored vehicle came tearing around the corner on a skateboard with the face of a crazed bull painted on it and intersected the space continuum curve exactly at the point where the Renegade intended to enter. From this nexus there emanated a peculiarly loud *bang* involving the boy, the boombox, the skateboard, six small coins in the boy's pocket, his three gold fillings, something that looked like a cat, and something that looked like a distorted blob of jaundiced mercury.

The boy was thrown clear across the street, where concerned passersby relievedly ascertained that his injuries consisted only of bumps and bruises. The boombox had been reduced to a mass of melted plastic and wiring that coated the smoking skateboard.

The odd little *bang* intensified as it rippled across the city of Manaus, reaching the proportions of a rattlingly good-sized sonic boom by the time it reached the metropolitan outskirts, where it confused the air traffic controllers at the international airport no end, since their screens showed no aircraft as being in the vicinity. The source of the noise was attributed to a low-flying air force jet whose pilot had decided to take an unauthorized joyride over the jungle. Curses in English and Portuguese filled the airwaves on the appropriate frequencies.

The cat which had leaped from the top of the telephone pole now relaxed in the center of the alley. Sitting back on its haunches it daintily licked clean first one paw and then the other.

A second cat materialized and the two briefly touched noses. Then it leaped; not onto a ledge, not onto a fence, not onto the empty garbage can sitting invitingly nearby, but straight up into the air. As it did so it changed, legs contracting to nothingness, ears flattening, color melting from tan and white to silver, eyes becoming twin pools of fire. It vanished, leaving in its wake a miniature echo of the earlier, much louder sonic boom.

The remaining cat turned and strolled down the alley until it stood beneath an open window. It leaped effortlessly through the opening to land on the hardwood floor inside. The room's three occupants were laughing and chattering and did not notice the arrival.

How pleasing to see them enjoying themselves, the cat thought. Much better than otherwise. She advanced across the floor to rub up against the right leg of one of the humans.

Carter looked down and a pleased smile spread across his face. "Hi, Macha. I wondered where you'd got to." Lifting the cat he carefully set her down in his lap, where she curled up contentedly.

"I see that stray is still with you," Fewick observed. "Most remarkable."

Carter stroked the animal's neck. "What can I say? Women find me irresistible. I suppose I'll have to learn to live with it."

"Such problems you have." Fewick glanced toward the open window. "I suppose Moe is still roaming around outside." He shrugged. "He will return when it suits him. He can vanish into thin air and return at the oddest times."

Da Rimini nodded understandingly. "Cats are like that, although I never cared much for them myself."

"I never thought about it," Carter said. "I've always been too busy for pets. Though if Macha's anything to go by, I've been missing something." As he continued to stroke the cat's neck she twisted her head around at an impossible angle to eye him approvingly.

For the first time in what seemed like an eon O'lal allowed herself to completely unwind. Once again they had trapped the Renegade and once more he had nearly escaped. After all his writhing and racing through the planes of reality, all his scheming and planning, in the end he had been undone by an accident, a twist of fate. It was true poetic justice that a human and not a Monitor had ultimately been responsible for his demise.

She was glad that the unaware young human had not been seriously injured. Her concern for her charges had always bordered on the maternal. His appearance at the critical time and place had been providential and the transposition had not proven fatal to him, so there was no reason for regrets. Nor did he have the slightest idea what had happened to him beyond vague memories of a collision with a cat.

The other Monitor had gone to rejoin his Boojums, whose development *he* was charged with supervising. In some ways his task was more difficult than her own, for the forgetfully superintelligent are more awkward to monitor than the merely undeveloped.

Best of all, the termination of the Renegade had been accomplished without the Shihararaneth having been forced to reveal their true nature to either human or Boojum. Things were once more as they should be.

She glanced up at the being called Jason Carter Humans had their problems, and they were going to require a lot more work before they could conceivably be thought of as mature, but in their clumsy, primitive way they were warm and agreeable creatures, and they had definite potential. Jason Carter in particular was a good example of his kind. She lowered her head to her paws.

The work of a Monitor was ever fraught with stress. Having a pet helped her to relax.

It was twelve years later that a Taiwanese fishing boat operating semi-legally in the isolated northwest corner of the Tuamotu Archipelago came across an unvisited island populated entirely by South American Indians.

These simple people raised their families, fished, cultivated wild fruits, and built houses in the style of the ancient Incas out of coral and coconut palms. They spoke Quechua and Spanish and claimed to have once had access to a higher civilization, but when queried they didn't press the point.

Norwegian scientists insisted that here at last was proof conclusive that the Polynesian islands had been settled by explorers from Peru. The rest of the anthropological community said nothing of the sort, often adding commentary of their own that was less than polite.

As for the islanders, who called themselves Contis, they enthralled the drifting clumps of visiting scientists with a unique Creation tale which described how they had found themselves transported full-grown from their homeland to the islands, whereupon finding their original attire much too cumbersome they promptly discarded it in favor of going about blissfully bare-ass.

As time passed they built boats and, delighting in their new home, proceeded to dump all reminders of their past into a deep ocean trough. Thus cleansed of any lingering guilt or sense of responsibility to their former lives, they felt quite able to settle back and enjoy the delights their little paradise offered them, and would the scientists, reporters, New Age freaks, and numerous other and diverse sensation seekers now kindly please go away and leave them the hell alone.

Author's note___

MANÚ National Park in the Madre de Dios region of eastern Peru contains what many scientists believe to be the greatest number of species of any comparable region for its size on Earth. While the Peruvian government has set aside this remarkable biota as a park, the same enormous size and lack of modern facilities which enable highly endangered species such as the giant otter, black caiman, and spectacled bear to survive within its borders create comparable problems of management for a society under considerable economic stress. Resources are necessarily spread thin and the danger from poachers and miners is great.

If you wish to contribute to the preservation of one of the world's great natural wonders, contributions may be made to the nonprofit *Friends of the Peruvian Rainforest*, 668 Public Ledger Building, Philadelphia, PA 19106.

The Manú is the Grand Canyon of rainforests. Perhaps the greatest wonder of all is that it can still be rescued from destruction and preserved intact for future generations to enjoy. I urge all of you who are concerned to contribute to its survival.

ALAN DEAN FOSTER
Prescott, Arizona